The
Square

SHAPE OF LOVE

HaUSS
jMcCLAIN

SHAPE OF LOVE

the Square

Edited by RJ Locksley
Cover Design by JA Huss

description

ALEC
Against all odds, we found each other.
And then a single moment of betrayal ripped it all away.
I thought Christine had forgiven me. I thought we'd moved past it. I thought she'd healed.

CHRISTINE
I loved them both and they loved me.
But then Danny left and our triangle was broken.
So was I really that surprised when Alec put it back together again?

DANNY
We are meant to be together. We all know that.
But what did Alec do after I left?
What could he have possibly done to make Christine want revenge?

CHAPTER ONE

There is nothing in life that cannot be conquered. Not even Death.

I should be dead right now. Indeed, I should have been dead a dozen times over. Death has come for me again, and again, and again along my journey. But I have conquered the art of denying her. Each time Death has approached and asked for my life, I have shown her that there is no life here for her to take. Because I understand something that others do not. I understand what she actually wants.

It ain't me.

It ain't him, or her, or them, or you.

It's fear.

Fear is the nourishing lifeblood that Death thrives on. She grows fat and full on the fear of those she visits. And that makes her seem powerful. But all one must do to drain her of her power is to starve her of her serving of fear. Then she withers, weakens, and is forced to look elsewhere for her supper.

Those who are intimidated by the idea of dying are simply unpracticed in the art of denying her their fear. They hand it over freely. When Death arrives and demands their soul, they believe they have no choice but to offer it up. Eish, man, most okes invite her in, let her sit at their table, and then feed her and feed her until her gullet is bursting and she has consumed them whole.

And I have discovered that the most effective way of avoiding this presumed inevitability is to see to it that there is no soul left for her to consume.

If you murder your soul before she can claim it; if you rip from deep within you that gnawing parasite that eats at your conscience and causes you to question what is right and what is wrong before Death arrives; then you become Death. And in so becoming, you can look her in the eye when she makes herself known and she will see that you have nothing left that she wants. You and she are the same. She will not be sated by sitting at your table, for you have already eaten all that was there. And Death will bow, and sigh, and look away and move along.

As I have said before: The only thing that can kill Alec van den Berg is Alec van den Berg. I am in control. Because Alec van den Berg… is death itself.

As I pull on the spill of yellow hair washing across the shoulder blades in front of me—twisting tightly and clenching hard like I'm holding the reins on a horse's bridle—my mind drifts, for just a moment, to a time, many years ago, when we were all in the Cook Islands. That yellow dress that Christine wore every single day. I bought her new dresses, crates of them, but she just wore that same yellow dress over and over again. Day in and day out until its tawny brightness began to fade and wash away.

I asked her why she was so attached to it. She said, "Because it makes me feel like I'm wearing the sun. And no matter what happens, as long as I have it on, it'll always be a sunny day."

She was such a precocious girl. A poem come to life and she didn't even know it.

The sound of, "Fuck me harder. Please, please, harder, Alec. Fuck me," in a posh British accent pulls me away from my brief reminiscence. To be sure, it is its own type of poetry.

I clench Eliza's hair tighter, force myself into her deeper, harder, as she asks. I smile at the request, because whenever she asks me to fuck her harder, I can detect the hint of her upbringing in her accent. She's worked hard over her life to cultivate the sophisticated, monied sound of upper-crust British society, but when she's tired, or drunk, or being fucked in the ass, the Essex girl creeps back in. Proper Purfleet spilling out from her pretty lips.

You can take the girl out of Essex, I suppose, but you can't take Alec van den Berg from out of her Es-sex-y ass. Not right now, anyway.

My forearm tenses as my fist balls tighter in her jumbled mane of blonde. I look at the veins bulging and throbbing and I grit my teeth. "Harder? Like that?" I ask.

"Yes," she moans.

I take my free hand and slide it around her hip, letting it find the throbbing bundle of nerves between her legs. With two fingers, I press on her and she squeals.

"You're going to make me come." She laughs.

"I certainly fokken hope so," I gasp in response. "Otherwise, I'm doing something terribly wrong."

She widens her stance, spreading her long, muscled legs as far astride as they will allow her, and in an echo of that movement, reaches her arms out as far as she can as well. She takes hold of the two posts at the footboard of the four-poster bed, and the force of our thrusting back forth causes the canopy to shake and the headboard to slam into the wall. Bits of plaster from the sixteenth-century stately manor cascade down onto the floor. I imagine someone will likely ask me to pay for that. When I rented this pozzy to lie low for a bit, the elderly oke who manages the estate went to great pains to emphasize the irreplaceability of the various knickknacks lying about. So I feel certain I'll be asked to reimburse for the centuries-old wash basin we just managed to knock off the bedside table and send crashing to the floor.

"Bugger," Eliza says, jumping at the sound of the smashing porcelain.

"I am, my dear," I say, letting go of her hair and slapping her ass with the back of my hand. She shrieks and slams her ass back into me, causing me to drive further inside her than I thought was possible. The muscles of her asshole clench my shaft as she attempts to hold me in place, lock me down, pressed against her. I draw back, slowly, wrenching myself from within as she tightens and resists. She hisses.

"Where do you think you're going?" she asks.

I don't answer. Just keep playing this tug of war between her ass and my cock until I'm almost out of her completely. Then, just as the tip is almost entirely free, I slam myself back inside her, pushing her forward and causing her to release. Her arms shake the bed, more plaster cakes off the wall, and I can hear the creak from the ancient bed frame as it struggles to maintain its structural integrity.

"Fuck! You!" she screams, full Essex emitting from her mouth in accordance with my full sex entering the other part of her. "Come now!" she shouts. "Come inside me, you right bastard!"

No demands made during sex sound as sexy as demands made in a rough, grimy British accent. And I can't deny the influence it has over me.

"All right. As the lady asks," I grunt out in the moment before I relax the muscles in my dick and allow a hot stream of passionate reward to gush inside her.

She moans and throws her head back, the long, blonde hair cascading down almost to the point where I am attached to her insides. She yells at the ceiling. Not in a cry of ecstasy, or a wail of pleasure, but in a roar. Anger is sewn into the fabric of her howl.

I reach up to her shoulders and rip her hold free from the bedposts. Drawing her arms back and handcuffing her at the waist, I force myself whatever remaining millimeters I can into her and mimic her screeching yawp. The manor echoes with our mingled voices bellowing in tortured joy. I imagine the sound escapes out into the vast acreage of the British countryside beyond these walls. I feel the devilish grin on my lips as I think of us scaring sheep.

Once I release her wrists, she throws herself forward on the bed, collapsing on the mattress with a plompf. The sudden exposure of my cock to the brisk air in our drafty haven makes me shiver all over. It's Spring, but in true British, vernal form, it's been raining every day, leaving us to explore the interior of our safehouse. And the interiors of each other.

I find myself hypnotized by the sight of Eliza now sprawled on the bed. Taut, lean muscles—all relaxed. This is the only occasion where I ever see her relax. The rest of the time, she is a helix of energy. A potential of action ready to erupt at a moment's notice, springing her into motion and sending her bounding into the world to fight or flee.

11

Her brothers are the same way. All wiry and anxious and alert. My devilish grin turns even more devilish when I think of her siblings and how, if they could see what I see now—my sticky come leaking from their sister's batty—they would lose their fokken minds.

It makes sense, them being the way they are. The childhoods they had. The lives they've led. In that regard, they remind me of Danny and Christine. It makes sense why they *all* are the way they are. In fact, the only one for whom the life he leads don't make sense—is me. But that's why I am who I am. I am the unique progeny of this universe, the lone creature on this planet who can live as I live and do as I do.

And whether or not that's true… I choose to believe it.

Eliza rolls over on the bed, props herself on her elbows, and looks at me.

"What're you thinking about?" she asks, her proper British accent having returned. It's the voice that allows her access to all the fancy galas, and high-end homes she gets into. The ones that, once inside, she and her brothers rob blind like they was in some goddamn Tom Cruise movie. Five scruffy kids from just off the M25 who learned early on that the best way to get something you want in this life is, as they might say, "to fuckin' nick it."

"Thinking that I might just buy this place," I tell her, looking around.

"Yeah?" she says, lifting her leg out to touch my cock with her toes. "Why's that?"

I shrug. "Seems like a nice place to have. Quiet. Remote. Secluded. A good spot to lie low and recuperate."

"I'd like to hope that you won't be having to recuperate quite so often that you'll need a place specially dedicated to it."

"I'd like to hope that too. But I also live in reality." Her digital fiddling with my softening cock is causing it to find its strength again. "Besides," I say, "given the amount of shit we're going to break while we're here, it's probably just as cost-effective to own it as it is to keep replacing the goddamn antiquities."

She laughs a tiny laugh, then her eyes narrow and she tilts her head.

"What?" I ask.

She lets out a small sigh and says, "Christine."

"What about her?"

"Last night. In your sleep. You said her name."

"Did I?"

She nods.

"OK. And?"

"How long do you think you'll stay here?"

"Here in this house?"

She shrugs. "The house. England. With me. Whatever. Don't you think, at some point, you'll need to go back to her?"

"Not sure. The last time I saw Christine, she didn't seem all that happy with me."

"Alec," she says, dropping her foot and sitting up straight, "that's entirely because of me. Are you sure you know what you're doing?"

"What I am doing," I say, stepping toward her, "is protecting everyone."

She takes on a skeptical, amused, smoldering smile. "Are you now?"

I nod. "I am."

13

"And how do you see yourself doing that?"

"As Graham Greene once said, 'You cannot conceive, nor can I, the appalling strangeness of the mercy of God.'"

She laughs, "So you're God now?"

I glance down at my re-inflated cock, come back to life as I have. Over, and over, and over. Thought dead and resurrected. Lazarus. Indestructible. Undeniable. Eternal. I smile at her in response and say, "No. I'm not God."

And as I crawl onto the edge of the bed, looming over top of her, and lower myself slowly to enter her properly, looking into her awe-struck face as my full girth slides into her still-throbbing opening, I add, "God works for me."

CHAPTER TWO

She's been reckless.

I've seen her like this before. It's a type of mania, I think. That all-powerful, no-one-can-touch me feeling of strength that comes with a plan. Or no. A purpose. A plan implies you know what you're doing. And hey, maybe she does. But I don't think so.

When she found me in the yacht that day she came back, I was ready to leave. Ready to just take my fuckin' medicine and accept my future. It was a bleak future. I realize that now that I've had a month to separate from the depression.

I had a purpose too. Kill Brasil. But I didn't have a plan either.

So I'm not gonna judge Christine. Hell, I haven't even asked her what the fuck we're actually doing. Why bother? We're on the other side of the world from the hellfire that's coming and we've morphed into ocean time.

I like that about yachts. The way they slow the world down and break it up into things like sunrises, and sunsets, and, _Hey, look at the dolphins!_ I bet a train is like a yacht. That rick-rack back-and-forth motion is nice too.

Next time we run away I think we should do it by train.

So I'm OK with the whole purpose-over-plan thing.

But like I said, she's been reckless.

We did a minor arms deal in Suva, Fiji and there was a... a hardness to her I don't think I've seen before. Course, I've missed her last four years and even though she hasn't talked about what happened during our separation yet, I get the feeling it was a whole lot more than just killing people.

Which is bad enough, I get that.

But that's just business—the way a small arms deal is just business—but this interaction we had with Nikhil for the guns in Suva felt very personal. We're definitely not gonna do any more deals with Nikhil again.

Which is unfortunate because I always liked Nikhil. He's not quite honest—who is in this business?—but he never ripped us off too bad and he wasn't being unreasonable this time either.

Christine didn't see it that way and by the time the deal was over one of his guys was dead.

Nope. Not gonna buy any more guns from Nikhil.

If it was just that I'd write it off. She *is* an assassin.

But it's more than how aggressive she got in Fiji. It's the way she stands on the deck in a storm, daring the lightning to strike her down. Or the way she studies the map, leaning over it at night under a soft beam of light jotting down notes while I cook us dinner. Notes that say shit like, *Stop here to see Jin, and pick up supplies from Matthew North.* And one that has a little circle around Hilo, Hawaii, that says, *Make phone call.*

We're not there yet so I'm not worried about it. We did see Jin. Stayed on land that night too. But whatever went down I had no part in it. Never saw the actual exchange, never had anything more than casual

16

conversation with Jin, and the next morning we were up with the sun and back on our way.

I didn't even see Matthew North. So whatever she was doing with him—well, it had nothing to do with me, I guess. But she came back with a black eye.

If I had known she was meeting up with Matthew I'd have gone with her. But I was sleeping when we arrived at Wallis Island and by the time I realized the catamaran was docked, she was gone.

The black eye was the only thing she came back with. There were no supplies—which we didn't need anyway. It felt like we were island-hopping like the old days instead of making our way to the West Coast of America. We had plenty of supplies. Hell, the actual ocean crossing hadn't even started yet. But there were no guns, either.

Which means she went to see Matthew on Wallis for information.

Information she didn't share with me.

I didn't ask. So it's not like she's keeping shit from me on purpose.

I just don't want to know.

I don't think I need to know.

Alec is alive. I know that much. And maybe that's all I need to know?

But as we approach Hilo this detachment I've settled into over the past few months begins to make me nervous. Not that something bad will happen—bad shit happens all the fucking time—but that her purpose, like her, is maybe a little bit too reckless and perhaps we need an actual plan.

So when she gives me the slip on Hilo to make her phone call I do the same.

She goes that way, I go this way and it takes me seven calls, actually, to find Russ. But on the pay phone outside a little bar called Alika's, which I kinda like the sound of, I finally get him

"Danny Fortnight," Russell says. It comes out sardonic, but I don't take it personally. Last time I saw Russell and his crew we'd just stolen a couple hundred thousand dollars from them.

"Hey, Russell. You're pretty fuckin' hard to find these days, aren't ya?"

"You know me," he says, his British accent clipped. "Always here, never anywhere. Whatcha need, mate?"

"How much have you heard?"

"Mmmm-hmmm," he drawls out. The world is kinda big, but our world is actually pretty small. "Yup."

"Which means… everything?" I laugh.

"I heard you three might be back together. Should I be worried?"

"Hmm," I say.

"What?"

"We're not quite back together yet. Which means you haven't heard. Fuck, man, I was really hoping you had some info for me."

"Info? Well, I can always scrounge something up if you really need it. But it'll cost you."

"I got money. But I don't got time. Russell, I'm sorta in the middle of something."

"Oh, yeah. I did hear about that."

"What?"

"Brasil, yeah? Oh, everyone knows about that."

"No, not Brasil. Not yet, anyway. And I don't need info on that shit."

"Then what?"

"Christine."

He laughs. And it's not sardonic, either. It's possibly a little bit sympathetic. "Nothing ever changes with you three."

"Nothing ever changes with anyone," I reply back.

"True. But…" He kinda laughs again. It's clipped and curt. "What about Christine could I know that you don't?"

"I'm missing the past four years."

"Oh, right. That."

"And she's keeping a secret. Something about Alec. You know anything about that?"

I can almost hear him think for a moment and then shrug. "Not any more than you do, probably."

"Seriously? I mean… Alec and Eliza—"

"No, mate. Sorry. Can't tell you anything."

"Can't? Or won't?"

"Does it matter? I'm not gonna give anything out about Eliza. So you can just tell Alec, 'Nice try.' But—"

"It's not Alec, it's me. Alec is… missing."

There's a long silence on the other end of the phone.

Eliza is his sister. They're a crew of five. Eliza, Russell, Theo, and the twins, Brenden and Charlie.

"Why don't you just ask Christine?"

"I already told you, she's keeping a secret."

"Yeah, well… sorry, Fortnight. Can't help you there."

I think about that for a moment.

"Anything else?" he asks.

"You haven't seen him, have you?"

"Alec? No. Been a couple years, actually." I'm silent again so he says, "What's going on, mate?"

"I don't know."

"I find that highly unlikely, Danny. It's your lot. You know more than nothing. Tell me and maybe I'll try a little harder to scrounge up whatever details you're missing."

"Is Eliza there?"

"Bru," he says, mimicking Alec in a way that hurts me. "Already said, not gonna say. But I'll tell you what. Give me a contact number and I'll look into Alec's, uh, whereabouts. With the understanding that if I find anything, the price for the information will be what you stole from us."

Two hundred and fifty grand. It's not a lot of money in the grand scheme of things. Not to him, not to me. And it's not like I didn't know he was gonna ask for it back when I made this call. But it feels kinda wrong for some reason. Like I'm betraying Alec and Christine by giving it back.

"Done," I say. Because I really have a bad feeling about this whole thing. What could possibly make Christine turn on Alec the way she did? What?

"Brilliant," Russell says. "Where can I reach ya?"

"Same way as always," I say.

"I've tried that a few times," he says. "Never worked out."

"It'll work next time, don't worry."

"Right then," he says. "I'll let you know."

"Right. I'm gonna be out of touch for the next week or so, but if you miss me, I'll call you back at this number when we reach port."

Russell *tsks* his tongue. "Fuckin' Triangle. Jesus. Never changes. Just get a bleedin' jet, mate."

"Later," I say, ending the call.

I don't know if I trust the guy. We did steal money from them. But they've stolen from us too. And yeah, to most people this is a big red flag. But stealing on our level is more of a gentleman's sport than a crime. I mean, everything we stole from each other was already stolen in the first place, so it's not personal.

"Danny?" I turn to find Christine looking at me, perplexed. "What are you doing?"

"Making dinner reservations. Remember that place we went to last time we were here?"

She crinkles her nose. Yup. She remembers.

"I didn't make them there."

She tries to hide a smile.

"I made them at the yacht club. It's been a while, ya know?"

She nods. "Yeah."

"So what do ya say? Wanna go on a date with me tonight?"

She tilts her head, eyeing me suspiciously. "What's gotten in to you?"

I shrug. "I dunno. Just… maybe things'll be OK."

She nods. Slowly. "They will, Danny."

"Good," I say, pulling her close to me. I slip my hands around her hips and lean in for a kiss. She kisses me back immediately. Whatever hesitation she was feeling a few moments ago is gone now. It's one of those kisses that are filled with longing and sadness. The kind where you can't quite make eye contact. Where there's a little bit of *Don't do this* but a little bit more of *Keep going*.

Funny, now that I think about it. Because back at my apartment that first day I was the one doing the *Don't do this, keep going* thing, not her.

I feel like that's just how it is when Alec's missing. So much push and pull. Too much hesitation. Just enough surrender.

Because we can't help it.

At least I can't help it.

21

"Come on," I say, taking her hand and leading her across the street to some boutiques. "Let's look the part tonight."

We shop separately. Her idea. She wants to surprise me.

And that's OK. Everything seems OK right now.

Not excellent. Not terrible. But OK. And ya know, sometimes OK is OK. You gotta take what you can get, when you can get it.

So that's what I do.

I didn't actually make reservations at the yacht club so I do that while I wait to be fitted for a suit. We're not members anymore, but we were once and it's enough to get a table.

Funny how it feels like those missing years never happened. How I didn't stop going out to dinner because she was missing from my life. How I didn't morph into someone else while she was away.

And maybe I should feel guilty about that. Taking her out in Alec's absence. But I don't. He had her to himself for four years. Four perfect years.

So I rationalize. I deserve one night.

The Holo Moana Yacht Club is small and private. One of the reasons we always liked to stop at this marina. They have a few private bungalows on the south side that they only let out to international members passing

22

through. White sandy beaches in front with tall, sideways-leaning palm trees and enough lush jungle around to make you forget the city is close by. That alone was was worth the yearly dues to Alec. He had places like this all over the world. It's like the whole planet was his home—and by extension, our home.

It occurs to me in this moment just how many memories we made those years we were together. More than a lifetime's worth. Several lifetimes, maybe.

For the first time in almost two weeks I let my guard down and think about him. Wonder what he's doing right now.

Is he still alive?

Christine thinks he is—and that's why we're heading back to the West Coast—but she's been cagy about what she knows and how she knows it.

I trust her. She's been right about impossible shit before.

But she's been wrong before too.

I shove my hands into the pockets of my new slacks and stare out at the water. No sunsets on this side of the island, but there's a reflection of light in the smattering of clouds that kinda tints the whole world orange and pink.

"What are you thinking about?"

I turn to find Christine walking down the dock. Smile on her face. Long, bronze limbs striking against her short white dress. Dark hair catching the reflected sunset, setting off red and gold highlights that only show up in moments like this.

Her body moves seductively and it reminds me that she's a killer. She prowls through life like a lioness. Stalking, and hunting, and completely at ease with her natural instincts.

I want to twirl her around, lead her back to the yacht, and fuck her brains out on the deck under the light of a half moon and a million stars.

We haven't done that yet. Not since Alec disappeared. We've been too focused on fixing things.

But it's gonna happen tonight.

"Alec," I say, replying to her question.

She pouts her lips — which drives me mad with lust — and sighs.

"I just…" I start to say. "I just hope he's OK."

She presses her lips together and nods. "He is. I know he is."

She says this all the time but I can't make out if it's wishful thinking, or actual knowledge, or a mantra she recites to keep going.

And I don't want to ask too many questions right now because I'm not ready for too many answers.

Tomorrow, I decide. When we leave tomorrow I'll be ready for answers. I just need this one night to draw a line. Some kind of clear boundary between then, and now, and what's yet to be.

"You look handsome tonight," she says, taking my hand in hers and swinging it a little. "We should get a picture."

"Yeah," I say, pulling out my phone. "We should."

"Hey!" she calls to a marina staff member. "Excuse me! Do you mind taking a picture?"

The teenager stops and looks at us. Then smiles, takes the phone and the picture.

But what she hands back is more than a phone and much more than a picture. It's documentation that *we* really happened. Something that can't be erased by bullets or forgotten by separation.

This picture might be the only one in existence of just Christine and me.

"We look damn good," Christine says.

"Yeah, we do," I mumble, studying the perfect couple we make.

Her, leggy and tan in her short loose dress.

Me, all broad shoulders and big biceps the perfectly-tailored, light gray jacket can't hide.

I look massive and strong next to her wraith-like frame. And she looks fragile.

How easy it is to believe this lie.

We always counted on that, of course. Our marks never saw Christine coming back then. Just a gum-cracking teenage girl. Sometimes she even had pigtails.

But there was always a gun tucked into the waistband of her jeans. Always.

"Oh, I love it," Christine whispers. "Send it to me."

I grin down at the screen, fingers tapping keys and buttons until that little whoosh sound happens. Her phone chimes the incoming photo and just like that, we're connected again.

Not that we've ever been untethered, because there is no way to break that link. But we've been apart and tonight feels like the night we're bonded again. This picture feels like the beginning of us.

Not we. Not three.

But just us.

The way it used to be.

And even though I miss Alec and there's nothing that will keep me from finding him, I like this. I like how Christine and I make the perfect pair.

Time does that, I decide. It really does change things.

"Ahh," Christine sighs. "I love it so much."

I lean in and kiss her neck, allowing myself to enjoy her scent and her softness. She's not often soft. Not anymore. So this is another sign that we've both gone back in time as we've moved forward over the past several months.

"Come on," I say, taking her hand. "Let's go inside."

She smiles the whole night. The entire night is nothing but grins, and easy laughs, and a comfortable settling in to the newness of the next step in our journey.

We order the prettiest sushi. Dozens of rolls wrapped in seaweed, and cucumber, and filled with rice, and avocado, and tuna, and salmon. Some of them are works of art, almost too pretty to eat.

We laugh, and drink a little, and talk about the trip. Not the destination, just the journey. We talk about sails, and wind, and storms, and waves. We reminisce about other ocean crossings over wine and dessert, which is a pink guava mousse encased in a tiny, dark-chocolate cup.

I feel like we're normal. Just two people in love.

And I don't think I've ever had that feeling before. I didn't think it'd ever be possible to feel normal.

Still, it's just an illusion. I know this. The whole thing is a dream and tomorrow, when the salty mist of the sea hits us and the sun bakes the deck until it's too hot to walk barefoot, we'll have to put on shoes. We'll have to put on sunglasses and hats. We'll have to get out practical things like Chapstick and a few days from now we'll be straining our eyes looking for land. Wishing for a real shower, and the stillness that comes from a bed not rocked by the motion of waves.

We'll be over it.

We'll be ready.

But we're not there yet.

We still have tonight

"Thank you," Christine says as we slowly walk the length of the dock back to the boat. "I needed this more than I realized."

"Which part?" I ask through a smile.

"All the parts. The new dress, the photo, the dinner, the drinks, the dessert..." She sighs. "I'd forgotten we used to live like this."

I parse that last statement as I help her onto the yacht, totally getting her point but wanting to know more at the same time.

"Lived like this... as in you and me? Or lived like this with Alec?"

She turns her back to me, the wind picking up her hair as she stares out at the ocean. "Both, I guess." She faces me again, soft smile on her serene face. "We're gonna get him back."

"I know," I lie. I don't even know if he's still alive. Not really. The answers she came back with when she left me back in the Cook Islands weren't definitive.

"But it's OK to enjoy tonight, ya know?"

Oh.

I mean, that was my plan, but I didn't know if she was thinking the same thing or if this was just a nice distraction.

She reaches for my tie, fingertips nimbly climbing the length of it until she gets to the knot and begins to loosen it away from my neck. She gazes up at me as she pulls it through my collar and drops it onto the nearby chair. She drags the jacket down my shoulders and drops that onto the chair as well.

It wasn't that long ago that I'd have stopped her. I'd have insisted that this wasn't what we are.

But it is what we are. This is who we are. A couple connected.

And I *am* gonna fuck her tonight.

It will take me two seconds to get her naked. Two more to sit her down on the overstuffed deck chair and spread her legs open. One second after that my tongue will lick her pussy and the whole thing will begin.

But I don't want to rush it.

She must not either because she pulls my white shirt out of my pants and begins to slowly unbutton it from the bottom, her eyes locked on mine as her fingers open me up and the warm wind blows across my bare chest.

She unbuttons the shirt cuffs next. My diamond cufflinks disappearing. Some secret pocket of hers, or maybe she drops them onto a cushion. Doesn't matter. They mean nothing to me. Diamonds have no value in our world. They are things we use, and steal, and trade for favors. And they don't belong here in this moment. Because time is the only thing with value right now. Time is the only thing we can't use, or steal, or trade. And I don't want to waste any of it thinking about diamonds.

I close my eyes when she drags her nails over my shoulders, pulling the shirt down my arms. She lets it hang there, billowing out behind me in the tropical breeze as she begins to kiss my chest. I picture her lips on my tattoos. And when I open my eyes again she's dragging her mouth across a red skull with black eyes.

"There's something dark about you, Danny," she says.

I nod. Because there is. There are lots of really dark things about me. Things she probably thinks she knows, but doesn't.

Her eyes dart up to meet mine. "But I don't need to know them to love you."

I thread my fingers into her hair, palming her head as I gently pull her up. We linger like that—lips not yet touching, but close enough to count. Close enough that even the slightest movement will connect us, mouth to mouth.

I don't have anything to say about what she needs to know. There is very little light inside me. Very little. She's poked me with that stick enough times to understand I'm not blue inside. She knows the truth even if I never explained it to her. But she's keeping her secrets so I'm keeping mine.

None of it matters anymore, anyway.

"So I hope you don't need to understand my dark side to love me," she finishes.

Ah. I get it.

The betrayal.

And it goes both ways, right? Alec somehow betrayed her and we all know how she betrayed him.

"I would never do that to you."

"No," I say. It comes out as agreement but that's not how I meant it. I meant it as, 'No?' Because she already did betray me. When she stayed behind with Alec after I left. Finding that out fucking hurt. Such jealousy. Such rage. So much darkness inside me in that moment.

I wanted to kill him.

I still feel the sting of that deception.

But I let it fade now just like I did back then. There's no time for regrets. Not tonight.

This will be the first time I'll ever have her alone. Truly alone. And I don't know how long I'll get to have her to myself.

Because Alec.

Because we'll either get Alec back and be us again... or we'll die trying.

CHAPTER THREE

Christine

I know what he's thinking about. That's why I'm trying my best to make him forget.

I need this. I need him. Just him, right now.

"We need each other," I whisper, lowering my face to his neck. He breathes in. Holds it. My lips flutter against his skin and he breathes out.

And I don't know why, but I like that. I sigh as I kiss him, enjoying his reaction as I softly drag my fingernails against the hard muscles of his waist. His shirt is billowing out behind him in the wind. Unfinished. Just like us. And I want it to stay like that forever. I want to capture this moment and hold it tight. Keep it to myself for as long as possible.

But, inevitably, the wind takes it past that point of no return and it slides the rest of the way down his arms and drops to the deck, leaving him bare from the waist up.

The sun has been gone for a while but the moon is out and it's bright and big, its hazy glow spilling out into the navy-blue night like the fog of a dream. Illuminating the hills and valleys of his chest and turning him into some supernatural thing. Some fantastical thing from a legend or a myth. A hero. My hero.

I lift my head up again and find his mouth, saying, "You have always been my hero," as we kiss.

And oh, God. It's a great kiss. Even though he chuckles about the hero thing.

"Please," he breathes back. Kissing me. Little ones. Just lips and no tongue. "I'm no hero."

But he is. And even though the kisses are perfect, he's not touching me. Not the way he should be. His fingers are pressing lightly against my head, threaded into my hair. But there's no desperation in his touch. We are not panting heavily. We are not in the agony of lust.

It's too calm. Too easy. Too perfect.

So I reach up and take his hands and place them on my hips.

He gets it, or does the next thing on instinct. Because they slip around to my back, encircling me and tugging me close. My breasts press against his chest and I melt.

Just melt into him.

We've been together for months now. Alone on this boat. And we have weeks of togetherness left.

I need those weeks to make up for the months.

The betrayal is still fresh. The lapse in loyalty still real.

And I need him to forget.

But even though he's not pushing me away, and that's a good sign, and I know with such certainty that we will be together tonight, he's not embracing it the way I need him to.

So I say, "Danny…" Because I need to tell him this. I need to explain everything. But the words leave me in that moment and the whole act is just another bit of unfinished business.

"Christine," he says, his voice low and throaty as he kisses me again. His mouth opens up and his tongue slides

up against mine. And I expect him to say something like…
I want to fuck you now. Or, *Everything will be OK.* Or, *Take off your clothes.*

Or maybe he'll just rip this little dress off my body, toss it overboard, and throw me down onto the overstuffed pillows of the deck couch and make me obey him.

But he says, "You need to lower your expectations."

And I don't know why, because this is not the way this night should be going and that should worry me, but I laugh.

"I'm serious," he says, his fingertips slipping under the strap of my dress and dragging it over my shoulder, leaving it like that. Unfinished, just like I left his shirt when I started the process of unburdening him. He looks down at me, his blue eyes catching the moonlight, making them sparkle in that supernatural way. Convincing me that he's wrong. That he is my hero. Even though he says, in the same moment, "I'm no hero. You know what comes out when you poke me. Blackness."

I stop breathing and study him. Shaking my head. Because it's not true. He's the bluest thing in the entire universe. But I don't want to waste time explaining why he's so perfect or how I know he'll save me—save everyone—when the time comes. So I reach down and grab his cock through his slacks and squeeze.

Which makes him close his eyes and smile.

And reach for the other strap of my dress.

And drag that one over my shoulder too.

Unfinished.

But it's enough to keep things going. Because the dress is loose. Just a simple shift that hides what's underneath with soft white silk. So when I pull my hand away from his hard cock, it falls. Right down to my hips, exposing the lacy, white, strapless bra that covers my breasts. And one more slight tug from him is all it takes to make the white silk slide over my hips and fall to the deck. It flutters for a second, catching the night breeze the way his shirt did, and then settles at my feet in a puddle of brightness against the dark.

He stops and looks at me.

And I wonder what he sees. A beautiful, young woman in matching white lingerie?

A friend? A lover?

His goddess who will save him—save everybody—when the time comes?

Or… does he just see me for who I am? The traitor.

I wait. Time stops, I swear it does. It gives him the gift of an eternal moment so he can make that decision.

Why is everything so slow? Why can't we just go fast?

But I know why. And there's nothing I can do about it.

We are in between things. In the middle of our story. And there's no way to rush the end that's coming.

We shouldn't even want to because there's a very high probability that none of us will be saved. That our enemies have another god waiting in the shadows. Some hero who will rip our world apart and tear everything to pieces.

And I'm just about to give up and turn away, accept this as an inevitable, forgone conclusion, when he reaches around and unfastens my bra.

It drops to the deck at my feet, joining the dress. I stare at it for a moment, holding my breath again. Because I was wrong.

And when I look up at him, he's smiling. Eyes still bright and blue. Still filled with the power to save us.

I realize in this moment that time, or the universe, or whoever runs this miserable fucking place, is giving me a second chance and I should not waste it.

So I don't.

I reach out, unbuckle his belt, unbutton and unzip his slacks, and slide my hand inside. Wrapping my palm around the thickness of his cock.

He growls a little and that makes the hazy dream world we've been stuck in for the last several minutes fade away. Brings reality back into focus.

And when he responds by palming my breasts, squeezing them with just a little more force than he should, the relief I feel is real.

He presses up against me so the length of our bodies are touching and now our kissing is what it should be.

Desperate, and heated, and filled with lust.

And our breathing is heavy, our excitement coming out in huffs as our tongues twist together. And he's backing me up. I almost trip over the discarded silk dress, but there's no chance of me falling. His massive arms hold me tight and carefully until my knees hit the back of the couch and I break our kiss so I can sit.

I gaze up at him, hoping he sees what I see.

My Danny. His Christine.

"Hi," he says, laughing a little.

"Hey," I say back, tugging the front of his pants down so I can pull his hard and ready cock out and hold it in my hands.

His fingertips are in my hair, then he fists it, tugging my head closer to him.

I open my mouth, eyes still tracking his, and take in the tip of his cock. Wrapping my lips around it, holding his gaze.

Then he gives in and sighs.

And so do I.

I take him further. Deeper into my mouth, all the way to the back of my throat, which makes him tug on my hair and I love that.

I love that he wants me. Wants more.

So I give it to him and begin bobbing my head in a back-and-forth rhythm. Taking him deep, then pulling back, letting my tongue slide along the underside of his shaft.

It's one of those messy blowjobs and I don't care. It's hot. So fucking hot. Saliva is pooling in my mouth until there's so much it begins to drip down my chin. And when Danny grips my hair again, tugging me backwards, he smiles at the mess.

This is a side of him I don't know, I realize. This erotic side wasn't part of who and what we were before. And for a moment I'm filled with jealousy that he's done this with other women.

But I'm stupid. I know I'm stupid. Because I've done this with other men. And he could be thinking the same thing right now, and he's not. I know he's not.

He's smiling at me. He's enjoying himself.

And then he's pushing me back into the couch cushions. A little too hard, but I giggle at that. Because I like it. I like the dark beast inside him. Because I know that beast is blue and no matter how much he wants to lose control, he won't.

Maybe I wish he would? Maybe I should push him harder? Make him?

But before I can finish that thought he's kneeling down with his hands under my knees, pushing them up towards my breasts, legs open as he lowers his head between them and brings me out of this introspection and places me squarely in the realm of unthinking ecstasy.

"Oh," I moan. Because the little flicks of his tongue against my clit are slightly overwhelming. "Oh, God," I say.

I can feel his smile too.

And that's it. Even if we stopped right now my night would be complete.

Because this has never happened before. We have never been this alone. Never this together, this excited—while not in the presence of Alec.

Is that bad? I wonder.

"Christine," he says, his words vibrating the soft folds of skin between my legs. "Stop thinking so motherfucking hard."

He pulls back, grinning wildly.

Which makes me grin too. "Sorry," I say.

But he just shakes his head. "Nothing to be sorry for, darlin'. You're too perfect, that's true. But I don't mind."

A laugh escapes. Because in no possible reality am I the perfect one in this couple.

He reaches down for his cock, fisting and pumping it a few times, then looks at me and frowns. "I'm gonna fuck you now," he says in a gruff, heated voice. "Because I can't wait another second. But I'm gonna fuck you again later and we'll do it right next time."

And with that he thrusts inside me. Filling me up. So deep it hurts, making me squeak out a little cry of pain.

But he doesn't stop or apologize or ask me if I'm OK.

He doesn't need to.

He knows.

He knows I love every moment of blissful agony when he's inside me

CHAPTER FOUR

Danny

I know what she's thinking.

Something along the lines of... *How did we get here? Who are we? And should we be doing this without Alec?*

Maybe also... how much of me has she missed out on?

The equal and opposite question can be asked of myself.

But I'm not gonna do it. I'm not gonna torture myself with regrets. I don't regret walking out. I don't regret letting her grow up into the woman she wanted to be before we got together.

This... right now... it's a gift of patience on my part.

And with that thought I let it all go and just fuck her.

I lean forward to kiss her mouth. Let her get a little taste of herself on my tongue. She sighs, and it's a lovely sigh. I cannot imagine a more perfect night.

She reaches up, placing her hands on my cheeks. Still kissing me. Still letting me pound her. And it's almost too much. It's almost too perfect.

But every one of those thoughts begins to drift away. Just silently drift away as the feeling of being deep inside her takes over. She's breathing hard now, little squeaks and moans spilling out of her mouth as I thrust inside her with such force, I push her backwards, squishing her head up against the pillow with my forward momentum.

She drops her hands to my shoulders, nails digging into the hard muscles of my flesh, and pants out, "Yes. Yes. *Yes*," each time. And I know she's close. And I know I said we'd do it again, softer next time.

But I'm not done with the hard fuck just yet.

I pull out and she whines, "Danny!"

But I just take her hand, pull her up, then twirl her around and push her forward. Hell, if we're gonna fuck hard, might as well... you know. Fuck. Hard.

Her hands reach out and stop her fall, pushing down on the top of the couch back. Her ass is up, and her back is arched, and even though there's just the glow of the moon for light and I'm desperate to be inside her again, I have to stop for a second. Stop and enjoy the view of her pussy as she wiggles her ass in anticipation.

I slide my fingers up and down her folds. Pushing inside just the tiniest bit. Which makes her groan with frustration.

"Stop teasing me."

I laugh.

"I'm serious. You don't want to piss me off."

"What will you do?" I ask, continuing my tease.

She looks over her shoulder, grinning at me. "Test me," she hisses. "Test me and find out."

"Maybe I will. Just to get your reaction."

"Danny!" she squeals.

I raise my hand up and drop it down quickly, slapping her ass.

"Ow!"

"Behave, Christine."

"Make me," she says, eyes sparkling with mischief.

I slap her ass again, wishing there was more light so I could watch her skin turn pink.

"You want this?" I ask, pushing two fingers inside her. She's so wet they slip right past her tight muscles. She clamps down on them in response and that almost sends me over the edge and I'm not even fucking her right now.

But I like the tease. I want to drive her wild with anticipation. I want to make her wait. I want to withhold her climax for as long as possible. I want to drag the ecstasy out of her, drip by drip.

"I want it," she says. "Please. Give it to me."

I want to. Badly. But not enough to give up this power I feel over her. She doesn't hand over power often. Never to me, in fact. And when we were together with Alec it was a give and take. Had to be or it wouldn't work.

But this is different in so many ways.

I crouch down, hands gripping her ass cheeks so hard there'll be bruises tomorrow, and push her forward until her breasts are pressed up against the back of the couch and her chin is resting on the top of the cushion.

"Yes," she says, as understanding floods through her. "Yes."

And even though I'd like to prove her wrong, do something else and keep her on edge, her pussy smells delicious and I can't stop myself. My tongue licks her. Pushes inside her, flicking back and forth, trying to get more than just a taste.

She gives in. Her shoulders drop, and her back goes supple, and her arms, though spread wide and appearing relaxed, aren't. I can tell because she's fisting the edge of the pillow. Gripping it with whatever strength she has left in this moment.

And that thought leads me to why I'm teasing her like this.

I like her powerless. Christine Keene is all power, all the time.

I like watching her give in to me.

"That's better," I say, sliding a third finger into her dripping wet pussy. "I like you like this."

She huffs out a few unintelligible words that are most likely a litany of fuck-yous.

I pull my fingers out, waiting for her protest, and when she stays silent I feel more satisfaction than I should.

And now it's time for a decision.

Do I want her to know me like this?

Do I want to be this guy with her?

Do I want to risk everything by showing her just how *not-blue* I am on the inside?

Probably a bad idea to make this choice when I'm so rock fucking hard I can barely see straight, but whatever.

And it's not really a choice anyway, is it?

We're here. Doing this. And there's no Alec to keep me in check.

I reach out and grab her hair, pulling it so hard she has to sit up and bend backwards. I stand up, pulling until her back is flat against my chest. She's panting now, probably surprised. Maybe a little off balance.

"Are you sure?" I growl into her ear. "Are you sure you want this?"

She breathes in and out three times. And what could've been thoughtful consideration or just a heat-of-the-moment *yes*, turns into hesitation.

I like that more than I want to admit.

I tug her hair again. Hard. So hard her head jerks to the side. "Answer me or I'll stop and walk away."

"Danny—"

"I don't want to walk away," I whisper, taking a moment to bite her earlobe. She squeaks out a cry of pain. "Believe me, I want nothing more than to stay right here and finish what we've started. But I will if you can't take it."

It's bait. I know that. And it's not fair. I know that too. But I don't care.

"Yes," she hisses, frustrated and... what? What else? Scared? No, Christine doesn't scare easily.

Angry.

I smile and let out the breath I was holding.

"Good girl," I say. Which makes her huff.

Oh, yeah, she's pissed off right now.

And that's all I needed.

I reach down and fist my cock. Squeezing it hard and pumping it a few strokes just to make the building excitement inside me build a little more.

Not that I need it. Because this is the real reason why I never wanted to fuck Christine when we were younger.

I am dark. I am dangerous. *I am Danny.*

And she's never known the real me. I've kept him hidden around her. All these years I've kept him in check.

Until now.

I let go of her hair and grip her hip, digging my fingers into the bone as my other hand positions my cock up to her so-wet pussy.

She moans, her anger temporarily tabled, and begins to breathe heavy again. Waiting. Waiting. Waiting for that moment when I...

Thrust deep inside her so hard she bends forward. I grab her hair again. Just in time to make her head yank back from the opposite force. She says, "Oh, shit!" But I don't stop. I push myself deep inside her, place the heel of my hand between her shoulder blades and shove her face into the pillow.

And then I fuck her for real.

I fuck her so hard there's no way everyone in this marina doesn't hear her moans, and groans, and screams.

And I don't care.

Not when I'm like this.

I just do not care.

We'll be leaving in a few hours anyway. And when they wake up in the morning and look around, trying to figure it all out, the only thing these strangers will know is that someone got the life fucked out of her last night.

They just won't know who.

I'm so fucking ready for this, my head goes blurry and my eyes go fuzzy. My dick is thrusting in and out of her so hard, so fast, the sound of slapping skin echoes off the water before being carried away into the night.

But I won't come before she does.

No way.

That's never part of my plan when I get a chance like this. I want her to remember all of it. The fear, the pain, the way my thick cock fills her up and stretches her wide.

But most of all I want her to remember how she felt when she came.

I want her to love it, want it, *crave it.*

So I reach around her belly, my fingers slick with her juices as they slide across her skin, and slip between her legs so I can play with her clit as I fuck her from behind.

She goes stiff. Her back goes straight and her head drops into the crook of my neck even though I'm no longer pulling her hair.

She gives in.

And this... this is the best fucking part.

Because she can't help herself. She might hate me right now, but she can't help herself.

She comes.

The muscles of her pussy spasm against the shaft of my cock and I almost lose it in that moment. Almost.

But I make a decision to hold it in.

I will give her this one gift. And whether or not she understands it, I don't care.

I do.

When she's spent she flops forward onto the pillows, breathing hard and sorta laughing. "Oh, my God. That was intense."

I smile. I nod.

She looks over her shoulder at me, grinning. But her grin fades when she sees the expression on my face. "What?"

I shake my head slowly. "Come on."

"Wait. What? Aren't you gonna—"

I pull out of her, taking her hand, and tug her upright. Her legs are quivering, so I pick her up in my arms and carry her downstairs.

"What's—"

"Shhh," I say, making my way through the skinny hallways toward the master bedroom.

"Oh," she says, thinking she gets it. Thinking I'm gonna finish on the bed.

But I ease my way past the bed and take her into the bathroom, flicking on the light as I pass by.

"What are we—"

"Shhh," I say again, setting her down inside the shower.

I turn on the water, and it's cold. Freezing cold.

"Holy—what the fuck!" she squeals when the ice water hits her overheated skin.

But I just push her backwards until her knees bump up against the bench on the far side of the shower. She sits as I crouch down, picking up her foot and untying the cotton ribbon of her sandal that winds around her ankle.

I slip the shoe off and do the same for the next foot.

She just stares at me, open-mouthed, as I finish.

I still have my pants on and I'm soaking wet. But I don't take them off. That's what normal people do and I'm not normal, I'm Danny.

I pull her back to her feet—her eyes are trained on her sopping wet sandals now—and then we change positions. I sit, tug her into my lap as I fist my cock again.

By this time the water is hot. Very hot. Her skin is already pink, and the stall is filling up with steam.

Her hair is damp, but not all the way wet. The kind of hair that sticks to skin, making dark lines along her cheek, and her upper arms, and her neck.

"Danny—"

But I have her legs spread, and my cock is hard and ready. So she doesn't finish. Just closes her eyes and sits down onto me. Lets me sink inside her.

She places her hands on my shoulders, not gripping tight anymore. No fight left. And just melts against my chest, her head on my shoulder, looking away from me, at the wall.

I grip her hips again, gently this time. And begin to rock her back and forth.

It takes her a while to get excited again. Which was the whole point of the cold shower.

But everything about this excites me.

And eventually, through no real decision of her own, she is moving herself and I'm no longer helping. She sits up a little, wrapping her fingers around my neck as she opens her eyes and stares down at me.

I shake my head, telling her not to say anything. And she sighs, but gives in. Because she begins to lift up and down on top of me. Forcing me out of her, almost completely out, before dropping herself back onto me.

Now it's time for me to close my eyes. I let her take over. I let her fuck me and she does it soft, nothing like the way I did her.

She kisses me. Breezy, gentle, probing-tongue kisses.

I lean back a little, so my ass is on the edge of the bench, and I'm just a little bit supine. Just enough so she can really dig in and fuck me a little harder.

"I like it hard," I say, opening my eyes just long enough to swipe a piece of sticky, almost-wet hair away from her cheek.

She nods. Maybe understanding. Maybe not.

But it doesn't matter.

She fucks me perfectly.

CHAPTER FIVE

In one of the great ironies of our lives, it was actually Christine who brought Eliza and her brothers into our world. Danny, Christine, and I were on a tour of the Tower of London during one of Christine's final winter breaks before we just gave up on school for her entirely, and upon exiting the building where they house the Crown Jewels, she started ruminating, not quietly, about how one might go about pilfering St. Edward's Crown. It wasn't a serious consideration (I don't think—one never can tell with Christine), but she wouldn't let it go.

She kept talking about it and talking about it. For hours she went on about how one might infiltrate the tower. How one might overpower the guards and make off with the jewels. How one would scale the walls. How one could get away clean. Danny and I just let her talk. Both amused, I think, by what animates her.

And later that evening, at a nightclub in Soho, Danny and I lost track of her. One minute we were all dancing together and the next, she was gone. I recall that the club was packed. We weren't *worried*, per se. There's never been a need to *worry* about Christine. But her being there one second and the next second gone was a jarring feeling that I don't think Danny nor I were expecting.

We searched through the throng of people for her and when we finally found her, she was outside, sitting on the curb, having a smoke with a gorgeous, leggy blonde who looked to be about two or three years Christine's senior. (Turns out she's four years older. Same age as me and Danny. Despite how different we all are from one another, on some deep, atomic level, Christine clearly has a "type.") Christine and the blonde, whose name we would learn was Eliza Watson, were continuing the conversation about the Crown Jewels. Apparently, Eliza was taking Christine's enthusiasm on the matter much more to heart than either Danny or I.

"That's not what would be hard," the blonde called Eliza was saying as she blew out a long stream of cigarette smoke. "What would be hard would be figuring out how to do it without anyone knowing it had been done." I remember her accent sounded posh. Very stick-in-the-ass upper crust. But there was something hard undercutting it. Something that belied the authenticity of its provenance.

"What do you mean?" Christine asked.

"I mean," she said, "you wouldn't want to pull off something like that only to be hunted for the rest of your bloody life. First things first, you'd need to have replicas made. And having forgeries like *those* made… well… that's quite a task indeed."

"What are you kids jabbering about? Hi, I'm Danny," Danny had said, extending his hand to Eliza. Danny was always the nervous one when it came to talking about our, um, lifestyle with people we didn't yet know. Or I thought it was nervousness. I came to realize it's just that Danny's far more naturally gifted at keeping his secrets secret than either me or Christine.

It is something that we would all come to be much, much better about over the years. Frequently, and unfortunately, to the detriment of the three of us.

Eliza shook Danny's hand, but never took her eyes off me. I pretended not to notice because I'd gotten very good in my life at pretending not to notice people staring at me. But the intensity of her glare is something that I could have felt even if she was on the other side of the room.

Inevitably, the question of, "So what kind of work do you do?" came up. I don't remember who asked it first. I just know it wasn't me. I'll admit that I tend to forget most people in the world have to "do" something. Typically, the unspoken conclusion to that question is, "for money." *What kind of work do you do... for money?* That's what's being asked. Whereas for me, Christine, and Danny the work we did was just for the thrill of the doing. Or it was for me at least.

Regardless, when it was asked by whoever did the asking, the energy on the sidewalk outside that nightclub in London shifted dramatically. Eventually, after some shuffling of feet and pretending to check watches, Eliza said, "Do you know what parkour is?" I did know. So, I said so. "My brothers and I... we have a... parkour business."

"Oh. Like a gym?" Christine had asked.

More shuffling of feet. More glancing at watches. More smoking of cigarettes.

Finally, employing one of my various superpowers—in this case, knowing how to read the fokken room—I took the cigarette from Eliza's lips, put it in my own mouth, took a drag, and handed it back, saying, "I buy, sell, and steal diamonds, sometimes legitimately, sometimes not. These two are my associates. We travel around the world, getting into whatever adventure the particular moment carries us toward, and occasionally we've been known to kill people. Though usually only fokken kakky naaiers who deserve it, so don't worry about them. My name is Alec van den Berg, and that's who the fok I am. So. Eliza Watson. Tell us a little about you."

I'll never forget the looks on Danny and Christine's faces. Makes me fokken laugh every time I remember. Saucer-eyed shock. Never saw it before, probably won't ever see it again. God, I love them so much.

After enduring the requisite 'how full of shit are you' queries that Eliza had in the wake of my admission (and quite a bit more dissembling than was likely necessary at that point) we finally got her to come clean about who she and her brothers are and what they do...

They were born in Purfleet, Essex. Their mother was a seamstress, their father was a drunk, and at this point it began to sound to me as though they were fokken Dickens characters come to life. Two older brothers. Two younger. Eliza, the girl in the middle. (At the time, I couldn't have predicted the symbolism that would eventually carry.) The two younger were born just fifteen months after Eliza and were an accident. An accident that was supposed to have only been one at worst, but lo and behold, Mrs. Watson popped out twins that no one was expecting. And that was the point at which the elder Mr. Watson up and left them all alone.

The two older Watson boys, one just about a teenager and the other only slightly younger, realizing they had to do something to bring in money to pay for young Eliza's dance classes and, you know, baby formula and that type of shit, turned to the aid of a Jamaican drug lord who took the lads in and gave them jobs as runners. After the oldest of the bunch, Russell, was very nearly caught by the police, the benevolent Jamaican drug lord introduced the boys to his cousin who had been a champion sprinter and was into an emerging athletic scene which would many years later come to be known as *parkour*, and which blended martial arts, tumbling, and free-running into acts of physical achievement virtually custom-built for committing acts of second-story crime...

Etcetera, etcetera, etcetera, and they lived happily ever after.

A regular goddamn *Tale of Two Cities*.

In any case, in the years that followed, the family was able to move to slightly more desirable environs and no one asked any questions. That is until curious little Eliza was about six and began inquiring after what her brothers did all day. Now that I have come to know Eliza as well as I have, it is no surprise that her intense inquisitiveness and unrelenting energy finally wore them down to the point that they told her. It is yet another way that Eliza and Christine have always reminded me so very much of one another.

And so, now, all these many years later, what the Watson clan has is something resembling a family business. The two younger Watson boys, Brenden and Charlie, they're the muscle. Rightly so. I never met the elder Mr. Watson, but if the other three Watson children are, in fact, his, then Brenden and Charlie are not. There's no way the same DNA that produced the three older Watson children produced the Herculean monsters that are Brenden and Charlie Watson.

Russell, the oldest, and his younger brother, Theo, are long and lithe, like Eliza, and are the ones who do impossible things like scale walls and bound across rooftops. And then, of course, there is Eliza. The actress. The seductress. The glue that binds them all together.

It is Eliza who keeps heads turned the other direction while the boys are doing whatever the boys are doing. It's not hard for her. Turning heads, that is. It would be hard for her not to.

Even so, I don't think I ever would have fallen into whatever it is I fell into with Eliza were it not for her brothers. Free will is free will and we all make our own choices in life, but it was the brothers Watson who decided that it would be a good idea to start playing a little game of "who can steal it better." And ek gee nie 'n fok nie who you think you are... no one on the earth can steal better than Alec van den Berg.

And that is why, as our little game wore on over the next couple of years—sometimes them capturing the flag, sometimes us—somehow Eliza got thrown into the mix of things that I had to prove I could steal from underneath everyone. And that was my entire motivation. My whole focus. I didn't think about how it might affect anything else.

Gaan kak in die kaap, man. I didn't think about how it might affect Christine.

And honestly, man, by the time we had stolen the quarter million pounds from them, and Danny had left, and Christine and I were on our own, and...

Shit. I don't feel regret. I truly do not. But if regret has an illegitimate stepchild, perhaps that is what I feel, standing here watching rain streak down the windows of my hidden castle. I've been here for a few weeks now. It's been raining the entire time. I wonder if that's an omen of some kind. Probably not. I'm probably just making connections where connections don't exist.

Eliza and I have had a deal: We will only be together when I'm in England. And then only if Christine is not with me. The thing about that, of course, is that it's not hard to find my way to England. And it's not hard to send Christine off on a mission or task of some kind somewhere halfway around the world. I could have picked a place to regather my strength anywhere on the planet, but I chose here. Along with not feeling regret, I do not second-guess myself. But...

With everything that...

And with what Christine just...

And with what I have...

Suddenly, a hand tracing the tattooed triangle on my back pulls me out of my contemplation.

"Hey," she says, kissing me on the shoulder. We just had sex. Again. That's all we've done since I arrived here however many weeks ago and called her to come join me. There is something desperate and frantic about our lovemaking. Always. It's simply because we're acutely aware that every time could be our last. That's true for all lovers anywhere in the world, but we are conscious of it. "What's in there, just now?" she asks, tapping me on the temple.

"Do you remember the night we met?" I ask.

"Of course. You tried to act like you didn't see me watching you."

"Did I?"

"Mmm-hmm."

"Was I successful?"

She shakes her head.

"Shame. I thought I had put one over on you."

She sniffs a laugh. Then, "What about that night were you thinking on?"

"You told Christine that the hardest part about stealing the Crown Jewels wouldn't be the actual stealing but figuring out how to do it without anyone knowing it had been done."

"That's right," she says, resting her head on my shoulder and staring out the window with me.

"Putting aside for a moment that I might disagree that that's the *hardest* part"—she laughs—"it's advice I should've heeded."

She lifts her head. "What do you mean?"

"I mean... when Danny, Christine and I stole my father's diamond—the one that got him and my mum killed—you know the one I mean..." She doesn't say anything. "It was impulsive. I was angry with my father. I mean, I was always angry with him, but... fok die kak. I don't know. The whole point was that I *wanted* him to panic. I *wanted* him to lose his shit. I just didn't know that those fokken Russian okes he owed the diamond to were gonna..." I trail off.

She turns me around to face her. She's also still naked.

"Hey. Look, I mean, I don't know what I don't know. I wasn't there. I didn't know you then, but... what's done is done, yeah? We can't none of us change the past. Can we?"

"Can't we?"

"No, Alec, we can't. So, I mean, you can dwell on this if you like—it's very sexy and broody and all that—but I need to tell you something that..." Now she trails off.

"Yeah? That what?" I ask. "What is it?"

"Well, that's more about the future, if you like."

She bows her head and looks down toward her toes. I tip her chin and point her eyes back at mine, saying as softly as I can, "Fok does that mean?"

I don't know why I say it that way. It's just what comes out. Because suddenly, I have this odd feeling in my chest. It's that feeling that comes in a crisis just before I breathe into myself and that Hulk fokker emerges.

But there is no crisis here.

There's no threat.

There's just me and Eliza.

Isn't there?

"It means," she says, taking a breath, "Alec... I'm pregnant."

CHAPTER SIX

Christine

I caught him with a girl once.

Danny, I mean.

We were staying in downtown Reykjavik for a few weeks waiting on new passports to come in from Copenhagen. We had this skinny, blue townhouse with a top-floor terrace, which was my favorite part.

I was... I dunno. Seventeen? Maybe? We'd just finished a job in the Southern Hemisphere and decided, hey, we've never been to Iceland, why not lie low there for a little bit?

So that's what we did.

Alec was gone, mostly. I don't even know if he was really in Iceland the whole time because he'd disappear for several days, then come back, then leave again.

But Danny was there.

This was during summer break from school and it was relatively warm and I was trying to practice some parkour moves that I'd seen these guys doing in England a few months earlier.

So I was clinging to the side of the severely-pitched roof when Danny came home that night with a woman.

It was about three in the morning. Though the sun was still hanging low on the horizon in what's called "the white night."

Which I sorta loved. Both the fact that the sun refused to set and the name for the phenomenon.

It was weird and I wasn't used to the light, so I had a hard time sleeping those few weeks we were in Reykjavik.

Anyway, Danny came home with this beautiful Icelandic girl. Just picture it in your head for a moment...

Right. That's what she looked like.

Pretty much the opposite of Christine from Dirty City, America.

So of course, I hated her immediately. Not even because she was so blonde, and blue-eyed, and beautiful— but mostly just because she had Danny's full attention.

They were kissing in the kitchen. The townhouse was four stories tall and I'd claimed the top floor as my bedroom, so I'm going to assume that Danny figured I was sleeping or far enough away that he didn't need to worry about me hearing them.

But I scaled my way down the side of the house, plopped silently onto the patio in the back garden, and peeked through the window to spy on them.

He had her pushed face first up against a wall. Her hands were pressed against it, arms and fingers spread wide, and he was fucking her from behind as he pulled her hair with such force, her neck was bending back in a weird way that momentarily made me forget that I was watching him fuck and made me worry that he was gonna kill her by accident.

Because, by this time in our little round-the-world adventure with Alec, he'd killed plenty of people.

As had I.

I'd had sex plenty of times too. That boy in New Zealand was my first back when I was fifteen but there were lots of them since. And they were all older than me by years. Like Danny's age.

I guess I have a type.

But they'd never fucked me like *this*.

And he had this look on his face like he *wanted* to kill her. And the window was open so even though they were trying to be quiet, I could hear him murmuring things as he pressed his face up against her ear.

Dirty things. Angry things.

And I kept thinking, *Why is he so angry?*

But he wasn't angry. I get that now that I'm older. He's just… that kind of lover.

I'm thinking about this now, lying here in bed in the cabin on the yacht, because I just had sex with him like that.

Sorta rough. And not at all like the sex we had with Alec months earlier.

I'm not complaining. I kinda like it rough. It's just… I'd forgotten about the night I caught him in Reykjavik. I'd forgotten that he had secrets.

All this time I figured I knew Danny. Knew everything there was to really know about Danny. Sure, we'd been apart for a few years and he's done all kinds of things I didn't know about—like the motorcycles and that Brasil asshole. But building motorcycles is just something he does and Brasil is just someone he knows.

So it had slipped my mind that there were private parts to Danny I'd never poked before. Deep parts inside him, maybe beyond the blue parts—maybe more like purple parts or red parts—that I had no clue about.

It unsettles me.

And it unsettles me more that I'm awake and he's not in bed beside me like he was when I fell asleep.

And that's the moment I realize we're moving. We're no longer docked at the marina in Hilo.

Catamarans are famous for their relatively smooth ride, so I'm not surprised that I didn't notice we were moving. But now that I'm awake and aware, I can hear that the low rumble of the engine is different than it was earlier.

After we'd finished fucking in the shower Danny put on a pair of cargo shorts and went to start the water maker. We wasted a lot of water for the shower sex. So I fell asleep to the rumble of the engine because that's how we run our water maker.

Still, it's yet another example of something catching me by surprise.

I should've noticed these things. So now I'm wondering… what else did I miss?

I swing my legs out of bed and get up. Search for something to wear, find one of those white sleeveless t-shirts Danny likes to wear in a pile of clean clothes on the nearest chair, and tug it over me.

Funny how it fits him so different than it fits me. My breasts fill out the top but the part below my breasts flutters all the way down past my hips. Then I fish out a fresh pair of panties from the pile as well.

Upstairs it's very quiet. Just the sound of the engine and that subtle creaking boats have.

When I get up top I can see the control station next to the kitchen, but he's not there. He'll be on the upper deck, sitting in the captain's chair. So I walk past the living area to the stairs and go up.

His back is to me, bare and browned from these past few months in the tropics. His hair blonder and longer than it was when we left the States.

This is the old him, I realize. The one I knew.

And yet it's not.

"Did I wake you?" he asks, without turning.

"No, not really. I just noticed the engine," I lie.

"Figured we should get a move on." He swivels the chair so he can side-eye me, his profile backlit against the glow of an approaching rising sun. "But it would be nice to know where we're going."

I huff out some air in a half laugh. "Only you would start a trip across the Pacific Ocean with no destination in mind."

"I figured LA. Am I wrong?"

"No," I say, stepping lightly across the teak floorboards toward him. He swivels the rest of the way toward me, arms opening as I approach. I accept his invitation and climb into his lap, acutely aware of just how sexy this man is.

We bump foreheads and he pulls my long hair out of the way so he can look up at me.

"Aren't you gonna ask more questions?" I say.

"Funny," he says. "I was just about to say the same thing to you."

Oh. Yeah. I bet he was. Well, why not? "So…"

"Yeah," he says.

"And…"

"Yup."

I laugh, I can't help it. "Mind-reader much?"

He shrugs. "Did you not like it?"

"I loved it," I say.

"Any more questions?"

"Not at the moment."

"Good. Now it's my turn. Where the fuck is Alec?"

I consider this, trying to decide how to answer that question. "We're gonna go to LA, then get on a plane and head to London."

"Oh," he says.

I nod. "Yeah."

We're both smiling now. Caught up in the shorthand two people have when they know each other so well, words almost aren't necessary.

Except... we don't really know each other, do we?

And even though there are a billion questions hanging in the air between us right now, and even though we've made up our own answers for all of them, we're never going to ask or answer those questions.

He places his hands on the top of my thighs, sliding them up and under my shirt until he's palming my breasts.

I close my eyes and think...

Maybe we'll get stuck on ocean time?

Maybe it's not so bad to be two?

He pinches my nipples. Hard. And I suck in a breath. I feel the heat stirring inside me. The throbbing that begins between my legs.

We both know how we're going to spend the next week.

It's going to be sex, and eating, and maybe some swimming if we want to drag this trip out a little longer.

But one thing we will not do is talk about the questions.

I don't know how I know this. Call it intuition. Or maybe I'm just picking up the obvious leftovers from the non-existent conversation we just had? Or maybe it's just wishful thinking on my part.

Who knows?

Who cares?

Because I'm right.

Because he lifts the t-shirt over my head and tosses it aside.

Because he lowers his lips to my breasts and begins to nibble.

Because he slips a finger between my legs, pulls my panties aside, and plays with my clit.

Who cares?

I have him, like this, all to myself, the good and the bad… and I'm gonna enjoy the fuck out of it for as long as I can.

I smile at his face, which has a blueish tint to it from the reflection of the GPS screen. I can almost see the maps in his eyes. All the places he can go. All the possibilities.

That's why he likes maps. He's always needed to be heading somewhere.

"Stop thinking," he says, still playing with me with one hand, while the other pops the button on his cargo shorts and drags down his zipper.

So I do.

Him. And me. Alone.

And it's not like I don't still want Alec, because I do. And I know he does too. But until last night I've never had Danny's full attention the way that Icelandic girl did back in Reykjavik.

He stands up, taking me with him, and I automatically wrap my legs around his middle as he carries me over to the teak table and sets me down. Pushes me backwards with fingertips pressing against my clavicles.

I grin at him as I lower myself.

He doesn't even wait to appreciate the grin. Just slips his hands under my knees, lifts my legs up and places his mouth on my pussy. His eyes are open, locked on mine until the flicking of his tongue feels too good to hold his gaze and I close them, shutting out the world.

He hits my sweet spot and I close my legs against the sides of his head on instinct. His beard is just a little too scratchy so it rubs against the inside of my upper thighs, but I don't care. I grab fistfuls of his too-long, too-blond hair, and push him deeper.

He responds by gripping the underside of my thighs. Pressing his thumbs into my flesh like he wants to leave marks.

I think he will.

There will be bruises tomorrow. But I don't care.

And just as I think that, he pushes me, my back sliding on the smooth teak. And when my eyelids flutter open, he has that look again. That gleam, or sparkle, or hint of red or purple lurking behind the blue of his eyes.

He's jacking off as I watch. And then he leans over, all the way over me, and kisses my mouth. But at the same time his free hand takes my hand and brings it up over my head until it bumps up against the railing that surrounds the u-shape of the seating area around the table.

"Grab on to that," he says.

I do.

"Both hands," he clarifies.

I reach my other arm up, grab the cold metal, and grip it tight.

"Now," he says in his new, not-blue voice. "Do not let go. No matter what."

CHAPTER SEVEN

She holds her breath. And even though I can't hear it, I know her heart speeds up. Her grip on the railing tightens and her back goes stiff.

She's wondering who I am and what I'm doing, and if I had an answer for that I might offer it up.

But I don't.

I have no idea who I am anymore.

I did. Not too long ago. I was Danny Fortnight, maker of custom motorcycles, partner to Brasil Lynch. Thief. Loner.

Then Christine came, and Alec came, and that Danny—he's just gone now. But I'm not old Danny either. I'm something new. Some sick combination of the two.

I pump my cock a few more times, getting ready. Christine's gaze wanders down to catch a glimpse. She's already so wet.

It's only been a few hours since we last fucked but it feels like we've been apart forever and we've got things to make up for.

Which isn't far from the truth, really.

"Don't let go," I remind her.

She swallows, licks her lips, and nods her head. Silent submission.

Which makes me grin. And with that grin, in that same moment, I thrust my cock inside her, sliding her along the table's surface with such force her head bumps into the railing.

She does not let go. She does just as I hoped. Stiffens her arms, pushing back on me so when I pull back and then thrust forward again, there's resistance.

Not that I could push any closer to that railing. Her head isn't even on the table anymore. It's suspended in mid-air over empty space. Just the very bottom of her shoulder blades and the force of her arms, now bent at the elbows, keep her from being pounded over the edge and disappearing into the depths of darkness. So she has no choice but to resist.

I do it again, and again. Fucking her faster, harder with each forward push.

She grits her teeth, watching me. Nothing relaxing or soothing about it.

In fact she's so crumpled up against the railing that I have to kneel on the table, hike her hips up, and prop the underside of her thighs over the top of mine, just so I can keep fucking her.

It's a messy, messy fuck.

Nothing artistic about the picture we paint. Nothing slow, or sensual.

It's just… erotic and hard.

And she's probably thinking, *What the fuck, Fortnight? What am I? One of your little sluts you pick up in random cities?*

But if she is, she doesn't say it. And I don't stop.

She's not one of those whores.

This is just how I like to fuck when Alec's not around.

I reach forward, grab her hair with both hands, pull her upward, then place one hand across the middle of her back with fingers splayed wide and hold her there.

We breathe hard and heavy as I continue to fuck her. Her chin is tilted up, her eyes locked on mine, her jaw tight as sweat rolls down her face, and my chest, and her wet, wet, so fucking wet pussy swallows my cock and then... there's this moment when we stop.

We don't really stop. I'm fucking her harder than ever and she's gripping my shoulders with the tips of her fingernails like she's clinging to the edge of a cliff. She's hissing air through clenched teeth. Her hair is damp again, but not from the shower. It clings to the sides of her face from the hot, stuffy, humid tropical air that simmers above this salty ocean and wraps around us like a mist as the sun rises above the horizon and heats us up with the coming of a new day, and—

—we both explode.

I take her like that two, sometimes three times a day. Or night. And then in between, there's the soft fucks. The ones in the shower where the heat comes from hot water and not the hell brewing inside me.

I'm out of control. I know this. I'm a fucking fiend for her body. I don't even let her put clothes on anymore. I make her walk around naked. I'm hard all the time.

We don't talk much.

I'm not sure I have anything to say.

And she doesn't ask any questions.

Oh, every time I come at her she gives me this look like... *Again?*

But then one touch, one twist of her nipple or one pull of her hair and she forgets that she wasn't in the mood because she is suddenly in the mood.

And I don't know if it's lust, or the heat, or why the fuck she gives in like this. The only thing I know it's not is fear.

She likes it.

I think that's why we don't talk.

And I don't care anyway.

All I know is that the depression lifted back in the Cook Islands and I've got her to myself for a few more hours. Just a few more hours and then we'll be docking at the beach club in LA and heading to the airport, where we'll get on a jet to London, and then this whole thing will be over.

We might never talk about it again.

Or maybe we will?

Maybe she'll tell Alec all about it when we get him back and he'll say something like... *Fok, Fortnight. I need to see this side to you.*

And then we'll all become the same kind of freak I am. We'll all go dark, and get dirty, become purple instead of blue and do things that we'll never talk about.

I kinda hope it goes that way.

But it won't.

I know it won't.

It's late afternoon when we get to our boat slip at the very tip of the dock in the west channel of the LA Harbor. We're not members of this club anymore either, but that's not enough to prevent us from handing over a fat wire transfer to keep the yacht safe until such a time as we decide to come back for it.

Maybe we'll never come back for it?

These people don't care. They got their money and as long as that wire transfer comes in every month, they'll shut the fuck up and do what I tell them.

They even give us a complimentary room at the hotel next door so we can freshen up and wait for their concierge to arrange a private jet to London.

"We can just take a commercial flight," Christine says, once we're in the room. It's weird being on land again after so many weeks on the sea.

"Fuck that," I say. "I've been frugal for years. Time to spend that shit."

She's brushing her hair, looking at me via her reflection in the bathroom mirror.

"What?" I ask.

"You," she says.

"So?"

She shrugs. We're doing that shorthand thing again.

What she's really saying is, *Who the fuck are you, Danny Fortnight?*

And what I'm really saying is, *I was always this guy, Christine. I just hid it really well. And that's why I never wanted to touch you when we were younger. But fuck it. We're not kids anymore, and you said you wanted this, so here you go. You got it. This is me.*

She stops brushing her hair and turns around. Waits there, on pause, for a few moments. Then she walks over

71

to me—stalks me like a fucking lioness looking to take down a baby gazelle on some barren, too-hot savannah—and when she reaches me, she slips her hands around to the back of my neck, resting her forearms on my shoulders, and says, "I love you."

Which means… *I get you.*

So I say, "I get you too."

A limo takes us to the jet. I'm still wearing cargo shorts and a sleeveless white t-shirt even though it's gonna be cold as fuck when we get to London. I'll change before we disembark. I'm just not ready to let go of what we had just yet.

I cling to it. The way you cling to a moment after waking up from a perfect dream.

Maybe Alec's dead.

Maybe I'll die, or Christine will die.

Hell, maybe we're all dead right now and we just haven't figured it out yet.

So I wear cargo shorts and a t-shirt until we're circling around London and there's no way out.

We must go forward and meet our fate.

CHAPTER EIGHT

"I'm pregnant."

Fokken perfect. Just fokken perfect, man. That's exactly what I fokken need right now. I know precisely how to deal with Death. But *new life?* Eish, man. And that this is happening now, just when Christine…

"Where are you going?" Eliza asks.

"Out," I tell her, shrugging on my jacket. The rain has finally stopped.

She smirks at me in a way that I have seen her smirk before. It's a manner that suggests she thinks she knows me better than I know myself. "How novel and very non-communicatively masculine of you," she says, with a not insignificant amount of condescension.

I spin to face her. "Is there something you need from me that I'm not giving you right now?"

"My God. Alec van den Berg. If someone walked in on us and didn't know better, they might think we're in a… oh, shit, what's the word? Ah, that's right… a relationship."

"What do you want?" I yell. Which I do not mean to do. She doesn't cower or retreat. Her smile just widens. She walks toward me, slowly, as she speaks.

73

"You were the one who summoned me here. Do you remember that? You called me here to tend to you while you healed. And hid."

"I'm not fokken hiding."

"You're not? Oh. Well, you see, I assumed that once your wounds closed and your ribs mended themselves and all that, you'd be back off into the world. But you're not. You're still here with me. Which, you'll pardon my confusion, feels like hiding."

She's almost to where I'm standing now. I wonder if she thinks I'm going to cower or retreat, myself. She can't possibly. She knows me too well. But lest there be any confusion, I step in toward *her* now, closing off almost all the space between us.

"You don't think it's probably just," I begin, "that I'm still here because I like being able to fuck someone in the ass whenever I feel like it? Without having to give a shit about what they want? Because that's what this is for me. And when seen through that prism, I'd be a daft fokker to leave until I grow bored. And I ain't. Fokken. Bored. Yet."

I stare down into her eyes, unblinking. She returns my stare, equally unflinching. This is the point where most others might turn and run, or slap my face, or scream at me, or any other of a dozen clichéd responses, but she is not most others.

So I grab her by the cheeks with one hand and force my lips onto hers. She doesn't resist, just kisses me back, grabbing my balls as she does. With my other hand, I reach around and find her ass. She's now wearing a light Spring dress and as my hand gathers the fabric into a bundle, I discover that she's not wearing underwear. My palm curves in between her legs and my middle finger slips inside her. She gasps, grabs my crotch tighter, and bites my lip.

Spinning her around, I lift her dress, slap her ass—hard—and throw her forward where she collapses at the waist over the Roman arm of the seventeenth-century tufted sofa. And it is at that moment that I stop. Stop everything. Stop moving toward her, stop feeling, stop breathing, stop everything.

Seeing her belly hit the grand, puffy arm of the chaise, I can't prevent my mind from landing on this new knowledge I have been given. There is a child growing inside her.

"How do you fokken know it's mine?"

"Well, luv, I'm no midwife, but you're the only person who's come inside me in the last six months."

"How long have you known?"

"Does it matter?"

"Why didn't you tell me right away?"

"Is that a real question?"

She's right, of course. I know why.

God fokken damn everyone and everything straight to Hell.

But, shit. Maybe God already has. And we're all already there.

She looks back at me over her shoulder. "What's happened? Why did you stop? You didn't suddenly find yourself *bored*, did you, pet?" She stands up, flattening her dress down. She faces me. "You know, Alec, it's not as if I expected you to pop a bottle of champagne and hand out cigars to all your mates…" She pauses. "Come to think of it, you don't really have any mates to hand cigars to, do you?" She sighs. Her shoulders rise and fall. "But I thought you might at least show something resembling, oh, I don't know, civility."

"How am I not being civil?"

"I don't know how they do things in Joburg, luv, but in Kensington, we don't imply that the mothers of our children are just there to be fucked in the arse until we tire of fucking them."

"Yeah, well, you ain't from Kensington, are you now?"

"It may not be where I'm from, babe. But it's where I'm at. And I got there by learning to do for myself. Not because I was fucking born into it with a silver bleeding spoon in my mouth. So maybe you'd rather save the 'crazy Alec doesn't care about anything' routine for someone who doesn't know all your bullshit quite so well."

I don't know what's happening. I don't know why she's pushing my buttons. I don't know why I'm still standing here, letting her. I should be gone. Off finding Christine and tending to her. Making up for… everything. And Danny. Fok, man. I miss Danny. It's moments like this, when I find myself alone with a woman, that I miss Danny the most.

I have all the fokken money a person could want. All the power in the goddamn universe, man, and yet here I find myself. Feeling completely untethered and adrift about what to do next. So I ask a modified version of a previously asked question. "What is it that you want from me?"

She steps back. Away. And sits on the puffy, Roman arm. "Why don't you ask what you actually want to know?"

"I thought I was."

"What you actually want to know is… do I expect anything from you? Money. Time. Attention. For you to be a bloody father to this kid."

"Yeah, all right. So. Do you?" She cocks her head to the left and then the right. Says nothing. "Because I can't," I say.

"I know."

"Do you?" I ask. She nods. "Do you know *why*?" She nods again. "Tell me."

"Alec—"

"Fokken tell me!"

She draws in a long breath, tilts her head back, closes her eyes. She relaxes her neck and shoulders again, lowers her head, opens her eyes to look at me, and says, "Because… I don't fit."

"Fit? Fok does that mean? Don't fit?"

"Into the geometry of your life, my sweet."

She stands and rounds the sofa to sit on it properly. She tosses aside a throw pillow and plops down onto the plush cushions of the settee. I wince as she does it. It's goddamn insane, man, but now that I know she's carrying a baby, everything she does physically causes me to feel a pang of anxiety. Because little babies growing inside their mother's tummies are fragile things. I don't know that I ever considered it much. Before. I've never been much of one to think about when life begins or what's right and what's wrong or any of that kak.

To my mind, we're all just a bunch of cells and blood vessels and bones and that. In that regard, I don't think anyone is anymore special that anyone else or that anyone has a right to life or a right to death any more than anyone else. We all begin and we all end. That's the only thing that's certain. How long one cheats the inevitability of their end is what makes someone who they are. Or, at least, that's how I see it.

Probably why it shocked me so, back when my mother and father were killed. My father always struck me as the type of oke who would live forever.

But my point is, I ain't precious about life. I haven't taken as many lives as some, but I've taken enough to have become inured to the idea that it matters all that much. But this... this is a baby inside a person I've also been inside of and that baby is partially mine. And that... that is a different matter altogether.

"What do you mean 'the geometry of my life?' Fok are you talking about, man?"

She doesn't look at me. She just stares ahead at the giant tapestry hanging on the wall in front of her. As if she's studying it. It's a battle of some kind. Some long-dead British king leading troops to their slaughter, it looks like. Has always seemed to me that the English are strangely keen to document battles they have lost.

"That piece on your back..."

"What piece?"

"The tattoo."

"What about it?"

"It only has three sides."

"Yeah. It's a fokken triangle. That's what a fokken triangle is."

She turns her head to me. "But that's not all it is. It's you. It's Danny. It's Christine. There's no room for anyone else. That's what I mean, my dear."

I stare at her. My chest heaves. I feel hot suddenly. "So what are you saying? You want me to add a fokken line to it? Change the dimensions somehow?"

"No," she says, slowly, as if she's debating it with herself but still stands by the answer. "No... that's not what I'm saying at all. Honestly, I don't think I'd actually like it much if I was drawn into your pattern. Fuckin' hell, mate, I know my brothers would lose their blinking Chinese blinds." She means 'minds.' And although the natural dialect that slips out is authentic, the Cockney rhyming slang is just as much affected as the posh, Queen's English that she uses the rest of the time.

I sometimes think that she's been playing a character for so long, she occasionally has to fumble around trying to find the real her.

I find it challenging that I am compelled to ask the question a third time: "So, then, what is it? That you want?"

She shrugs. It makes her look impish and younger than she is. "I dunno, luv. I suppose, what with us being here for as long as we seem to be stashed away, you should just be aware. In the event that I, you know, start to give birth or anything."

"Stop being so goddamn clever!" I bellow.

She breathes out. Closes her eyes. "I'm sorry. Truly, I am. I'm just taking the piss." She stands and walks to me again. Carefully this time. "Look, Alec, I just thought you should know. I don't expect anything from you. All right? I really don't. I don't even plan to tell the boys it's yours."

"Your brothers?"

She nods. "They'll want to kill you. But then you'll likely wind up killing them because you have endless resources and a private army and all that tosh"—she rolls her eyes—"and that would be terribly sad for everyone. So, I figure, best to just avoid the whole thing altogether."

I can feel my brow furrow as I stare at her. "So you're definitely going to have it?"

"I am. I've decided. And truth be told… that's why I'm only just telling you now."

"There was a point where you were considering not having it?"

She nods. "But then I thought"—she reaches up and strokes my cheek—"God forbid you should ever find out that happened. God forbid. Because who knows what daft fucking thing you might go and do then? Fragile as you are."

I grab her wrist and pull her hand from my face. "Don't you suggest that this is some grand act of generosity on your part."

"All right. Fine, Alec. I won't. Maybe… maybe it's just that I *want* to have a baby." She bows her head slightly and casts her eyes upward, looking at me intensely. "And maybe the real reason I debated saying anything is because I would never, in a million bloody years, luv, want that baby to be raised by you."

I can feel myself expanding. I can feel time slowing and the air getting thick. I can feel my fists balling. And so, before I can feel anything else…

I wrap my coat around me, turn on my heels, and walk out the door.

CHAPTER NINE

Christine

We stopped at the shops on Oxford Street to get some warmer clothes. Which seems indulgent both because of Alec's situation and because we spent a little over eight thousand dollars on just a couple of outfits. But Alec has been in his present situation for months and money hasn't mattered to me in a very long time.

So I just go with it.

We separate, as is our custom it seems, and meet up two hours later dressed like assassins.

I cover my mouth with my hand to hide my laugh.

"What?" Danny says, sliding his dark sunglasses down his nose so he can peer at me with those beautiful eyes of his.

"Why do we bother shopping separately," I ask, "when we turn up looking like twins?" I don't slide my dark sunglasses down my nose to allow him a look at my beautiful eyes.

He checks me out. I'm in all black. Black leather jacket—kind of a thin one so I can fight, and move quick, and draw guns in it. Underneath, which he can't see, is a black t-shirt. Just a simple one. And I have on dark jeans and a new pair of black sneakers that are quite literally the best shoe for what we're probably gonna need to do.

Danny has the same outfit, men's version. Little bit heavier black leather jacket. But he didn't get one with lots of zippers or metal studs like he usually does, and I can only assume that this is the stealth version of Danny's leather jacket. He's also got on dark jeans, but unlike me he opted for a pair of black work boots. Probably steel-toed. Danny was always partial to kicking people in the teeth.

He reaches over, pinches my cheek, and says, "You're cute. Now what, genius? You gonna let me in on your little plan?"

Here's the problem with my plan.

I don't actually have one. Not a solid one, anyway. I have ideas. Ideas about where Alec is, why he's there, and how we can get him out with the least amount of fuss.

But I don't want Danny to know how precarious this half-plan is just yet. Not until we get there, at least. Because it's gonna be touchy. Alec's with people and possibly involved in things I can't quite wrap my head around yet.

All I know is that something big is happening. Big with a capital B at the front.

So I say, "It's not far. About an hour outside London."

He opens his mouth to say something. Probably something like... *What's the address?* Or, *Who's he with?* Or, *Does he know we're coming?*

But he changes his mind. And because I know him— or at least I thought I did at one time—I deduce that he's decided not to give a fuck about these details.

We just motored a boat halfway around the world, jetted another five thousand miles to London, so what is the point of knowing or not knowing anything when we are so obviously committed?

Besides. I am Christine, and he is Danny, and together we can do just about anything we set our minds to.

But then he surprises me by asking, "Do we need guns?"

And I surprise myself by answering, "Not yet." But it's a lie. Because I don't actually believe that. I'm taking a chance with this plan. I'm hoping that the ties that bind are still strong and still matter, but I can't know that for sure until we get there.

He sends a text to the driver and we wait at the curb in front of Debenhams until the car pulls alongside and we get in, me handing the driver a piece of paper with the address on it.

Danny eyes that piece of paper, then eyes me, but he doesn't reach for it.

Is this behavior disturbing? Or comforting?

I go with comforting. Because it says he trusts me. And trust is the only thing that matters right now.

It takes forever to get outside London traffic, so then it's another hour to get to the actual place we're going. Danny's restless and silent the whole time. Sometimes playing on his phone, sometimes looking out the window. Sometimes rummaging through the backpack he brought with him from the yacht, which doesn't contain anything useful, per se. Like there's no gun in there. There's no knife in there. But he's got snacks. And at one point he offers me a water, which I take, and a pack of unsalted cashews he took from the jet, which I decline.

I am starving but too nervous to eat, not knowing who and what is waiting for me on the other side of this long, boring ride out into the countryside.

But it is quite picturesque. Quintessential English in all directions.

And then, before I'm ready, we're pulling up to the gate of the house, which is open. Almost welcoming. Which is a lie. But we pull through and continue down the driveway until all my time is up and we have to get out.

Which we do. Danny zips up his jacket, but I leave mine open because I'm suddenly hot and sweaty, even in the biting Surrey wind.

I wipe the palms of my hands on my jeans and walk toward the front door like I know what I'm doing. And when I get there, I stop, look over my shoulder to find Danny at my back, gather up all my courage, and knock.

CHAPTER TEN

"No," I say, returning from outside.

"No what?" Eliza asks. I find her in the kitchen, which has clearly been renovated and made suitable for the twenty-first century. Or else the First Duke of Whatever the Fok who once lived here was very ahead of his time. She's making a cup of tea, using the electric kettle. How very goddamn British of her.

"What you said. About the baby. No."

She places down her mug and squares off to me. "Which part? Can you be specific? I'd like to know exactly which thing you think you're giving me an ultimatum on, so that when I tell you to go fuck yourself, I can be precise."

"You said that there's no way you'll let me raise it. No. If it's my child, I will, by God, raise that kid in whatever way I see fit."

She places her hands on the massive farmhouse table in front of her and leans forward. "Will you now?"

"You'd certainly better believe I fokken will."

"Hm," she says, turning to pour the water from the kettle over the tea leaves in her mug. The steam rises as she pours, like some kind of genie in ethereal form, come to spy on our conversation. She turns back, pulls out a chair from the table, and sits with her hands around the sides of the mug. It's still drafty. While I was out, the rain started again. She's put on an oversized sweater. The sleeves are too long for her arms and they cover her hands and almost all of her fingers. She looks like an urchin from *Oliver Twist*. Yet another case in which her Dickensian upbringing peers out from behind her crafted façade.

"Hm? Fok does that mean? Hm?"

"Nothing. Where did you go?

"When?"

"Just now."

"Around. Down the lane. Why?"

"Did something happen?"

"What do you mean? Like what?"

"I don't know. Like Saul becoming Paul on the road to Damascus."

"Fok are those cunts?"

"Charming." She blows on her tea and takes a sip. "I guess what I'm saying is that I'm surprised you feel so strongly about wanting the responsibility of caring for a child."

"Why?"

"Because, my precious, you're the most selfish person I've ever known."

Sometimes I have to stop when Eliza talks to me like that. No one talks to me the way she does. Not even Christine or Danny ever talked to me the way Eliza does. But, for some reason, when she does it, it doesn't really bother me. I do not welcome it, and if she didn't, I'd be just as happy. But I don't have a problem allowing it.

She's never done it in front of anyone else. Nor would she, I don't imagine. She knows that if she did, I'd have no choice to take action. Action that no one would be pleased about. And so, for some reason, we've fallen into a pattern where she gets to do it in private and I allow it. I think it's the tacit agreement we have that lets her continue to know she's special in my world.

I take off my newly rained-upon jacket and place it on the back of the chair across from her that I sit down in. "I'm going to tell you what will happen next."

"Are you now?"

"Tomorrow, we're going to leave this place and we're going to Nara."

"Are we then?" She takes another sip of her tea. I choose to ignore her annoying and rhetorical questions and I don't say anything. After a moment, she asks, "Why Nara?"

"I have a house and no active concerns there at the moment. It's safe and I can have medical staff on site."

"Nara's the place where they have the park with all the deer, yes?"

"Once we're there—"

"Don't like deer."

"Once we're there—"

"Knew a lad once called Trevor. Got bit by a deer tick and developed Lyme disease. Nasty business that. Don't you have an apartment in Tokyo or someplace a little more cosmopolitan?"

"Will you fokken stop taking the piss?" I slam the table so ferociously that it jolts the mug sitting way across the other side. She sits back. Looks at me. Nods. I go on. "Once the baby comes, we'll make decisions about what happens then. But, for now, this is what we're doing. How pregnant are you?"

"Quite."

"You know what I fokken mean."

87

"About eleven weeks, I suppose."

I start working the math out in my head. "We've only been here…"

"It didn't happen on this jaunt, darling. I imagine it happened on that stopover between the States and Joburg that you took a few months back. Almost three months back, to be precise."

I pause to think about that. I barely even remember it. It wasn't official business. I was just getting away. Things with Christine were… complicated, and on my way back to South Africa, I had my pilot land at Heathrow. I called Eliza from the plane and told her to meet me at the airport hotel.

Savagely romantic.

"Yeah, all right," I say. "Well, this is what's happening now. So…" I stand, pull my cell phone from my jacket pocket.

"Who are you calling?"

"Whoever I need to. We can arrange for your shit to be sent, after." As I'm pressing 'send,' she steps around the table, pulls the phone from my hand, and ends the call before it can commence. "Oi, give me my phone," I say, reaching.

She places it down on the table and puts her arms around my waist. She kisses me lightly on the lips and looks into my eyes.

"Alec?"

"Yeah?"

"Do you love me?"

I squint. Not only was I not expecting the question, I don't have a ready answer. She's never asked me before. It's never come up. If I'm honest, I don't know if I've ever even considered it.

"What?" I say in response.

"Do you love me? Simple question. You love Christine. I know you do. You love her desperately and with your whole heart. I'm pretty sure you feel that way about Danny too. I know they love you." She starts tracing the back of my shirt with her fingernails. Roughly in the area where my tattoo lives. "They love you so much, they'd do absolutely anything in the world for you. They'd go wherever you ask them, do whatever you ask. Kill who you tell them to kill... Anything. And even though you'd never admit it, you'd do the same for them. So," she says, stepping back from me now and taking my hands in hers, "all I want to know is: Do you feel that way about me? Would you do anything for me? Go to any lengths? Kill for me?"

"Of course I would."

"OK, well, that's not really fair. You're a sociopath. I think you just like killing people. You don't need an excuse. But the bigger question remains... do you love me?"

"I... I feel like..."

"I didn't think so." She smiles. I would call it a sad smile, but it's not. It's just... accepting. "Which is fine. Because, honestly, Alec... I don't love you. I don't. And I know you don't care. Which is perfect. Because if you did, you wouldn't be you and this wouldn't work. But, dear heart, I'm not sure that I see us raising a child together and living happily ever after. Happily ever afters are for romantics and simpletons. And we are neither of those things. Are we?"

"I'm not trying to be something I'm not or suggest that I'm interested in living a fiction. I'm just—"

89

"You're just feeling guilty. But—and please consider seriously what I'm saying—you're feeling guilty about a whole raft of things that have nothing to do with me. And since you've gone and gotten your life right cocked up and aren't sure you can fix it this time… you're trying to fix it with me. And Alec, my angel"—she takes a deep breath—"I don't want to be someone's fucking consolation prize."

I'm just about to respond when I am reminded of a short-short story that I once heard described by an oke I knew. He said it was "the scariest thing he could of." He was a monstrous naaier who was unintimated by anyone or anything. Not even me. Which was a shame for him. Had he been more easily intimidated, he might still be alive today.

But in the moment right before my hands tightened around his throat and he took his last breath, he said, *"I ain't scared."*

"Good for you," I told him.

And then he looked up at me, smiled, and said, *"The only thing what's ever scared me is this thing I heard once… 'The last man on earth sits alone in a room. Suddenly… there's a knock on the door.'"* His smile widened and he continued, *"Just hope, bru, that—one day—when the knock comes, you ain't the one sitting in the chair."*

It was such a curious thing for him to say in that moment that I laughed slightly.

And then I choked him to death.

It's an odd thing to be remembering now. Except maybe it's not. Because here, in the middle of this isolated estate, miles from nowhere, alone with Eliza in this place that no one knows about…

Suddenly, there's a knock on the door.

CHAPTER ELEVEN

I wait, standing behind Christine, as the sound of footsteps approach the door from the other side. She's nervous. Been nervous this whole car trip. And I have a million questions, all of which I'm holding inside. But they are about to explode because I have a very bad feeling about what's happening right now.

The locks disengage.

Christine sucks in a breath of air.

The door opens inward.

Christine exhales.

And the woman on the other side is someone I know. Someone I was just asking about back in Hilo, in fact.

"Well, look at this," Eliza Watson says with a smirk. "I've been wondering when you would find us."

"*Expecting someone?*" Eliza asks, with a wry smile.

"Fok are you smiling at? What's going on?"

"Honestly, I smile when I'm nervous, and right now things feel like they could go any number of terrible ways, don't they?"

I stare at the main entry door all the way across the other room. It sounds like someone is pounding on it violently. And while that's likely just an illusion created by the reverberating bounce of sound in the wide-open space, it's also just as likely that there is some kind of violence fueling the knock. Violence fuels every moment that exists in my life.

No one knows I'm here. The only person who even knows about this place is Lars. But there's no way my brother has come.

Unless…

I snap out of my momentary stupor, realizing that whoever is here, if they wanted to do harm, they wouldn't be knocking. So they're probably not here to kill me.

Probably.

But before I can step to greet the arrival of this unexpected guest, Eliza is breezing across the floor and has her hand on the great, primeval doorknob.

Time slows. I can hear my breathing filling my lungs. Eliza's hand goes to turn the knob and she looks back at me over her shoulder with a shrug in her smile and a raise of her eyebrows. And when she opens the door…

There is Christine.

If you had asked me to lay odds on who it might be, I honestly would have wagered at about a million to one against it being Christine. After everything. After… all of it. She's possibly the last person I would have said would come looking.

And yet, for whatever reason, I am not surprised at all.

She looks a bit like a drowned rat. Her white sneakers are all muddy from having trekked up to the door in the rain. Her tight blue jeans look as though they're being shrink wrapped to her body. She has on a yellowish windbreaker that calls to mind the dress she used to wear every day. The dress that would allow her to pretend that no matter what was happening it would always be sunny.

Fokken irony, that.

Her wet hair is matted to her cheeks and the rain on her face makes it impossible to tell whether or not she's been crying. Neither that she has or hasn't would shock me at this point.

And now something that confuses me happens.

The knocking continues.

The door is open, Christine is standing here in the rain, and yet I can still hear the knocking. A bang, bang, banging that causes me to look around and see from where it's coming.

Christine and Eliza don't acknowledge it. Through the open passage to the kitchen, far across the great entry hall, they are just… talking. I can't hear what they're saying. I can't make out what's going on.

And quite without warning, I cannot see them as well as a moment before either.

I can't hear them. I can't see them. I only know that they are close.

And from somewhere I can't understand, the knocking continues.

CHAPTER THIRTEEN

Christine

She hasn't changed much. It's only been a couple years since I saw her last but from what I've heard she's been quite busy these past two years. And I don't know why I expected her to... I don't know... look more... *motherly*. Since she is now, in fact, a mother. As evident by the tow-headed, blue-eyed, pig-tailed toddler clinging to her knee at the moment.

But Eliza is Eliza is Eliza. Through and through. She might be more beautiful now than ever.

I hold in my jealousy and my rage. I check all my hidden feelings of betrayal because, like it or not, that's how we got to this moment in the first place.

She is why I betrayed Alec. And now she will be the way I get him back.

CHAPTER FOURTEEN

"Mr. van den Berg, sir. Mr. van den Berg? Are you all right, sir?"

That does not sound like Christine.

One: the accent is not American. It's very distinctly Saffie.

And two: it's an oke's voice.

Where am I? What the fokken hell is going on now?

"Mr. van den Berg, sir. Are you all right?"

My eyes spring open and I sit up. Oh, shit. That's right. I know where I am.

Fok my poepol.

My ribs remind me quickly that they're not all hundreds just yet, the hint of residual pain through my torso the last vestiges of the careening fall I took a few months back. Me and Lars, tumbling over the edge of that fokken waterfall back in the States like goddamn Sherlock Holmes and Moriarty at the end of *The Final Problem*.

Which one of us was Holmes and which Moriarty, I can't be sure. I think perhaps we were both Moriarty. Both of us the villain.

"Yeah, Liam, I'm fine," I call back through the closed bedroom door.

"May I come in, sir, and make sure?"

I sigh, because it's been like this for a while now. Ever since I awoke from whatever comatose state I was in for however long I was in it, Liam and the other laaities who have been tasked with looking after my wellbeing refuse to take my word for it when I tell them I'm OK. Whoever is responsible for my being here has instructed them to ensure that I'm "proper cared for."

They've apparently also been instructed not to tell me who the fok it is that brought me here, how the fok I was rescued from that tumble, or what the fokken plan is in my being here or for how long I am expected to stay. All I know for certain is that young men with guns are very eager to make sure I'm comfortable and well fed and seen to. And they're also nervously emphatic about not allowing me to leave the property. And since they're the ones with automatic weapons and I'm only armed with silk pyjamas, I suppose they get final say.

"Yeah, man," I say. "Come on in."

The door opens, gingerly, and the laaitie called Liam who has, I reckon, been assigned as my principal caretaker, peeps his face through.

"Everything's fine, sir?"

"Yeah, man. Aces. Why?"

"You were making… quite a bit of noise, sir."

"Was I?"

"Yessir."

"What type of noise?"

He looks down toward the ground, sheepishly, adjusts the rifle that hangs at his side, twists his neck back and forth a bit. "Sir… it just…"

"Liam, man, even though I do, in fact, have all day and am clearly not going anywhere, I still hate to fokken wait."

100

"It just—and I could be wrong, of course! But it sounded a bit like... like crying. Sir."

Under the pretense of scratching my cheek, I reach to feel if any teardrops seem to have moistened my skin. No. Feels dry, so far as I can tell.

"Does it look as though I've been weeping, man?"

He studies my face for a moment. "No, sir."

"Right then," I say, tossing the sheets off myself onto the mattress of the four-poster bed and sliding my legs over the side. I pop my feet into the slippers that wait for me on the floor and stand. "What's for breakfast, Liam?"

"Whatever you like, Mr. van den Berg. Is there anything special you'd like to have?"

"What time is it?"

"Almost noon, sir."

I nod, considering. I scratch at the stubble on my chin that is now approaching proper beard status. Someone else shaved me while I was unconscious, but when I awoke initially, it still hurt to lift my arm. And then I just grew lazy and decided to not care. It's the first time in my life I've had anything resembling a beard. I think I hate it.

"Erm," I mumble, "let's have pap and wors, yeah? Do we have Rhodes gravy?"

"I believe we do, sir."

"All right." I nod and Liam withdraws his head and begins closing the door. "Liam?" I say, just as it's almost shut.

"Sir?" he says, poking his head back in.

"How the fok did I get here, man?"

This is a script we play out every day. Every day I ask the same question and every day he gives a variation of a non-answer. Today's version is...

"Pap and wors with gravy, sir. It'll be just a few minutes." And he goes.

I take a breath. Let it out. Allow my hand to drift down the post of the bed next to which I'm standing. It's been two years since I was here with Eliza. But then again, I was with her here just moments ago.

I've had the same dream every night now for the past few nights. Or possibly the past few weeks. It's become impossible to tell. Or perhaps I've been here for all of eternity. Perhaps nothing is real and I am simply a figment of the universe's imagination.

Whether I am or not, the pinch in my ribs feels real to me and I suppose that's all that really fokken matters.

How, though, am I here? Here in the manor I purchased after my last time here with Eliza? After my last time with Eliza at all? The last time I saw her. The last time…

Is *she* the reason I'm here? Did she somehow save me and bring me to this place as some sentimental homage to our time together?

No. The simple answer is no. That's the most absurd fokken thing imaginable. But, then again, my life has become fokken absurd. So I'm not ruling out any theory, no matter how ludicrous.

Perhaps I didn't deny Death this last time, after all. Perhaps this is what Death is. For me. Stuck in the last spot I ever visited before it all came unglued. Life. Quietly and without my awareness, but unglued nonetheless.

Sartre mused that "Hell is other people." I might suggest in return that Hell is actually their absence.

Fok, man. All this convalescing is causing me to become soft and ruminative. And that ain't no good for nobody.

I shuffle over to the window and look out on the estate I own, the former haven that has become my unexpected prison for reasons passing understanding. A light mist has begun falling outside. The smell of pap cooking on the stovetop is starting to waft throughout. And the awareness that I'm being held here—by someone—as a virtual prisoner; the awareness that somewhere in the world right now, my business is not being run by me; the awareness that I have no clue what's become of Christine and Danny; the awareness that… fokken hell, man… that I've become soft, and ruminative, and have begun making noises in my sleep that sound to Liam as if I'm goddamn crying… bring me to a probably overdue decision.

I ain't staying here much longer.

CHAPTER FIFTEEN

"Listen," *Christine says*, hand up, palm out. "Before you slam the door in my face I just wanna say we've got mutual business and I'm not taking no for an answer, so just get off your high horse for one second and hear me out."

Which seems like a lot of preemptive protest from Christine seeing as Eliza hasn't made a move to either slam the door in our faces or reject us outright.

But then I look down at the little, pig-tailed girl, who is staring up at me making a 'come here' gesture with one tiny forefinger, and decide—yeah. There's a lot I don't know about this fucking situation.

"Business you say?" That's Eliza.

"Pssst," the little girl says, still beckoning me to bend down to her like she's got some secret to share. Which is stupid because I'm fairly sure people this tiny can't possibly talk. "Pssst," she says again.

"It's Alec," Christine says. "So…" And then she loses a bit of her steam and just shrugs.

Eliza sighs. Long. Loudly. And then directs her eyes to mine. "Danny."

"Uh, hey, Eliza. How's things?"

"Things are perfect, mate. Quite literally." But then she redirects her gaze to Christine and adds, "Or at least they were."

"High horse," Christine reminds her.

"What do you want?" Eliza snaps. Because... yeah. I think I'm getting this now.

"Pssst," the tiny one says again, still making that little 'come down here' motion to me.

"We want..." And then Christine starts getting into details. They spill out of her mouth like a runaway train. Like she can't talk fast enough.

The little one is tugging on my pant leg now. I look down, then up again, where Eliza is making that *what the fuck are you going on about* face as Christine gets to the part about the waterfall, conveniently skipping over the reason Alec and Lars went over the damn thing in the first place—which is Christine—and then ends the whole thing with... "And he's been missing ever since."

"Oh. Well. Bloke is dead," Eliza deadpans.

"No," Christine protests. "He's not. He's here in England, in fact. Which is why I'm here in England, knocking on your goddamned door." Then Christine winces, looks down at the tiny one, and is suddenly unsure if she just fucked up the whole thing by swearing in front of the child.

We both stare at Eliza, waiting for a proclamation. And when none comes, Christine continues.

"Pssst," the insistent tiny thing says again. Still tugging on my pant leg.

So I bend down, but keep my gaze trained on Eliza as Christine goes on about how she left me in the Cook Islands to "recover" and went looking for answers about Alec's fate after that tumble, and how she went to the local authorities back home—which has me momentarily distracted because that was a stupid move on her part. Fucking Brasil is there and she could've been captured, or tortured, or raped or any of the other dozen nasty things that are always running through my mind about how people can hurt Christine—but I snap out of it just as Christine gets to the part where she says she came to England several weeks back, just doing a cursory check of all known safehouses once she realized no dead bodies turned up after the "incident", and found him—

"What?" Eliza gasps.

"Yeah," Christine continues. "He's here. At that goddamned estate."

By now I'm face to face with the tiny one, but still looking up at Christine and Eliza. So, the little person pats my scruffy cheek to make me focus.

"What?" I ask her. Which is absurd, because as I've mentioned, people this tiny can't talk.

"I'm Alecandra," she says. "Come play with me."

She's got a weird accent. So I'm not sure if I heard her right, but then again, I'm pretty sure I heard her right.

I don't get to the part where I say no, I'm not going to play with her. Because I stand up and look at Eliza. "She's—"

"Yes," is the answer, but it comes from Christine.

Which makes me turn to look at her. Then back at Eliza. Then down at the tiny person who is still very busy tugging on my pant leg and spouting off a whole litany of things we're going to do when we stop this all this nonsense grown-up stuff.

She talks quite well, even though for some reason she sounds like a life-long Brooklyn-er with her weird tiny-person speech patterns. Because she says things like 'have tea and biscuits,' and 'play hopscotch and jacks.' Which comes with a disclaimer that she's not good at jacks but she can hopscotch well. And do I know how to hopscotch?

I picture myself hopscotching. I know what it is but never in my life have I given it a try, and so, just to shut her up, I say, "Sure," but then look at Christine and say, "This is why?"

And she knows the question I'm asking, even though I haven't asked it. Because she nods, but in the same moment, she shakes her head no, too, like there's more to this story that isn't self-evident, and gives me one of those *later* looks.

And then Eliza says, "That's not her name. She just can't say it right yet. It's Alexandria. But we just call her Andra."

Because of course they do. "And who is we?" I ask.

"Everyone calls me Andra," Andra says. "Even my Uncle Theo, but he sometimes calls me 'pigtails.'"

"Uh-huh," I say. "So listen, Eliza. I get that this is unexpected and whatnot. And I didn't know we were coming here—hell, I haven't even thought about you in years—but I have been in touch with Russell and—"

"When?" Christine interrupts.

"Hilo," I say. "And I've already made a deal with him for help anyway. So if you could just put all of this"—I make an all-encompassing motion with outstretched arms—"aside and let us in so we can discuss a plan of action—"

Which is when she cuts me off with a very loud laugh. "I don't give two shits what deal you have with Russell, I'm not getting involved with saving Alec van den Berg. He can rot in bloody Hell for all I care."

At which point Christine must decide swearing is not forbidden in front of the tiny one and says, "You fucking *owe me*," in the meanest, most serious, I-will-kill-you-where-you-stand voice she can muster.

Which is pretty good, I think. Because my heart skips a beat in the wake of her threat and the tiny one even stops her tugging.

Eliza leans back on her heels. Not in a taken-aback way either. But in a I-bloody-dare-you-to-try way, complete with wide, incredulous eyes and a smirking grin.

And here we are.

The impasse.

CHAPTER SIXTEEN

*I was with a woma*n from the American South once. Long, long ago. Mississippi, I believe. Or South Caro-Bama or some fokken place. I remember her now, as I eat in my luxurious prison quarters, because I recall that she insisted on calling pap "grits." I explained to her that the dish I enjoyed that she referred to as "grits" is, in fact, called pap. She thought "pap" sounded disgusting. I thought "grits" sounded disgusting. I was right. She was wrong.

I threw her over the railing of a bridge.

Not because of the grits thing. I'm not a lunatic.

It's because she got quite hysterical on me, threatening to tell her "daddy" that it was I, the oke who was seeing his daughter, who stole the necklace he kept in the safe in his study. The family heirloom that dated back to the eighteenth century. I don't know why I told her I took it. I was a teenager. Teenagers do stupid things.

I have always had complicated feelings about her accident. The necklace had actually been stolen by slave traders from an African village that was plundered sometime in the seventeen-hundreds. Through a long and circuitous turn of events that involved a Xhosa oke I was friends with and a story that had been passed along through the generations about some appropriated jewels, I found myself in the right place at the right time to make something resembling reparations to a greatly appreciative tribal chief.

I mean, I must be honest, I'm no great philanthropist or humanitarian. I had arranged for an appropriate finder's fee, but still… stealing from the descendant of a slaver and throwing his daughter off a bridge feels like it's doing God's good work.

But that's not why I did it either.

I did it because in the heat of her hysteria and threats, she turned to the backseat of the car I was driving at the time, where Christine and Danny were sitting, and called Christine a whore. In her piercing Ala-Tucky accent (or whatever the fok it was), she yelped at me, "Fuck you, you African piece a' shit! And fuck this low-rent fuck boy and dirty little street whore you hang around with too!" She then leaped into the rear of the car and began striking violently at them both. She wasn't even drunk. Or high. Just… herself.

I had not known Danny and Christine long at that point. We had only just begun our adventures together. So it was confusing to me that I found Misty's particular verbal assault so personally offensive. But I did.

I always knew what Danny and Christine are to me. Always.

Now, in fairness to her—and I strive to be fair—Misty had just found out that I had no intention of bringing her along with us on our next departure and was quite emotional. So, the more mature, more patient Alec van den Berg that I am today might only have dragged her back into the front seat and, I don't know, smashed her head into the dashboard or something equally non-lethal.

But being the hotheaded young Alec that I was at the time, I pulled the car over to the side of the road, got out, and dragged her from the passenger side. And—and even though through the gauzy haze of memory one can romanticize one's recollections, I don't believe I am—I honestly had no intention of harming her. I really did not. I had planned to just sort of abandon her there and then flee the country as swiftly as possible, assuming that there would be other ways to avoid ever dealing with her again.

But, unfortunately, Christine had not taken kindly to being struck and called a whore, and she got out of the car as well. Sweet, little, equally-hotheaded and unintimidated Christine who, though smaller and arguably cuter than Misty, was about five times stronger and more vicious. She went after the poor girl with a horrifying vengeance. Like the legendary Biloko—a dwarf-like creature that attacks the unfortunate and unsuspecting soul who passes by their lair in a hollow tree—Christine was on her.

And in the process of separating them, I wrenched them apart and lofted the dear girl over the guard rail of the bridge we were on at three in the morning.

We watched her fall into the river below, all three of us a bit stunned at the turn of events. The water washed her away and she struggled to stay afloat. But, truthfully, I didn't even consider her for more than half a second before I had my hands on Christine's shoulders, asking her if *she* was OK. She nodded, then started crying, and Danny and I sandwiched her between us, telling her it would be all right.

I wonder if, when I went over the falls, Danny held her in his arms in the same way and told her, once again, that it would all be OK.

No way to know, I suppose.

Misty managed to survive as well, it turns out. In my opinion, it's less impressive than what I survived. She hadn't also fought her way free from capture by a small army and then been shot by one of only two people in the world she believed she could trust, but still, I'm glad she made it.

Some years later, I believe I read that she and her entire immediate family were sent to prison for insider trading. Or something equally banal. Shame.

In any case, this bowl of pap and wors I'm finishing right now actually isn't half bad.

I'm about to call for Liam to come take the dirty dish away when I look out the window again. The weather is clearing, and the sun is creating shadows across the great lawn outside. And there, from the corner of my eye, I see something that looks like… that looks like… that looks like people I know.

It isn't.

Upon closer examination, I can see that it's just some trees casting Christine- and Danny-shaped illusions onto the earth. But for a moment, it felt as if they were here. Or at least close.

I've been thinking about them more. Not more than any specific time. More than at any other time I've ever thought about them in my life, since knowing they were people whose feet trod the same earth as mine. It don't seem fair, man. It don't seem fair that Christine and I worked through all the struggle with Eliza only to discover that we hadn't. That she was harboring a hatred close to her heart that I didn't know about.

It don't seem fair that Danny was back in both of our lives for less than a proper twenty-four hours before I was ripped away from him again. I wonder if he's indeed with

Christine. I wonder if they're happy. I'd like that, I think. I'd like it if through me, they found their way back to each other. That would make *me* happy.

It don't seem fair that I'm here in these silk pyjamas, enjoying a perfectly serviceable bowl of pap and wors while my baby brother is very likely dead at the bottom of a waterfall. Or, more likely, washed away somewhere, never to be seen again. If only he had found it in himself to *talk* with me, maybe... maybe... fok. At least maybe I could've killed him myself. That would feel just and right somehow. Better than the way it all went down, I reckon.

Eish, man. But when has anything ever been fair? Come along now, van den Berg. You're starting to sound like other people.

All right. Enough of this kak. Time to go. I can't claim to know what about today in particular is causing me to decide that I cannot stay here any longer, but something in the air—or more probably, something in me—is pulling me toward an exit strategy.

The time that I was at this estate before, it was so that I could rest after a near-death scrape. Somebody who knows me knows that. That's why I'm here again, I have to assume. It's some perverted commentary on my life that whoever has chosen to keep me alive has chosen this place to hold me hostage. It's a fokken allegory. Or metaphor. Or some cocksucking thing. Whatever it is, it ain't cute, and I'm done.

I think the part that I really can't tolerate any further is not having answers. Staring down uncertainty does not make me uncomfortable. It fokken hacks me off, man. I refuse to believe that I denied Death her claim on me yet again for me to sit here in thousand-dollar sleepwear, wondering about what the hell is happening. I aim to find answers.

Now.

"Liam, man! I'm done, bru!"

It's not the disarming him that hurts. That's actually somewhat easy. He lets the rifle slide down his arm when he takes up the tray, and I'm not in optimal shape, but I'm still quite quick. No, what hurts is knocking him out with the butt of the rifle. Whatever it is that's still pinching on my ribcage seems to tighten a bit. Or possibly tear. Not sure. Medical school was not for me, so I didn't go. All I know is it stings.

I'll need to be conscious of that as I make my way out of here. I've only seen about a dozen okes around the premises, but I've also only been around a limited amount of the premises. The good news is that this is my place. I bought it after having lived here with Eliza for probably a good month and a half. And until the day that she spoilt everything by getting pregnant—or, accurately, *telling me* she was pregnant...

Kak, man.

But until then, we had good fun in just about every corner of this citadel, so I should be able to sneak out through some of the less easy-to-spot passageways round the back. It would be a delight to free myself into the countryside sunshine while killing as few people as possible.

And, as if on cue, the rain starts pattering against the window again as I lean my head into the hallway to make sure no one is watching my door.

Yes, it *would be* a delight. It certainly would.

But, unfortunately, something niggling inside me tells me that this day is not fated to be a delightful one.

CHAPTER SEVENTEEN

Christine

I'm standing in the corner of Eliza's kitchen—which is quite nice. In fact, the whole fucking place is English-countryside quaint and perfect. So perfect I feel like gagging—while Danny and Eliza sit at the kitchen table overlooking a massive back garden where Alec's daughter is busy drawing a hopscotch grid on a dark, slate pathway which I can only imagine leads somewhere magical. Like a smaller-sized, but dimensionally correct replica of this estate, hidden in the woods and surrounded by those wood fairies—what do you call them? Pixies. Yes. There's a fucking mini-mansion playhouse out there at the end of that path surrounded by pixies. I'm sure of it.

The storybook childhood home. That's what this place is.

I am seething with rage.

Also, possibly, jealousy.

But definitely rage.

I don't hate many people. I don't, in fact, give any fucks about most people one way or the other. So having feelings of rage and hate towards Eliza is a big deal for me.

Russell has been called. Courtesy of Danny, not Eliza. Because Eliza is still going on about how in no bloody dream world is she lifting even a pinky finger to help Alec out of whatever mess we're all involved in.

But in between those declarations—which come with side-eyed glances my direction, like I'm the reason for her feelings about Alec and she is not the reason for my feelings about her—she has mustered up a pot of tea in an actual fucking china teapot (like, come on, OK?) and a plate of cookies that appear to be, yes, you guessed it. Homemade.

I'm drunk on rage.

Because she has the nerve to answer that door looking fucking fabulous. Like the years haven't touched her and there's been no falling off rooftops, or hidden guns under floorboards, or losing one's memory of betraying one of the two people you love most in the world, since she gave birth two-something years ago.

And—*and*—she has that beautiful little child playing out there in her magical back garden of this huge, quintessentially English estate like she's never known a life of strife, and hardship, and disappointment.

Rage.

Also, possibly, jealousy.

The Watson twins, Brenden and Charlie, show up first, not Russell. And there's a big production as mini-Alec comes running in to wrap her arms around her uncles' knees and blabber on about hopscotch and jacks, and do they know her new friend, Danny? Who can also play hopscotch?

I think I'm the only one listening to her, because Brenden is shaking Danny's hand, like they are old friends and not old enemies, and Charlie is, along with Eliza, side-eyeing me as I keep my distance in the corner.

But that's because Charlie and I had an almost-thing once upon a time, and he's probably wondering if I ever told Danny about that.

This shit is gonna get complicated.

Gonna?

I laugh, which makes everyone turn to look at me, not just Eliza and Charlie. And Brenden says, "Hey, Christine."

And I manage a small wave without uncrossing my arms from their defensive position across my chest.

Because the fact of the matter is—all this is my fault. I have no delusions about that. This whole thing is my fault.

Mostly for taking up with Lars, even though I still don't really remember that part. But also because things got messy a couple years ago when I found out Eliza was pregnant with Alec's baby.

Really. Fucking. Messy.

And then the whole goddamned production starts all over again when Russell arrives, then again when Theo comes. Only when Theo comes, mini-Alec jumps up into his arms and he twirls her around as she giggles.

So I guess Theo is the favorite uncle.

What must it be like to grow up with a favorite uncle? And giggle when he showers you with love?

I wouldn't know.

Rage.

But my rage is tempered when Russell says, "OK, let's get down to business." And he looks at Danny for... what?

I don't know, but Danny nods and says, "I told you, I'm fine with it."

Which makes me feel even more like an outsider because they have some deal going that I wasn't a part of and even though I'm the one who brought us all together, I'm the one who's forgotten now.

But then again, I'm the only one with information, so the moment after I think that thought, every one of them turns to me with expectations.

So I spell it out.

"Alec's at the country estate," I say. "But not by choice."

This is news to everyone, even Danny. Because as far as I was aware, he had no interest in where Alec was before this moment right now. He was in some kind of denial and never asked me for details. Which I totally get. Denial is something I've practiced for over two decades. Which is why I indulged him.

But there's this little stab of hurt that he called Russell without telling me.

I discard that hurt and morph back into business mode.

"I went there several weeks ago, just checking to see if maybe, possibly, he'd choose that fucking place, of all fucking places, as his regroup base—"

Which earns me a snarl from Eliza, but I don't care. I just continue.

"—and it's surrounded by guards. I'm talking AK-toting fucking mercenary-type guards."

"So you didn't get in?" Eliza asks.

"No, I didn't get in," I snap back.

"Then how do you know he's there?" Danny asks.

And here it is. The moment when I have to make a decision to keep my end of a fucked-up bargain and risk the consequences with Danny and Alec, or risk the help of this fucked-up bargain and remain loyal.

But who am I kidding, anyway? Apparently, I haven't been loyal for a very long time.

"I saw him. I was lurking in the woods at night and I saw him through a window. He's there."

"Maybe he wants to be there?" Eliza says.

And I know what she means. She means, *Maybe he's done with you two and he's rethinking that decision he made two-plus years ago?*

"He doesn't," I say. "He fell. Over a fucking waterfall. He didn't just pick himself up and cart his ass across an ocean afterward. OK? Let's all be real here. Someone picked him up from that river, took him to England to recover, and now he's being held against his will."

Silence.

Then—"I don't know." That's Russell. "Sounds crazy to me."

I look at Danny for backup and thankfully he obliges. "Doesn't matter. We're doing this. You in or not?"

This is when the Watson crew look at each other the way they always look at each other when a crew decision needs to be made, and then Russell says, "Give us a minute?"

And Danny, who has now taken over, says, "Sure. Come on, Christine. Let's go check out the back garden."

Which makes me roll my eyes as I follow. Because of course we need to wait out in that perfect back garden, where favorite Uncle Theo has sent perfect little mini-Alec to play again with her chalk on the slate pathway that leads to the magical playhouse.

It's not that I hate children. I do not hate children. I actually love children. And Alec's child is adorable in every way imaginable so there is no possible way to dislike her.

What I dislike is her mother.

Oh, hell. Who am I kidding? I dislike her father too.

Not Alec, as in Alec, Christine, and Danny.

But Alec as in Alec and Eliza.

Danny gets out his phone and starts checking for a GPS signal or whatever. And I take a seat on the stone wall that surrounds a flower bed and watch the little girl grab a jump rope from a colorful wooden toy box next to the ivy-covered trellis which climbs all the way up the side of the stone house to the authentic thatched roof.

Who the fuck has a thatched roof in the twenty-first century?

I feel like vomiting.

"So we should talk plans," I say, turning away from the house and the little girl to focus on Danny.

"What's there to talk about?" Danny says, kinda distracted by his phone.

"Like, how we're gonna get in there?"

He glances my direction and shrugs. "They steal priceless jewels and artifacts from museums. I'm pretty sure they have a whole playbook of plans to choose from. That's why we're here."

"Eliza's not gonna do it."

"She will."

"No." I shake my head. "She won't. And she's the one we need because she's the one who gets inside first."

"Let Russell handle Eliza."

"What did you promise him?"

"Not much." Danny shrugs. "Just that last job we stole from them."

"What? Hell the fuck no. We do not give back stolen money."

"We do now," Danny says. "I set up the wire transfer on the drive out here."

"That's just wrong," I say. "We earned that money."

"We stole it."

"Yeah, but we got away with it. So we earned it."

"Not this time. We're giving it back."

"They don't even need money."

"It's not about money. As you well know, otherwise you wouldn't even blink at giving back two hundred and fifty grand."

I sigh. Because it's true. If they had said, *OK, we'll help. Our price is a million dollars*, I still would not have blinked. This is Alec and we need him back.

But whittle that amount down to one quarter and then tack on the understanding that this is *them* stealing something back from *us* and that changes everything.

"It's dumb," Danny says. "And we don't have time for dumb. So the understanding is… they won that round."

I want to explode with rage. "They didn't win. We did."

"And now we lost and they won."

I say nothing.

"Christine, it's stupid. This whole rivalry thing the two of you have is stupid. He loves you, not her. How do you not see that?"

I glance over at mini-Alec without meaning to and, of course, Danny doesn't miss this slip-up.

"Come on," he says. "So she got pregnant. Guys get girls pregnant all the time. It's got nothing to do with feelings."

"You should shut up now," I say. "Because you have no idea what you're talking about."

"Well, it's not rocket science."

"It doesn't bother you?" I ask, trying to change the subject. "That he has a baby and you didn't even know about it?"

"I mean…" Danny says, kinda thinking this over for a moment. "No. It doesn't."

I'm just about to say something I'll need to immediately take back when Charlie comes out from the French doors.

"Hey, Andra. Uncle Theo wants to see you inside."

"OK!" mini-Alec says, throwing down her jump rope.

"And Russell wants to talk to you, Danny."

Danny nods and walks over to Charlie, giving him a sidelong glance that Charlie doesn't see as he passes.

Charlie doesn't see because he's looking at me.

"What?" I ask, irritated.

His gaze remains locked with mine for a long second, but I look away first. He's very handsome. Light brown hair, light brown eyes, and a perfect fucking body that should never wear clothes.

Which means Brenden is equally as handsome. Because they're twins and all. But Charlie has something that Brenden doesn't. I don't know what it is, we just… click.

I'd like to say that was the whole reason why we had an almost-thing back when I was younger, but it's not. Charlie was my friend. He was there for me.

"You OK?" he asks, walking over to me and taking a seat on the stone wall.

"Just fine," I snap. "Just motherfucking fine."

He's silent for a second and then he huffs out a breath of air. Not a laugh. Not a sigh. But something more like... a sense of resignation. "I don't get it. What were you expecting?"

"I don't know what you're talking about."

"Come on. Don't play dumb with me. I was there."

"Shut up, OK? Just shut the fuck up about it."

He's quiet for a minute. And just as I'm about to get up and go back inside, he says, "I heard some things about you three."

"Yeah? So?"

"Things about you and Lars."

"I'm not discussing it, Charlie. So don't bother asking me."

"I already know. And I told the lot of them just now, so Russell and Eliza know what they're getting into if we agree to this."

I want to cry. Just break down and... be sad. For as long as it takes to stop being sad.

But I've never really had the luxury of sadness. I can count on one finger the times I've been able to stop and just *feel* things.

And now is not the moment to pick up that habit. So I take a deep breath, stand up, look down at Charlie—who is looking up at me with an expression of pity or maybe, probably, just disappointment—and say, "You're going to agree. We all know you will."

Which is a lie. I'm pretty sure Eliza will say no just to spite me. But I soldier on. "So what's the plan?"

He smiles at me. A very charming Charlie smile that heals my heart just a little and makes me glad we were only ever an almost-thing and never a real thing. Because he is my friend. Has been my friend. Has been by my side.

JA HUSS & J McCLAIN

And he's still here.

"You know I said yes and even though Eliza is the one who must say yes, she will because I told her she owed me."

I deflate at this news. Not in disappointment, but with relief. Like all the stress I've been holding inside since that night out at the waterfall leaks out and relieves all the pressure.

"Thank you," I whisper, unable to look him the eyes. "I guess I owe you twice now."

He stands up, takes my hand—which makes me look up at him in surprise—and says, "There are no debts or favors between us, Christine. Ever."

CHAPTER EIGHTEEN

I feel like fokken Bruce Willis in that Christmas movie he made a long time ago. The one where he's trapped in that building and ain't got no shoes on. I should have thought through what was going to happen next. I should have considered my plan of escape. I should have at least put on shoes. But, oh, well, I suppose I'm in it now.

I laugh to myself a tiny bit as I peer around a corner to make sure that there's no one standing in the hallway. Because this is exactly the kind of thing Christine would do. Go off on some undercooked plan of action. Just plunge headlong into a dire circumstance with no particularly strategic course of remedy.

I blame myself. I taught her to be that way, I think. Although she always had it in her. That trip to the Tower of London. Her obsession with charging in and stealing the Crown Jewels. It's proper insane. Nobody muses over that kind of thing. Or, if they do, they don't ever intend to act on it. Christine did. I really believe that if neither Danny nor I were there to put the kibosh on it, she might have ended up enjoying the rest of her life trapped behind the walls of Bronzefield Prison. So I chuckle, thinking about how I'm being moved by the spirit of Christine Keene.

Still and all… I wish I had on shoes. Or at least clothes. I'm like that oke Holden Caulfield in the book *Catcher in the Rye*. The little mental fokker who gets beaten on in his night clothes while trying to have sex with a prostitute. The difference, of course, being that I ain't mental and I don't have the pleasure of being with a gentoo. I'm quite sane and am escaping an unknowable situation with the intention of discovering if the only two people in the world that I feel true love for are alive and together and at all willing to allow me back into their lives.

No. I ain't mental at all.

Ach, man. Ek gee nie 'n fok nie. Ek loop.

I don't see anyone lurking about, so I begin working my way down the corridor. It's actually probably quite all right that I have no shoes now that I think on it. Quiet. The pitter patter of my steps is well muted. Which is useful in this moment, as it allows me to hear the sound of heavily booted feet coming from around the next corner in the direction I'm headed. Shit.

I turn and head back the way from which I just came. Which seems like a goddamn waste of a lot of energy, but I really do want to have to use this weapon only as a last resort. Because very few things in the world call chaos upon you like the sound of automatic rifle fire. If conflict is unavoidable, then one must do what one must. But in my current state, I'd say the odds are not in my favor.

I dart around the corner leading back to my bedroom-cum-holding cell. And just as I do, I hear, "Oi! Liam. Whatsit, bru?"

Shit.

I make it back into the room before the approaching oke spies me, I think, because the pace of his steps doesn't accelerate and the ease in his voice remains the same when he says, "Liam? That you, man? What's happening, bru? Everything hundreds? You need something?"

I have to assume that they (whoever "they" are) all have their own posts. In the small bit of meandering I've been able to do, I've tended to see the same faces in the same places over and over. Very much exactly like sentries on prescribed posts, guarding a fortress. And for the flashiest of flashes, I again wonder... why the fok am I here and how?

But I've got no time to indulge the notions, because as I dart back inside my sleeping quarters, I see the laaitie Liam, still on the floor where I left him. Snoring. Actually snoring. Like a goddamn cartoon character. I knocked him out and now he's making more noise than he was when he was conscious.

Jesus Christ, man. This has got to be the most cocked-up escape attempt in history.

I close the door behind me and run to where young Liam is sawing logs, as they say, on the ground. Just as I reach him, a knock on the door...

"Liam? You in there, man?"

I don't respond. Just stare at the closed door, as if by willing the oke to go away, he will.

"Liam?"

He doesn't.

"Mr. van den Berg?"

I start to respond, when suddenly I have what is quite possibly the stupidest idea of my life. I don't fancy myself a particularly stupid oke, so it's not as if I have a vast barrel of stupid ideas from which to choose. But even if I were a right ninny and had a bottomless pit of dumb from which to pull, this might be way, way down there below all the other dumb ones as the inanest.

"Mr. van den Berg, sir? May I come in?"

It's an odd feeling to be held prisoner but still very clearly be regarded as the boss.

I kneel down, sliding the rifle under the bed, and grab Liam up under the arms. I hoist him to his feet, discovering that he is sturdier than he looks. My ribs virtually moan in protest. But I manage to drag him to the side of the bed where I drop him and force his crumpled body underneath as well.

And then life starts happening in slow motion.

I can see the door handle starting to turn. I return my gaze back down toward the snoring Liam. His arm and booted foot protruding out from the side of the bed frame.

The door handle spins all the way round and the door begins to crack open.

I kneel down and force Liam's appendages underneath and out of sight.

My ribs strain and I moan.

The door is ajar. "Mr. van den Berg? Sir?"

A head is visible in shadow as I spring onto the mattress and pull the covers over me.

Liam continues snoring.

I slide the sheets to the side of my face just enough to see the head of the laaitie make its way into the room. Arno, I believe he's called.

"Mr. van den Berg?"

Liam snores, loudly. And as he does, I move about under the sheets and make noises suggesting that I'm not going to be easily awakened.

"Mmmm," I moan. Liam snores. It times surprisingly well.

"Oh, I'm sorry, sir." Arno, half-whispers. "I was looking for—"

Liam snores *very* loudly and I toss in the sheets in concert.

Arno stops talking and begins backing out of the room.

Fok me, man. I cannot believe this might have gone over.

And just as I'm about to throw the sheets from me and count my blessings that the absurdity of this recent turn of events seems to have worked out in my favor...

Arno opens the door and reenters the room.

Fok die kak, man. Are you kidding me right now?

I continue peering from under the sheets as he steps into the space.

Liam snores. I rustle.

Arno makes his way toward the bed.

I had really, really hoped to make it through today without killing anyone. I truly had. But if Arno takes two more steps in this direction, he'll be leaving me with limited options.

And then, at the very last moment before he lands at my bedside, he curves away from the foot, takes up the empty bowl of pap and wors, and makes his way back to the door. He pulls it open, steps into the hall, looks back into the room once last time, and closes it behind him.

Jesus. Christ.

If I read that sequence of events in a book... I would cry bull kak.

I cast the sheets off, make my way to the door, open it a crack to make sure he's gone, and then close it again. Liam continues his symphony of sleep.

Goddamn it, man. This may well wind up being harder than I thought. And my next thought is… is it even worth it? Even if I do get free from here, what do I think I'll do? I'll still have to escape into London, find clothes, charter a plane, and then set about figuring out where Christine and Danny are. *If* they are.

And it occurs to me that that's entirely the wrong order. The wrong sequence. The first thing I should be attempting to do is to determine if Danny and Christine are. Out there. At all. If they aren't, then…

I should just determine if they are.

I dart back over to the bed, reach underneath, and start rummaging through the pockets of Rip van Liam. I find his mobile and retrieve it.

Several years ago, Christine, Danny, and I set up root numbers. Numbers that the three of us could memorize and that I would see to it were forwarded to whatever mobile devices we happened to be using. In perpetuity. That's how I was able to reach Danny back on the plane from Cape Town. However many… weeks? Months?… ago that was. I took a gamble that it would still be active. And it was. And now, I have to take that gamble again.

I could reach out to Christine, I suppose. But when last I left them, Danny and I were on far better and less being-shot-at terms. I start to dial, but then think better of it.

I don't know what kind of service Liam and the assembled crew here are using. Commercial, private, secure, unsecure, monitored… I have no idea. Calling is far too risky a proposition.

I choose to text.

Danny. Bru. It's Alec. Really. I'm sure it's hard to believe, but it's me. Here's how you can tell: It may be time to improvise. If you're alive and able to receive this, do let me know.

I hit 'send,' and then I wait. And wait. And wait. Liam's snoring feels as though it's getting louder. I have no idea how long he'll be out, but if the snoring thing doesn't abate soon, I may have to suffocate him.

Just as I'm considering planting a pillow on Liam's face, he is miraculously spared by the ding of a text.

Alec?

Yeah, bru. It's me.

Jesus

Indeed

You're really alive

It would seem. I'm going to try to work myself free and come to you, yeah? Tell me where you are.

A few moments go by. Tiny bubbles appear on the screen. I have no idea what's going to come my way. He could be anywhere. Honestly, if he told me he was on holiday on the surface of the sun, I wouldn't be shocked. Nothing would surprise me at this point.

Well… almost nothing.

Finally, after almost half a minute, his response pings through.

We're here

It was a proper plan. I will give the Watson crew that much. But there were two things wrong with it from the start.

One—we had no clue where Alec actually is. It was weeks ago that Christine was here spying, so there's no evidence that he's still here, or still alive, or any of that crucial intel most people gather before they attempt a crazy break-out-your-friend scheme.

But now we know.

Because I got a text.

What a crazy turn of events.

Three hours ago, when we put this whole thing together, it was all faith. Turns out Theo is sort of the interim hacker for the crew at the moment because when they go out and do a job someone has to stay with the tiny person.

That tiny-person sitter can't be Eliza—she's a critical part of the crew's success rate. If she's not the sexy distraction then she's the lead sneak because even though the whole family can fling themselves on and off buildings like howler monkeys on crack, Eliza is the nimblest and can fit in spaces her over-muscled brothers can't.

So Theo is the tiny-person-sitter-slash-crew-hacker for the time being.

Theo was setting himself up in the home base with Eliza, pulling up the security system for the estate, and Christine stood in a corner watching. Rage written all over her face as Eliza demonstrated just how familiar she was with Alec's English home.

I thought for sure Christine was going to kill her before we left the house, but she checked herself, and just stood silent in the corner.

And two—the plan was to have two phases, and both of them were based mostly on improvisation. Which is not how this crew normally works.

Normally they plan for months, not hours.

It was intended to go like this:

Part One—Brenden and Charlie cause a distraction at the front gate, as delivery men. Which is so cliché and will never work for more than half a minute at most. Which is becoming really obvious, as at this moment we are in front of said gate. Brenden and Charlie are in the front seats of a refrigerated meat truck—the only delivery truck the crew could procure on such short notice— Charlie in the driver's side holding a clipboard, Brenden in the passenger side. They are doing their stupid brother routine. AKA arguing like dumb, muscled blokes with only half a brain between them.

It's funny. The insults are perfectly timed, there's a little physical comedy like slapping each other on the side of the head, and of course, it's all done in that thick Cockney accent, complete with rhyming slang, that's both hard to take serious and deadly serious at the same time.

"Oi, mate! Eyes on the frog and toad, boy! You almost clipped the bloke!" says Brenden.

"Who you fink you're talking to? I'll put my foot up your bottle and glass!" responds Charlie, taking a swipe at Brenden.

"Don't get nasty with me, me old son. I'll bop you right on that fireman's hose o' yours," Brenden shoots back, slapping back at Charlie.

"Oh, will you now?"

"Adam and Eve, mate. Adam and Eve."

And now they're in an honest-to-goodness, goddamn slap fight.

I have to be honest, I get a kick out this shit. I really do. Even if I have no fucking idea what the hell they're saying.

"Hey! It's fine, man," says the guard they're talking to, in his thick Afrikaans accent, which—at least—confirms that we're in the right place. "Calm down and say again. What do you have in the truck?" He says the last part very slowly and with a fair amount of suspicion.

I'm hunkered down in the back seat—which isn't an actual back seat, just a small space for shoving leaflets and trash, apparently. And I wouldn't actually call it hunkered down. Wedged is the word that fits. There is no way I can help these two dummies should things go wrong and I'm not gonna lie, I'm a little bit claustrophobic at the moment because the mercenary at the gate is waving an AK around like an idiot.

And then the text comes in.

I have my phone on silent, but I'm holding it in my hand because Christine and I have a call going so she can hear what's happening and the three of them—she, Eliza, and Russell—can get over the fence on the west side of the property, run across the lawn, and then scale up the side of the house and get on the roof.

All this has to happen before the asshole with the gun at the gate decides to spray us with bullets.

And—to make things even more complicated—we have to get him in communication with however many other mercenaries there are on the property in order to make the distraction big enough to give the three of them time to do all that.

We're about twenty seconds into all this when my phone notifies me of an incoming text from my root number—the phone number that Alec, Christine, and I set up years ago just in case things get so fucked up, we have no other way to communicate.

Only two people have that number. And one of them is on the open phone line, so it's not her.

Jesus Christ.

And just as that happens, I hear Christine whisper into my earbud, "We're going up now. Are we good?"

But the twins are deep in their current distraction routine—

"It's right here on the manifest, mate! Thirteen hundred pounds of prime rib to be delivered today. Just give us your Hancock and we's off!"

—and there's no way to relay this new piece of information to them, or Christine, without giving myself away and getting our heads blown off.

The merc at the gate pulls up the walkie clipped to his shirt and says, "Does anyone know anything about a truck of prime rib that was to be delivered today?" He puts his hand to his own earpiece and listens. "I don't know, man, two giant fokken chops who say they're here for us."

"What'd that geezer call us?" shouts Brenden.

"Oy! Watch who you's calling a 'chop,' my china," says Charlie, pointing his finger in the guy's face and half-mocking his accent with that last phrase. (Which is one that at least I know.)

And that's when the asshole at the gate gets fed up and grabs Charlie by the coat collar and tries to drag him out of the truck via the open window.

CHAPTER TWENTY

Christine

We're as prepared as we can be for a plan this big brought to life in under three hours. Theo is manning the now-hacked security system, talking to us via earpieces, and the whole time I can hear mini-Alec, back at her perfect country estate, talking about how Danny is gonna hopscotch with her when he gets home from work and what time is that gonna be? Seventy-one thirty?

Seventy is her thing. Everything that has to do with numbers with this child comes in seventies. They are gonna jump rope seventy-two times. And eat seventy-nine biscuits as they drink seventy-four pots of tea. And that little hopscotch grid on that dark-slate path all had various numbers between seventy and seventy-nine. Some repeated more than once.

This makes Russell chuckle, but I'm just annoyed. And I hate that I'm annoyed because it is cute, but for fuck's sake. I'm on a goddamn mission to save one of the men I love—even if I did try to kill him, which makes it all the more important, if you ask me—and I do not need a reminder in my fucking ear that he has a child with another woman, OK? I just don't.

Meanwhile, we're in the woods on other side of an electrified gate, waiting on Theo to confirm that he's got the voltage turned off, when up ahead, we hear the mercenary closest to us radioing the gate guard to "just shoot the fokkers and hide their bodies."

It's not looking good. Because A, the fence is still hot, and B, it doesn't appear that this asshole is gonna go help out his friend.

And that's when luck intervenes. Because the asshole starts asking his front-gate friend things like, "What? What's going on? What the fok is happening?" and takes off at a hard run toward the front of the property.

Several guards are now running across the property toward the gate. And for sure, this plan is shit and it's never gonna work, but at least things are now going our way.

And that's when Theo says, "Go!"

So there's no time to think, or wonder if Danny will be alive when this is all over, let alone Alec, because Theo can only turn the fence off for nine seconds without triggering another alarm. So we jump up, grab the fence, and hurl ourselves over. Dropping to our feet and running across the lawn in the same instant.

Theo says, "And we're back online. No one got fried, I hope."

And mini-Alec says, "Seventy-six thirty? Uncle Theo? Or seventy-four thirty?"

But there's no time to be annoyed about that just now, because we've reached the side of the house and Russell makes one of those stirrup things with his hands, Eliza puts her foot in it, and he flings her upward. She latches on to a window ledge and is already climbing her way up when I put my foot in Russell's stirrup hands and get flung up as well.

I'm good at this parkour shit, but these Watson siblings—this is their main routine. So, two seconds later I'm still climbing up, grabbing on to things that don't qualify as handholds, when both Eliza and Russell pull themselves up and over the edge of the roof.

Russell reaches down, grabs my forearm, and drags me up the rest of the way while Eliza looks at me like I'm an amateur.

I decide right then and there I'm going to kill her one day.

CHAPTER TWENTY-ONE

Fuck do you mean *you're here? Here where?* I text.

From underneath the bed, young Liam gasps in a snort and moans a bit. I really don't know how much longer he'll stay out. I consider going ahead and suffocating him just for good measure, but I'm still clinging to the fading hope that today will be one of those rare days where no one gets murdered.

When no text comes back my way, I try again. *HERE WHERE MAN?*

And now, from someplace that appears to be the front of the estate, I hear a horn. Not a trumpet. A horn. A car horn. And shouting. Liam snores and moans. And there appears to be some commotion inside as well, as I can hear boots running toward the main entry hall.

I dart over to the door and pull it open a crack. Sure enough, down the way a bit, I see some of the laaities who've been placed here to keep me held captive, making for the front of the manor.

HERE DUDE FUCKIN HERE THEYRE

That's the text that comes through as Liam's phone vibrates in my hand. Shit. Fokken hell, man. He's *here?* Here here? How? And is Christine with him? And what does *THEYRE* mean? "They're about to catch me?" I have to

145

assume that's what he was intending to write, because the one sound that I desperately wanted to keep from hearing today… I hear.

Gunfire.

Automatic gunfire.

What have you fokken done, Danny?

Well, it now seems I don't have a choice, do I?

I reach under the bed to grab for the rifle and make my way out to see just how kind fate actually is, and when I do… Liam grabs my wrist.

He moans out something that sounds like, "Mr. van den Berg?"

Kak, fok, piss. Why couldn't you just have stayed asleep, boy? He's leaving me no choice. He's grabbed my free arm, so with the arm that's holding his rifle, I turn the barrel toward his stomach, hoping that I can just tap the trigger and put him away swiftly. As opposed to making a freight train of noise and lighting up the whole room in the process.

But just at the very moment that I'm about to apply pressure on the firing mechanism, he moans, "Are you safe, sir? He said to keep you safe."

I am not usually distracted in a moment of crisis. One of my greatest superpowers is my ability to maintain my focus. But I have to be honest, I find that statement attention-getting.

"What? Who? Who said to keep me safe?" He doesn't respond. "Hey, man! Eyes on me! Who said to keep me safe? Safe from what? How did I get here?"

It is a heightened version of our usual script. And, just as usual, I get no satisfactory reply from him. It would appear that he had just enough petrol left in the tank to make that gasp of effort before falling back into a state of unconsciousness. I double-check to make sure I didn't actually shoot him after all. Nope, still has a pulse, he's just a sleepyhead.

Danny? Is it Danny who somehow got me here? Is that who it is that the laaitie meant? Is Danny the one who is trying to keep me safe?

That don't make any sense, though. Danny is, if all is to be believed, currently outside and possibly taking fire. What in the name of holy fokken Christ is happening?

And then, just at the moment when events cannot become any more baffling...

They do.

I grab up the rifle and phone, stand, ready myself to sprint outside and presumably shoot a bunch of people, and as I glance in the direction of the window, I see...

Eliza Watson. Standing three meters away from me.

I can't be sure for a moment that she's not an apparition of some kind. I thought I saw Danny and Christine in the bushes before, but it was just shadows. Wishful thinking perhaps. Figments of my imagination.

But then it turns out Danny's actually here. So was it a fiction after all?

My doubts about whether or not Eliza is really here are quickly put aside when I see the look on her face. It's something like exhaustion blended with disgust and a hint of resentment. Yes, it must really be her. I don't believe my fantasy version of her appearance would be so precisely authentic and not sugar-coated.

I'm sure I must look to her like the proverbial deer in headlights. Of all the people on earth I could have imagined seeing today, she is likely at the end of that list. She shakes her head at me a tiny bit in a way that is very familiar. It's the way that says, without words, *Oh, Alec, you stupid fucking twat.*

This oddness that is swirling around me keeps getting odder.

And odder.

Because as, once again, I feel we have reached the apotheosis of preposterousness, I am proven wrong.

Russell Watson, the eldest brother of the Watson clan, drops into view next to her. I need to repeat that to myself. He *drops* into view. As if from a roof. But, when I stop to consider, Eliza and Russell scaling a roof and plopping down somewhere they're not supposed to be is far and away the least curious thing about now.

Russell lifts his hand in a totally casual salutation. Out of some kind of reflexive instinct, I return the gesture. And then Eliza and Russell both look up. It causes me to look up in kind, although all I see is the ceiling. And I wonder, what in the great wide heavens is going to happen now?

And when I lower my chin to face the window once more…

Christine.

Christine Keene drops into view beside Russell and Eliza Watson.

And I drop to my knees.

I'd like to tell myself that my ribs began hurting too much. Or that, perhaps, someone has just burst into the room and shot me in the back. Something dramatic, and heroic, and not simply the result of my normally immutable steadiness being stripped from me, incomprehensible event by incomprehensible event, until I just no longer have the power to support my inexcusably human form. But that's what it is. My mind cannot process this moment and my body follows suit.

Seeing me drop to my knees, Eliza kicks at the frame of the French-style shutter and it smashes open, ripping free of the latch. She bounds through the window, Russell and Christine behind her, and lands in front of me. She looks down and says, "Hello, luv. Nice PJs. Very Hugh Hefner of you."

CHAPTER TWENTY-TWO

Christine

"Is this really happening?" Alec asks, looking up at us from where he's knelt on the floor. It's very strange. Very, very strange. I've known him for almost half my life, and I've known him in almost all the ways it's possible to know someone. But I've never known him like this.

Confused.

Muddled.

Vulnerable.

He doesn't look scared. That's a look that I've never seen from him, and doubt I ever will, but what he's projecting right now is the closest I imagine it'll get.

"Yes, Alec, this is real. And it's time to go," Eliza says.

"What…? How…?"

"Ah, yes, you're as charming a conversationalist as I recall. But all that for another time. I don't know how long Brenden, Charlie, and Danny can keep your friends occupied without getting someone killed."

"Brenden and Charlie are here too?" Alec asks, even more confused-sounding than before.

"Yeah, mate. They's here. That's what all the going-on outside is about. Shall we?" Russell extends his hand to help Alec up. Alec stares at it for the briefest of moments before reaching out and being assisted to his feet. He winces as he stands. And something inside me winces as well.

He's hurt. He doesn't look like he's been beaten or tortured or anything. In fact, he looks pretty well taken care of. Apart from the fact that he's unshaven, which I've never seen on him before and never really even imagined as a possibility. It's odd. Being scruffy is such a Danny thing.

But otherwise, he looks exactly like himself. Apart from the scruff, the bafflement on his face, and the fact that he's in pain. So. Actually. No. Nothing like himself.

And I get sad. Because I have to conclude that the pain is a remnant of what happened with us at the waterfall. So I did this to him. I put him in this place. In this state. In this position. And I still don't even have a full understanding of exactly why. I don't have a complete picture of everything. There are still holes in my memory. Ones I really can't afford to have.

My long-term memory seems okay. All the things that led up to that night on the roof are pretty clear.

I think.

But I don't know exactly what happened that night. And I don't know if the things I do remember are accurate. Or true. Or how I should feel right now. I thought I had worked out all my emotions and gotten clear that I just wanted that day back. That perfect day that Danny, Alec and I spent together. That brief moment we had where it looked like everything was going to be OK and we were finally all three going to just… be together. The triangle.

But seeing him now, a flood of feelings wash over me. Especially when I see Eliza, who is two steps closer to him than I am, go to help Russell pull him to his feet. She takes him by the other arm and puts her hand on his side, saying, "You all right there, luv? Can you walk? Or do I have to carry you?"

She says it with a smile and an almost wink. He smiles back, as if by impulse. Like an old record that has been dusted off and is being played once more.

And I have to remind myself again. I did this.

"I'm fine," he says. And then, quicker than a flash of lightning, he remembers himself and who he is. He steps back, free from the both of them, lifts his hands in a broad gesture and says, "I imagine that now that we're all jolly and reunited, someone has a plan to get us the fok out of here."

"There he is," Eliza says with what can only be called shit-eating sarcasm.

"Well," says Russell, "the plan is fuckin' shit, mate. But so far, it's maybe kind of working. Christine... what's happening out front?"

I'm still just staring at Alec when he says it, so it takes me an extra beat before I answer, "Hmm?"

"You've still got Danny on the mobile, yeah? What's happening out there? Sounds like it's quieted down."

He's right. It has quieted. I hadn't even noticed. I pull out the phone with the line I have open to Danny and whisper again, "Danny... what's happening? What was all the gunfire?"

After a moment, he whispers—so quiet I can barely hear him—"Yeah, one of the guys was shooting at the sky to get everyone to shut up."

"He was shooting at the fucking *sky*?"

"Yeah, they're... emotional, these guys."

"What the hell's happening now?"

"Um... well, I can't fucking believe this, but Brenden and Charlie actually started blaming each other for the fuckup, started wrestling—"

"Fucking *wrestling?*"

"What I said. And then the mercs started laughing at them, and one of them—who looks to be in charge—broke it up, asked for the manifest, shrugged, said, 'Top grade eats for us, my boets,' and then, once they looked in the back and saw that it's really beef and not, like, a truck of assassins or something, started helping unload it. They're all taking it into the kitchen now."

Un. Be. Lievable. "And what are you doing?"

"Still fucking pinned down, hiding in old Chinese food wrappers, wondering why I agreed to come along."

I turn to Russell and say, "We're good. I guess. Tell Theo to be ready to kill the fence again. We'll get out through the woods and meet the truck by the main road." I step to Alec and say, "Can you climb?"

"Climb what?"

"Whatever. Can you get up on the roof so we can get back out through the fence?"

"Nunu, that parkour thing is not mine. It's all of you. And besides, I'm not hundreds. My ribs still need some tending. Maybe if I had some pain muti, I could work through it, but I don't. They have the laaitie dole it out to me."

"Brilliant," Eliza says. "Well, good to have seen you, I suppose. Cheers." And she makes her way toward the window again. I don't think she's really going to go. I think she's just being Eliza. But you never know.

"Which laaitie?" I ask. "What do you mean?"

"Him," he says, and gestures to under the bed. Russell, Eliza, and I bend down to look. There, under the bed, is a young man dressed like the other guards. And completely knocked out. Snoring.

"What did you do to him?" I ask.

"Well, before I knew everyone was coming to retrieve me, I had decided that today was the day I planned on leaving. I even sent Danny a text to see where he was in the world."

"You did?"

He nods at me. "I did."

"Today?"

"Today, nunu. Just around the exact same time that you all were coming for me, I reckon."

He grins and I can't help the feeling I get in my stomach. I can't stop it. And I don't try. "That's…"

"Yeah. It's a coincidence, ain't it?"

He smiles at me. I smile back. We *are* connected. Always and forever.

"Charming." Eliza's voice breaks through. "But none of us are successfully out of here yet. Since Mr. van den Berg here can't climb, do we have an alternate course of egress?"

We all look to Alec, who says, "I had planned to use the passageways."

"Passageways?" Russell asks.

"Yeah," Alec says, "there's underground passageways. Like catacombs leading out underneath the property. Eliza remembers."

We now all look at Eliza. "Yes," she says. "I do remember." Then she puts her hand on one of the posts of the four-poster bed. "I remember a lot of things about this place."

Rage.

Whatever feelings I was having in my stomach are now replaced by my friend, rage.

"Super. Let's fuckin' go," I say, making my way to the door.

"Wait," calls Alec. "How do we know it's clear?"

"I'll go up," Russell says. "You two stay on comms, stay with him, and I'll do a quick perimeter check from the roof. If I see a bunch of blokes hauling meat, we'll assume that they're all preoccupied with that."

"How can we be sure that there's no more on the main floor?" Eliza asks. Russell shrugs. "Brilliant," she says.

"I'm not sure it's any better an idea, us just mucking about here waiting on someone to walk in though, is it?" Russell says.

"Good point." Eliza sighs. "To which end... what about him?" she asks, referring to the kid snoring under the bed.

Russell says, "What about him?"

"If they come in and don't find Alec, but instead a groggy lad on the ground who's been stripped of his rifle, there's a *tiny* chance they might become a wee bit hostile."

No one says anything for a moment, and then, since it would appear that nobody plans on stating the obvious—a tactic that calls back to the very first conversation I ever had with Eliza—I offer it up.

"Replica," I say.

CHAPTER TWENTY-THREE

Young Liam is about three inches shorter than I am, so his clothing is an imprecise fit, to say the least. And his shoes didn't fit, so I'm still in proper Bruce Willis mode.

Conversely, the silk pyjamas in which he is now swaddled make him look as though he is a tiny, happy, paramilitary baby. We left him bundled in the bed, snoring safely, blankies pulled up around his face, and now we can only hope that if anyone enters the room, he stays that way.

By everyone's admission, this entire endeavor is one hastily thrown together absurdity after another. But, so far, it appears to be working, and my hopeful dream of making it free of here with no bloodshed is somehow maintaining. Eish, man. This can't be real life. Not because it's ludicrous—life is fundamentally ludicrous. All life. That we are here, breathing oxygen on a geological exception to the laws that govern the rest of the galaxy, is ludicrous. But it can't be real life because there is absolutely no way Eliza, Christine, and I would ever occupy the same place at the same time again.

Even less probable that her brothers would be helping, and that Danny would be waiting to receive me and Christine back into each other's loving arms again.

157

Which is why I'm not so certain that I'm not still dreaming. It's all just a little too perfect. As perfect as imperfection can be, anyway.

I am strangely comforted by the fact that I still don't know how I got to this place. How I was retrieved from the bottom of that abyss and brought back to here, to the site where the beginning of the end... began. I am comforted because it allows for a virtual Sword of Damocles to remain hanging over my head. And I am at my most relaxed when I know that catastrophe very likely awaits.

When one is born into a world of chaos, one can either be made subject to its unpredictability, or become its master. I thrive on the mayhem.

"This is fucking mayhem," Christine says as she, Eliza, and I scurry through one of the underground tunnels that web their way below the property. There is no radio signal, so we're fully out of communication with the rest of the world for the moment. It is just us three as far as we're concerned. We have only each other for now. "How did you get here?" She follows up, as though the question has been simmering inside her and has now reached a boil and spilled from her mouth.

"I don't know."

"You don't know? How can you not know?"

"I don't know."

She lets out a breath of frustration and pushes past me. "Yeah, OK."

"Glad to see each other, are you?" Eliza asks. I ignore the question and run up to catch Christine.

I take her by the arm to slow her down and whisper, "I wish I had an answer. I truly do. But, sadly, I do not. But I'm glad you found me."

I mean it. Not because I'm glad to have been found. I would have gotten free one way or another. As long as I'm still alive, I will find a way to do as I like. But because I'm glad *she* is the one who has come for me. She and Danny. I can't help that in my dreams the memories that came to me were those final moments when Christine and I were challenged by my relationship with Eliza. I write that off to being back in the same place where it all came undone.

But in my waking hours, as I would amble about the parts of the house I was not restricted from, I would think only of Christine and Danny. Their touch, their voices, their bodies pressed against mine. My will to survive does not need a great deal of encouragement, but if it did, the love I feel for Danny and Christine would be more than enough. And it is love. Which is a remarkable thing for me to feel. Because I didn't believe myself capable of feeling such a thing. Triumph, exuberance, a certain jouissance, all of these things felt possible to experience. But love…? Unexpected.

I am suddenly overcome with an urge to tell this to her. Here, in front of Eliza. She needs to know, and I need to make it unambiguous. "Christine—"

"Which way?" she interrupts.

"That way." Eliza points. Reminding Christine, of course, that she knows this place better than Christine does and, in effect, dousing the flame of love I was about to express with an icy bucket of Eliza. Which is what she is. An icy bucket of reality. It's what she's always been. I'm curious to see what happens once we're all out of here. And by "curious," I mean fokken dreading.

We reach the end of the passageway and land at an old, wooden door that looks as though it might splinter into pieces if you put pressure on it. It has stood here for hundreds of years, unmolested, and the idea that our being here and pressing on it might shatter it into a thousand tiny shards seems symbolically fitting somehow. That is what we do. All of us. Break the things we touch.

"What the hell was all this? Was it used as, like, an escape route during a war or something?" Christine asks.

"Not sure," I say. "I never bothered to ask after its pedigree. I just bought it."

"My guess is that these were likely installed by some land baron for liasons dangereuses," Eliza says. And I hope that she'll just shut up and leave it at that. But she's Eliza, so... "You know, secret entry- and exitways through which the lord of the manor might shuttle his mistresses and whores. That type of thing. Probably." There is an extra amount of knowing emphasis on the last word.

And because there are automatic weapons available and no one would know... I would not put it past Christine to run outside, weeping, and telling everyone, "They didn't make it," after having laid waste to us both.

The sound of blood pumping furiously though her veins is very nearly audible.

"Lekker," I say, and push on the door. To my surprise, it doesn't splinter and fall apart, but retains a startling amount of integrity and requires quite a bit of shoulder to force open than I expected. I definitely feel pain throughout my side and look back at Eliza and Christine for a bit of aid in the pushing. They offer none. They both just stare at me.

All right. That's fair.

The door opens and afternoon country sunshine greets us. The rain has stopped completely, and the sky is beaming with the rays of that great, golden orb. There is a small set of steps that lead up and out into the pasture just beyond the fence that protects the property. A fence, I might add, that I did not have installed. I don't know who did.

I step up and into the meadow. Looking back, the manor appears to be about two or three hundred meters behind us. We've arced around and can see the front of the place spread out laterally before us. The great drive that leads to the front of the house ends just a bit ahead of where we stand and meets up with the road that passes us to the side.

Typically, these geographic details might not be important. But they are now, owing to two things that happen simultaneously.

One: I can see two bulky figures who bear a striking resemblance to the Brenden and Charlie I remember streaking from around where the entrance to the kitchen is to make their way into the cab of the vehicle. I also see Russell on the roof, sprinting to the edge of the house to, it would appear, leap down onto the escaping vehicle before Charlie and Brenden leave him stranded there.

And.

Two: The radios that Christine and Eliza are carrying erupt with sound. The sound of mingled voices shouting, "Go, mate! Fuckin' go, go, go, go, go!"

It is immediately evident why.

The various laaities who had been seeing to it that I stayed safely within their ranks are also running after the Watsons (and an as yet unseen Danny, I suppose), rifles aimed and firing.

Ah, yes. *This* is more what real life looks like.

Russell reaches the front edge of the manor just as the truck is pulling away. And as I am not prone to hyperbole, when I say that he makes a death-defying leap onto the roof of the vehicle as automatic weapon fire lances the air around him, I am not exaggerating. It is quite something to watch. I've never been impressed by acrobatic feats. It's just not something that interests me. But if Cirque du Soleil thought to incorporate small-arms fire into their acts, I might be forced to change my assessment.

The vehicle comes barreling straight toward us, Charlie and Brenden growing clearer in my view along with Danny, whose head I now see popped up between the twins. The look on his face is half-astonishment, half-anger. Russell is pressed flat to the roof of the truck, making himself as small as possible. The back of the cube is opening and flapping about, a couple of slabs of beef crashing to the ground as the lumbering transport weaves and jolts in our direction.

It makes its way through the only unsecured portion of the estate itself—the opening in the fence where the drive connects to the road. Two more guards wait there and my hope that no one will die today is looking increasingly unlikely. The bigger concern is that the ones dying will be us and not them. But, if we're lucky, perhaps not.

I raise the weapon I'm still holding and point it in the direction of the guards, who appear ready to fire into the windshield. My finger is on the trigger just as it was with Liam earlier, ready to pull away.

And then, as if in support of my global thesis that life is ludicrous… the firing stops. Their shooting ceases, entirely. Every one of them. The okes chasing the vehicle all stop, seemingly at once, and lower their weapons. The guards at the edge of the property also lower their weapons and don't make a move to stop the lorrie. Instead, they step aside and let it pass, unfettered. It comes squealing to a halt beside where we are huddled by a copse of English countryside and Charlie yells, "Get in, get in, get in!"

Eliza bounds to the open rear and in one feline pounce is up and into the back. I, in my barefooted, ill-fitting, and not-quite-yet-fully-healed state, attempt to do the same, but just like the guards, I also stop when I see that Christine is making no attempt to move forward. At all. She is just standing in place, looking ahead, impassive. Almost catatonic.

"Christine! Let's go! Come on, nunu!"

"Christine!" Charlie yells urgently from the cab. "Make moves, luv!"

But she doesn't. In the midst of the confusing chaos, she stands stock still. Looking back at the house, her chin lifted slightly.

"Christine!" I shout again, going back to take her by the arm and drag her if necessary. "Christine, we have to fokken—!"

And then I stop my forward energy once more. And see why she's inanimate. Because as I look to understand what it is she sees that has frozen her thus, I become frozen in exactly the same way.

Watching from a massive third-floor window that overlooks all that just played out on the grounds of van den Berg manor—unmoving, standing as still as Christine and I have become...

There he is.

Lars.

CHAPTER TWENTY-FOUR

"What bloody happened out there, bruv?" Theo asks as we all enter Eliza's.

"Somebody tried to fool the Queen's Guard with fake Crown Jewels, and it didn't go well," I say.

"Bloody hell does that mean, mate?"

"It means these three"—I point at Eliza, Christine, and Alec—"thought they could trick a team of armed mercenaries with the old mistaken identity routine."

"Oh, right, mate," Eliza says, wryly, "it's our fault. Not at all the fault of the two people who showed up here suggesting that we assault a virtual fortress in the hopes of retrieving a man no one would really miss in the first place." Then she adds, "I'm referring to you, Christine, and Alec, lest there be any doubt."

"Eliza," I offer, "I know we haven't seen each other in a while and that we don't really know each other that well, but I'd like to invite you to go fuck yourself."

"All right, all right," interjects Russell. "Let's all just take a breath, shall we? We got in, got Alec, and all made it back safe and sound. So, mission accomplished, yeah?"

There's general mumbling, in which I participate, because if you just look at the Xs and Os of the thing, he's technically correct. Still, something isn't sitting right for me…

"Why'd they stop?" I ask.

"Why did who stop?" Eliza responds.

"The mercs."

"How do you know they're mercs?"

"What-fucking-ever! The guys with the guns. They stopped shooting. Why? Somebody must've ordered it. Who? Did you see?"

"No, luv. I was in the truck wondering why we weren't moving."

I look at Brenden, who's at the fridge, opening a Whitbread Pale Ale. He shrugs. I step over, snatch the beer from him, take a sip, and hand it back. He scowls at me.

I look to Russell, who shrugs also, and Charlie, who doesn't seem to notice because he's focused on Christine, who stands in the corner, kind of hugging herself.

"Alec," I say, regarding him. He looks absurd in pants and a jacket that are three inches too short and no shoes. The beard also looks ridiculous on him. Some people are built for beards, some not so much. Alec is definitely in the latter category. "What the fuck happened? Do you know?"

He lifts his head, looks at each of us in turn, taking me in last, and says, "Lars."

"Lars?" I repeat. He nods. "What about Lars?"

"It's him. He's the one. He's the one who brought me there. He's the one who was keeping me there. It's him."

"Fuck are you saying?"

He shrugs. "Dunno, man. Dunno how. Dunno why. But we saw him. Christine saw him, then I saw him.

Standing there. Watching it all. He's the one behind it. He's the one who stopped it."

"I don't even understand how—"

"Yeah, I don't either, man. But I don't make the fokken news. I just report it."

There's a moment of silence before Eliza shakes her head, echoes Alec in an almost inaudible, sarcastic mumble, "You don't make the news..." and then says brightly, "Well, very good! Good luck to the three of you. Goodbye now. Charlie, Brenden, Russell, Theo... tea?" She goes to the stove and grabs up a kettle.

I rub my hand down my face and say, "Yeah, OK. We'll go. But you should too."

"What's that mean?" Theo asks.

"If Lars is somehow the reason that Alec is still alive then he's not done."

"Done with what?" Eliza says.

"Us. I guess. Christine gave you the highlights," I remind her, "so you know that he's got a vendetta that's not been settled yet."

"That's insane."

"Yeah. No shit," I say. "Have you met the van den Bergs?"

"Fair point," she accedes.

"And now, you're all implicated in this whole thing," I finish.

"Fucking hell," Russell says. "Are you taking the piss? I fuckin' hope so, mate. Because otherwise this is gonna cost quite a bit more than a quarter million quid, yeah?"

"Danny," Eliza says, touching my arm gently, "get the fuck out of my house now, please."

"Fine," says Alec, stepping between us, "we'll go. But he's right. You should protect yourselves. Just, at the least, be cautious for a bit. Until…" He drifts off, his gaze shifting over to Christine.

"Until what?" Eliza asks.

"Until I've killed him."

Christine looks up now, her eyes meeting Alec's. They hold each other's stare. There's a lot—an awful, dreadful lot—for us to unpack. It was already going to be a messy reunion with the way Alec wound up in this state.

Add to that the fact that the whole reason he wound up here at all owes to whatever happened between Christine and Lars—the details of which she still can't fully recall or just isn't willing to share—and now it seems that Lars is also still alive and behind Alec being alive.

Add to *that* the fact that we have included the Watsons into our adventure, and we have a history with them.

Add to *that* the fact that, apparently, there's a whole separate history between Eliza, Christine, and Alec that I wasn't even present for.

And then add to ***that*** the fact that this whole history between them that I wasn't present for appears to have resulted in…

"Hopscotch?" The tiny, curious accent comes from the doorway behind us. It's tinged with a hint of sleepiness. I turn to see Alexandria standing there, yawning, rubbing her little eye with her little fist. She holds a raggedy, brown teddy bear with part of its ear and one eye missing. Theo goes to her.

"Hey, hey there, pigtails. Whatchou doin' awake? You're s'posed to be napping."

"I heard talking." She points at me and says, "He's going to hopscotch with me."

And there's something in the way she says it. Something about the clear, decisive nature of it. The unwavering self-certainty that because this is what she expects is going to happen, it *is* going to happen. The way she points at me. All of it. That reminds me of…

When I look over, Alec has both hands pressed to his shaggy chin in what resembles a small prayer. His mouth is open, and his eyes are drifting back and forth between the tiny one and her mother. Eliza has her hand on her hip and her eyes closed. She sighs.

I look at Christine who doesn't move, consciously, but who radiates with an energy that causes her to look like she's vibrating. I know that vibration. Water gathers in her eyes. Not sadness.

Intensity.

Rage.

And when Alec then says, "Right. We need to make sure you're all protected," she stands, opens the door, and marches out, slamming it hard behind her.

Yeah… there's a lot to unpack.

CHAPTER TWENTY-FIVE

Christine

The door rattles the frame as I slam it shut. I don't look back, but I hope it knocks some of the precious shingles off the thatched roof.

Avoiding the slate pathway and marching straight through the garden, I step on and squash as many daffodils, or daisies, or pussy willows, or dandelions, or whatever as I can. I don't know what I'm stomping on, exactly. I don't fucking garden.

I trudge my way into a grove of trees just past the little stone wall and see the magical playhouse that I knew was there. Just beyond the playhouse is a proper guest house that looks like a larger version of the playhouse. The playhouse that looks like a miniature version of the main house.

This whole place makes me wanna puke.

From behind me I hear the door to the main house open and I turn, expecting to see Alec. Because Alec would come for me right now, right? After everything. After all we've gone through. After coming to rescue him, and admitting that we needed Eliza's help, and facing her, and all that, and the past... he'd come out to make sure I'm OK, right?

Danny and Charlie call my name at the same time.

"Hey!"

"Oi, Christine!"

… I guess not.

Charlie spies me across the way and trots over first, taking my elbow as he arrives. "You OK, luv? Is there something—?"

Danny comes up behind him and puts his hand on Charlie's shoulder, pulling him back. "Thanks, mate. We got it."

There's a moment.

Charlie spins on Danny, seemingly out of instinct at the sensation of being touched. It looks like they're going to—as I've heard the Watson boys says in the past—"have a tussle." If they do, I don't want to be here to watch it. They're well matched physically and neither one will ever back down, and I don't have any desire to stand here and watch them kill each other.

But then Danny tips his head toward Charlie with a resolute and knowing look and repeats himself. Slowly. "We got it, man. Thanks."

Charlie stares at him, looks at me for… I don't know what. Something I don't have to give. I look at the ground and Charlie huffs a breath, nods, and turns to head back inside.

Once Danny and I are alone, the sounds from Eliza's property settle in my ears. Bees buzz. Birds chirp. I'm pretty sure I hear Snow White singing to a motherfucking blue jay somewhere in the distance. I rip a bunch of roses from a bush, tearing them free and cutting my hands on the thorns.

"Hey! Yo! What are you doing? Don't do that. Stop."

I keep ripping at them anyway.

"I said, stop!" Danny repeats, grabbing my hands and holding my arms at my sides.

"Let me go."

"Not until you calm down. You're going to hurt yourself."

"Oh, I'm gonna hurt somebody all right. Let me. Fucking. Go."

He does. He releases his grip and I rub my palms together to get the stinging to stop. The blood smears.

Danny sits on the stone wall. He plants his hands beside his thighs and lifts his shoulders. "What else aren't you telling me?"

I cross my arms. I'm probably going to smear blood all over my clothes. I don't give a shit. "What are you talking about?"

"I feel like I've been pretty fucking cool and understanding about the fact that I'm in the dark on what's going on. I don't know a whole lot of other motherfuckers who'd travel all the way around the world knowing as little as I did about what the hell was going to be waiting for me when I got here, and not make a thing out of it. And I know there's still holes in your goddamn memory, but I also know there's shit you're just withholding from me, period. But y'know what?"

He lets that hang in the air for a second before he goes on.

"We're here now. We're here. And we did it. The whole fucking reason that we risked our lives—and are going to continue to risk our lives, it would appear—is so we could get Alec. When you left me, disappeared to I didn't know where, and then came back to say that you had found him, I said, 'Let's fix this.' Remember?

I nod.

173

"And that's what I thought we were doing. Fixing it. But now that we're here, shit still looks broken to me. So what's left? What's left to be fixed? Because I thought we were going to put our fuckin' triangle back together, but right now we still feel like three broken lines. So what else aren't you telling me?"

He lifts his hands and rubs his palms around and around each other. Like he's soaping them up. Like he's washing them. Like he's been holding on to something dirty and now he wants to get clean.

I take a breath, look at him, step over, place my bloody palms around his fists—in effect, dirtying them up again—and say as softly as I can, "Not now, OK?"

"Not now what?" he asks with exasperation.

"I'll get into everything. I will. I promise. I just… not now."

"Is it just the kid? He had a kid with Eliza. So what?"

"Danny—"

"I know you a little, Christine. Y'know? I do. So, is it that *her* life looks like this?" He gestures around us. "That she gets to have this and we're… where we're at? Because we could have this too. Y'know? We could have all this shit too. I mean, to be fair, life in the Cook Islands was pretty fuckin' plush. We could've just stayed there. So I'm saying, if it's some kind of suburban-ass, tea-and-biscuits bullshit you want, we can fuckin' have it. Just tell me and we'll fuckin' do it. Because we've been through way, way too much and paid way, way too high a price to not be a little bit happy."

I stare into his eyes. There's something urgent in them. Desperate. Wanting. I know that Danny loves me. I have always known. And I've known that he would do anything for me. But until this moment, here, now, I don't know if I realized how much.

He did come all this way, asking almost no questions and just trusting what I was telling him. He found out that I had been with Alec, without him, for four years, and I know that hurt him, but he still let me back in. He let us both back in. The way I've seen him in this time that we've been alone together again—dark, angry, intense in a way he doesn't show other people… there's still so much pain inside him. And he knows he can show me that part of himself and I'll still be here.

He trusts me. He loves me. And he came for me just now. He's the one who followed me. Not Alec. I know that Alec van den Berg believes he has special powers. That he wields some kind of control over people. Over me. But I didn't come for him because he's got some magical ability to control my mind or my heart. I came for him because it was the right thing to do. And because Alec, Christine, and Danny are who we are meant to be. I can feel it as much as I can feel my heart pumping the blood that oozes from my hands. The sped-up heartbeat that reminds me that I love Danny with everything inside me and would do anything for him, and despite his best attempts to make me hate him… I love Alec the same way.

"Is that what you want, Christine? Is it? Because we can have that. We can."

I stare into his beautiful, haunting eyes and I nod. "I do. I do think I want that."

He claps his hands. "Fuckin' A. Then let's make it happen. You, me, and Alec. Yeah? Let's make it happen."

I don't say anything. Just keep staring. Because… because… because that *is* what I want. That life I dreamed of once where I was an executive assistant or whatever and things were "normal."

"Christine?"

That's still what I want. Right? Me, Danny, and Alec. That's what I want. Isn't it?

"Christine? You, me, Alec. We'll make a life. Somewhere. Yeah?"

Isn't it?

"Christine?"

Isn't it?

"Christine…?"

Charlie came back inside, shook his head at his brothers, and all four of them exited into another room. Some telekinetic brother thing, I reckon. Now it's just me, Eliza, and a small human with eyes that look still a bit sleepy and also strikingly familiar.

"Mummy," the child says, "are you making tea?"

"I was."

"Can I have some?"

Eliza continues looking at me and after a moment says, "Of course, dear." She goes to the cupboard and takes out a delicate-looking miniature teacup and equally miniature saucer. As she pours, I approach the small human.

"Hello, little one, what's your name?"

"Alecandra," she says. It stops me in my tracks.

"Alexandria," her mother chimes in. "Trust me, I'll see to it that she learns to get all the syllables out."

"What's your name?" the little one asks. She's a bit tricky to understand, but she talks quite well, I decide. I know nothing about children, but she seems bright. I'm going to decide that she is.

"My name? My name is Alec, funny enough. Alec van den Berg."

She laughs. "That's a silly name."

I laugh too. "Yeah, I suppose it might be. How old are you, Alexandria?"

"Mummy? How old is I?"

"You're two, luv," Eliza says, setting the tea onto the table. "Two going on twenty. Now take a seat in your chair. Use both hands."

With some effort, Alexandria scrambles up into a chair and grips her tiny cup with her chubby little fingers. She attempts to drink and manages to spill as much as she lands in her mouth. Then she pours some tea onto the teddy bear she's still holding. The whole exercise is an adorable fokken mess.

I step to Eliza, who bristles as I approach.

"Nice kid," I say, my voice low.

"She is."

"Nice place," I note, looking around.

Eliza's eyes go cold and dead. Without taking her glare off me, she says, "Andra, dear. Go see what your uncles are up to, will you?"

"I was supposed to hopscotch with that other man."

"That other man has to go, luv. See if Uncle Theo wants to hopscotch. You know how good he is at it."

Alexandria giggles. "He is pretty good!" she says, with a giddy enthusiasm that I don't think I've ever felt about anything. And then she finishes spilling the rest of her tea everywhere and goes.

Once she's gone—"Why are you three still here?" Eliza asks.

"We've been here for five minutes."

"That's about seven minutes longer than you're welcome."

"Hey, you lot brought us here."

"Yes, well, in the absence of a plan, I'm not sure what we were supposed to do." She throws a dish towel down, saying, "Goddamn it, Alec."

"Don't blame me. I didn't ask for you to come after me. I was figuring it out fine on my own."

"Were you?"

I nod.

She shakes her head. "I must have gone right barmy to have agreed to assist in this."

I take a risk and step in just a bit closer. "But you did. And I appreciate it. I truly do. I know you think I'm—"

"You can't even begin to know what I think of you."

"Perhaps not. But I know it ain't nice. And regardless of what it is exactly, I know you think I'm incapable of gratitude. But I am. I'm grateful."

"Fine. You're welcome. Goodbye."

"You don't know what I'm grateful for."

She cocks her head. "Don't play games with me, Alec. I have four lads in the other room who would be just as ready to disappear you from the planet as I am. Stop pushing your luck."

I put my hands up in a gesture of surrender. "I'm not playing games. I'm trying to tell you…"

"What?" she asks, with annoyance. "What are you trying to tell me?"

I take a breath. "I'm trying to tell you that I'm grateful you stood up to me the way you did. About…" I lift my chin in the direction the little one exited. "Because you were right. I'm not a father. There's no way I could be. I had a terrible father for a role model, and the one chance I had to prove to anyone that I could be a better example myself was when I was left in charge of Lars. And we see how that has worked out." I close my eyes, feeling a deep sense of... something I don't like to feel. I continue, "So, when I say 'nice place,' 'nice kid,' I mean it. It's far better than anything I could have provided. So... thank you."

There's no kindness or forgiveness in her stare, but at least the dead-eyed threat of annihilation is gone. And she says, more sincerely this time, "You're welcome." Something almost approaching a truce feels like it could be emerging when she adds, "Whatever happened to those blokes you were hiding from? The last time. The time when I told you that I was pregnant with her?"

I have to think hard to remember. "Which ones were those?"

She rolls her eyes. "The ones that you were going to have to stash us away in Japan to hide us from? The ones who stitched you up and left you burrowed away in that silly estate?"

I squint. Still trying to remember. "I don't... I'm not sure. I honestly don't recall which group of okes it was. But, I mean, the answer is that they're dead. They're all dead. Anyone who has ever posed a threat to me is gone. That's how it works."

She purses her lips and nods. "You mean anyone who has ever posed a threat to you or your triangle. They're all gone. I know, because that includes me. And your daughter."

That stings. I'll admit it. But I can't blame her. "Well, now, the way things are, anyone who poses a threat to you two is part of that equation. So..."

"What are you saying?" she asks. Somewhat rhetorically.

"You know what I'm saying. I'm saying that I won't leave England until I'm sure that no one is going to come after you for helping today."

"We can take care of ourselves."

"I know you can. So can I. And look what happened to me."

She grinds her teeth and pushes her hair behind her ear. "Fine. Do whatever you like. But it has nothing to do with me. Or my brothers. Or my daughter. Do you understand?"

I nod. "I do."

"And if any part of it—and I mean *any* part of it—gets visited back upon me or them…" She pauses for a long time. A long, long time. I think she may be waiting for a prompt. When I don't offer one, she finishes her thought. "I'll kill you."

I raise my eyebrows, press my lips together, and nod. "OK."

"OK."

And then we stare at each other. It's a strange, strange thing. She's beautiful. Beyond beautiful, in fact. And I do care for her. I always have. But she was right, back then, when she said I didn't love her. I didn't. I don't. She's impressive and I always liked how much she felt like a challenge, but when all is said and done, the only two people I love are sitting outside right now. They are the only two people I feel anything for. Truly.

Which is why I find it so very strange that if you asked me if I would be willing to lay down my life for a two-year-old person who I only just met moments ago, the answer would be yes.

Funny that.

CHAPTER TWENTY-SEVEN

"Christine?" I say, feeling like I'm stuck on repeat. But she's not answering me, and this is making me very fucking nervous. "Fucking say something or I swear to God, I'll pick you up by your ankles, tip you upside down, and shake the words right out of you."

She smiles. Because I used to say this to her back in that first foster home where we met. I knew she was holding a lot of shit inside and I needed to know what it was. Because I was holding shit inside too and I wanted her to need my story as much as I needed hers.

But she didn't need anything back then.

It's scary to meet a kid who needs nothing.

I mean she needed food, and shelter, and all that other basic crap. But she was already at that late stage of neglect where one decides they don't need love.

I was there too. But I was fourteen and she was ten. It just felt like I should've been way ahead of her in the whole no-love thing, not on equal footing.

So I wanted her story and she didn't want to give it up.

This was my threat. _Gonna shake it out of you, Christine._

I never did of course. Or maybe once or twice I'd actually pick her up by her ankles and make her squeal.

But I never hurt her, and I never shook any words out of her.

The story came, eventually, but she was the one who shook it out, not me.

She sighs loudly in the here and now and says, "There's more."

And she looks ten again. No, she looks eight. Or six. Or four. She looks like some version of Christine I never saw but always knew existed.

"Yeah, no shit," I say, taking her hand and pulling her towards me. "I know that." She sits down on the wall and kinda… slumps into herself. I put my arm around her shoulder, and she leans against me.

"I can't talk about it here. I can't stay here." She straightens up again, turning a little so she can look me in the eyes. "I need to leave this place right now and never come back."

I nod my head. "OK. I mean, I never figured we'd be staying so I texted our driver to come get us. He should be here in a few."

"But I'm not sure Alec should come with us."

"Whoa," I say, putting up a hand. "No. We didn't just fucking break that asshole out of a fortress to leave him behind with Eliza fucking Watson."

"He needs to decide—"

"Fuck you," I say. "Just fuck you, Christine. He did decide. He's with us. These Watson assholes can do whatever the fuck they want, but he's with us."

She sighs again. "That's his daughter."

"I know that. He knows that. And if we go in there right now and say, 'Let's go, man. We're out,' he's gonna leave with us."

"You *can't* know that."

"Let's go test it out."

She deflates again. Shakes her head just a little bit. "I don't think I can."

"I'll do it."

"No," she says. "I don't think I can take it. I don't think I could stand those empty seconds where he thinks about it and makes a decision."

"He's gonna choose us," I say. So fucking sure of this.

"Maybe. But there's gonna be a part of him that wonders if he should stay and I can't deal with that right now, Danny."

"He doesn't love Eliza, Christine. He loves—"

"It's not about *Eliza*," Christine snaps. Rage in her voice. "It's not about her kid either."

"Then… what?"

"I just need to leave."

Now it's my turn to sigh. "Well, that's the plan. Let's grab Alec and go." I see her words before she speaks them and hold up a hand to shut her up. "Fuck you. We're not leaving him behind. He's not here for Eliza. Or the kid. He's here because we brought him here. I'm sure he's got lots of questions and I'm sure his answers will be coming. But I want my fucking answers too. Right the fuck now. And if you can't give them to me here, then we're leaving. So get up, put on your big girl panties, and stop acting like a goddamn child."

Footsteps on the path make us both look up. Christine tenses up so bad, I have a moment of panic that the interloper is Eliza.

But it's not, it's Charlie.

"Dude, I thought I told you I got this."

He doesn't even look at me. He only has eyes for Christine.

"You never told him, did you?" Charlie asks.

"Shut up," Christine snaps.

"Told me what?" I say. "Did you two—"

"No," Christine says.

But Charlie says, "Yes," in that same moment.

And I don't know how I know they're talking about two different things, so both these answers make perfect sense, but I do.

They didn't do what I was asking about. Meaning they didn't date, or fuck, or whatever.

They did something else. Something Charlie seems to want to talk about and Christine clearly doesn't.

How much did I miss in those four empty years?

"You got something to say?" I ask Charlie. "Because now would be a really good time to fill me in."

"Don't you dare," Christine seethes.

Charlie puts up his hands. A gesture that says, *I won't. But you need to.*

My phone buzzes a text. I glance down at the screen and read it.

"OK," I say, getting up and pulling Christine to her feet. She resists for a second, which is dumb—she's the one who wants to leave—but relents. "The driver's here. So we're going inside, grabbing Alec, and going somewhere else."

I don't wait for an answer, just tug Christine past Charlie and head back toward the house on the dark slate path. Inside it's quiet and we find Alec and Eliza at some sort of standstill in the kitchen. Christine yanks her hand from mine, picking up her pace, and marches on through towards the front door.

I say, "Come on, Alec. The driver's here. We're leaving."

And then the moment does come. The one Christine was dreading. I'm glad she's not here to witness it, because there is a split second where Alec considers this.

It's fair, his consideration. Because anyone, in any situation, even ones that don't involve ex-girlfriends and secret babies, would need this split second to decide if they were staying or going.

But I get her point.

To Alec's credit he just says, "Hundreds," and heads after Christine without a second glance back at Eliza.

She stares at me. Glares at me. A look of hate that's probably meant for Alec but lands with me since he's already gone.

I just turn and follow him outside. Christine is already getting in to the back of the limo, but Alec is saying something to Russell as he walks past. "Get them somewhere safe. I'll be in touch."

Then it's Russell's turn to glare at him.

Alec doesn't even notice. He's already reaching for the door handle on the opposite side of the car.

I slow my steps as Russell's eyes turn to me. "I don't know, dude." I say in way of explanation. "Lars, I guess."

"I got that part, mate. thanks. But the part I don't have quite yet is… what the fuck does he think he's doing?"

"I have no clue," I say, passing him by. "Just… get them somewhere safe." But then I turn and add over my shoulder, "And tell that tiny one that I'm sorry I couldn't stay."

I don't know why I say it and I'm pretty sure it was a bad idea. Pretty sure that Uncle Russell isn't too keen that Uncle Danny has suddenly shown up out of nowhere.

But fuck it.

Alec's kid, right?

And we're a team. So…

I just know what it's like to be left behind without a second thought and I made myself a promise many years ago that I'd never do that to a kid. Ever.

That was the whole reason I took to Christine in the first place. Someone bailed on her just like someone bailed on me and it's not right.

"I'll do that," Russell murmurs.

And when I reach for the door of the limo, I look back at the house. The seemingly perfect happily ever after that Eliza is living here. And I get it. I do.

This is something Christine and I never had but always wanted.

That has to be what's eating at her. That has to be why she's acting this way.

I tell myself that as I open the car door to find Christine's shattered emotions staring up at me.

"Scoot over," I say, motioning her to take the middle between Alec and me.

But she doesn't. And that's how I know I've got it all wrong. I'm missing too many pieces. This puzzle hasn't been solved.

She gets up and takes the seat across from us.

When I get in, we're a triangle all right. Each of us taking one point in the shape of our love in the back seat of this limo. But it feels wrong in this moment. Feels false. Because there's more to us now than there was before. A new shape has formed.

Some kind of square that includes Eliza and her daughter.

Three is hard enough to maintain in a relationship. Four… just doesn't happen. And five?

We're fucking doomed.

But that's not it either. Not all of it, anyway.

Christine is not missing her childhood or comparing it to the one Alec's daughter is living out. She's not worried about Eliza and Andra coming between us.

It's something worse.

Something much, *much* worse.

CHAPTER TWENTY-EIGHT

Christine

Never did I ever think that I'd have to confront these feelings again. I thought it was over. Convinced myself it was finished. That I'd moved on from that dark place I found myself in two and a half years ago. Gotten over it. Past it. Came out the other end stronger, more resilient, better than I was before.

But it was all lies.

I never got over it. I never moved past it.

I'm stuck inside it still. Every raw emotion that kept me up at night, crying—no, sobbing—uncontrollably, is back.

Like it just happened yesterday. Like it just happened today. I'm in that limo with Alec again as he took me home.

Home.

What fucking home?

That place wasn't my home. I have no goddamn home.

I look up, but not at Danny. I look up to find Alec staring at me. His mouth a tight line. His eyes sad. He looks like shit. The fucking beard, for one. So unlike him. He's pale too. Like he hasn't seen the sun in decades. That golden-boy persona has gone missing.

And you know what? This makes me happy.

So I say, "You deserve this," my voice low. So the words come out as a whisper.

"What?" Danny says, thoroughly confused. "What the fuck are you talking about?"

But Alec doesn't answer him. Doesn't even look at him. He just stares at me with that sad, defeated face. That same face he wore when he drove me home. He nods and says, "I know."

"You know what?" Danny says, almost shouting. "Someone fill me in. Please."

"Christine was—"

"Oh, fuck you," I sneer, cutting him off. "You do not get to start this story with my fucking name."

Alec sighs. He looks weary and weak. So unlike him. But that was me, two and a half years ago. And once again I find myself feeling happy about that. We've switched places. I'm the strong one this time. I'm the one in control. I'm the one with the upper hand and he's the one at my mercy.

I don't think I've ever hated Alec. Even back then when all this shit was going down I didn't hate him. I loved him so much. So fucking much it hurt. The love I felt back then was killing me. Eating me up from the inside out.

I never understood heartbreak until then. I never knew that love could hurt so much. Never thought that I, Christine Keene, would ever experience emotions so charged, so undeniable, so consuming that I couldn't eat. Or talk. Or hell, even get out of bed.

But I did. I felt those things.

And then it was all ripped away in an instant. One minute I knew what love was and then the next... the next moment changed me forever.

"Please," Alec says, pleading with me. "Let me say something."

I turn away from him, shaking my head. "No. You just need to sit there and shut up." And then I look at Danny. I look at Danny and a rush of air leaves me. The hate, and anger, and sadness all spill out with my breath. And I say... I say, "Just listen. Just let me tell it my way, OK? Give me that one chance, will you?"

"Of course," Danny says. He gets up, takes one step, and then he's in the seat next to me, his arm around me. Being the rock—no, the mountain—he always has been.

And I hate myself in this moment. Because I gave him up for *us*. This stupid fucking triangle. And why? For what?

I lost.

I thought we could work. I really did. I thought the three of us were indestructible. So when Alec and I decided to give Danny that ultimatum, we thought he'd cave. And when he didn't, we thought it was temporary. He'd be back. And when that didn't happen either, we mistook our infatuation for something else. We dared to dream without Danny. We dared to move on.

And this is what happened...

"Why are you smiling so big, nunu?" Alec is touching my face with both hands. His palms are cool and comforting, his amber eyes sparkling with mischief, like always. But with something else too. He loves me, I realize. And I love him back.

So much. I love him so much that I get this... this sick feeling inside my gut when he looks at me this way. Or when I just think about him. I love him so much my heart hurts every time I gaze up at his face. Or his fingers gently caress my arm.

I don't know what to do with this love. I don't know how to process it.

I love Danny this way too, but Danny is gone now. He'll be back. I know that much. But my love for him, that all-encompassing passion that ruled my life ever since we met that day I poked the blue beetle… it's died a little. Not died, maybe. It's just been tempered by the new love I feel for Alec.

I have some guilt about that, but not much. Because Danny is part of this love. He's not here now but he will be once I call him and tell him.

I almost did that yesterday when I got the news. I almost told him first but I stopped myself. Because there's this rational part of me that knows how Danny would react.

Oh, he'd get over it. I'm sure. But still.

"I'm pregnant," I say, still smiling up at Alec.

And he does everything I expected. His reaction is everything I could've hoped for. Elation. Happiness. And a litany of rhetorical questions like, "What? No? Yes? Oh, my God! I'm gonna be a father? You're having my baby?" And of course… "I love you, Christine."

We dressed up. We went out. We had dinner, and we danced.

We celebrated.

And of course, we talked about Danny. We would call him… eventually. Not tonight. Tonight was ours. But that call would happen, and he'd…

Did we really think he'd be happy?

That night we did. We really did.

But everything is different the next morning, isn't it?

So we didn't make that call even though Danny was the only other person I wanted to tell. He was the only thing missing in my life.

"Let's just wait, nunu," was Alec's reply the next day when I brought it up.

"But Danny loves kids," I said. "And he loves us."

"He loves you, yes," Alec replied. "But… I'm not sure how he'd feel about me as a father."

Which I acknowledged. Alec isn't really father material. I was actually counting on that to win Danny over. I'd plead with him to come take care of me. Come be the perfect father that Alec never could be.

And it's not even like Alec objected. This was just a fact we all knew. Each of us fulfills a role in this triangle. Each of us has a place. We knew how to share.

But as the weeks went on, I think we both realized that Danny was never going to buy into this idea. That Danny wanted me. And if there was a child, and if there was a relationship to be forged from it, then that relationship would be three people, yes. But not four.

It was never going to work.

I think this is why Alec continued his relationship with Eliza. I really do.

Not to hurt me, though he did. Not to get her pregnant, though he did.

This baby was his, but it wasn't his, not really.

It was mine and I belonged to Danny first, not him.

So we didn't call him.

Sometimes it makes sense.

It does.

I get it.

And then other times it's insanity.

It *is* insanity. The whole fucking thing from top to bottom is insane.

But love does that to people. It makes them irrational, and stupid, and impulsive.

I turn to look at Danny in the limo. He's staring straight ahead. Processing. "But you... you don't have a baby."

I shake my head, trying to stop the tears, but failing. "No, I don't."

And there's only three ways this ends, right? He's running this trio of possibilities through his head right now.

One. I gave it up. But he discards that immediately because I would never do that to my child. Ever. Someone did that to me once. And him. And not in the loving way, either. Not at birth, but later. After years of neglect, and violence, and drugs, and foster homes.

Two. I had an abortion. He thinks about this a little longer, but then finally says, "No. You didn't get rid of it."

I start crying. Because no, I didn't get rid of it.

He doesn't even think about the final option. Just reaches round with his other arm and hugs me tight. Then tighter. Then he buries his face into my hair and says, "Oh, Christine."

And I blurt, through tears and sobs, and snot running out of my nose, "I lost it, Danny. I lost it."

Nothing prepared me for the feelings that came after. Nothing could. I'd never lost something so wanted. Even when Danny walked out I always knew he'd be back. It was never final. It was just... a cooling-off period. Time to consider things and maybe learn a few things about ourselves and this new kind of love we were inventing. We needed space to remember who and what we were to each other. A few months to dream about what we could be if we tried hard enough.

And then we'd be back together. Better than ever. Stronger, more committed, more in love.

Except it didn't happen that way.

Alec and I grew apart in those weeks following my miscarriage. I was in bed. Recovering at first. I was in the second trimester. Almost five months when the miscarriage happened. So many hormones in my body at the time.

Then... nothing. They were all gone.

And we'd already bought a bassinet and a crib. We knew it was a girl. I'd had an ultrasound just one week prior to the miscarriage with no detected issues. 'Incompetent cervix' was the term they told me afterward.

So crazy how fast things can go wrong.

So we were decorating things in pink and white. Discussing names. All the things couples do when they're expecting.

And then we weren't.

It's like... we went from having so much to say to having nothing to talk about at all.

We were strangers. Which was something we never were before. We were never strangers. We were always Alec, Christine, and Danny.

So I knew that was why. Because everything had to have a reason. There had to be a reason for this, right?

And there was. It was because we didn't include Danny. We let him walk out. We kept this secret from him when he deserved to be there.

I didn't get out of bed for almost a week. And then I stopped eating. And then I just gave up. I wanted to call Danny, tell him everything. Beg him to come get me and take me back. Take me home. My real home. Which was anywhere he was. With him, I guess. That was all I wanted. To be with Danny.

Alec didn't know what to do.

He came back less. He stayed out later. He was gone more.

And then... so was I.

We were different. For now. And I was OK with that. At least I thought I was.

I went back to work. Took assignments—hell, started making my own assignments. Started running my own jobs.

The space we needed turned into distance over the next couple months.

But I was not in bed, I was sort of eating. And I was killing people.

I was almost normal again, I rationalized.

This was just who I was now. Christine, the assassin.

I was fine. Or at least, I was alive.

I was OK until I found out Eliza got pregnant.

And then I wasn't.

CHAPTER TWENTY-NINE

As I sit here, watching Danny hold Christine, a few things occur to me.

I should be pissed. She tried to kill me. She took up with my little brother, and for God knows how long plotted to bring my universe to an end.

Not only that, she did all this while still professing her love for me and standing by my side, and working with me, and doing terrible, violent things on my behalf even though I could have had anyone else do them instead. Because she said she wanted to. She is a very, very good liar, indeed. I have taught her exceedingly well.

Also, in the process of doing all those things to plot her revenge on me, something went horribly wrong and she was very nearly killed. But my girl is hard to kill and so instead, her fall just killed the parts of her memory that reminded her she hated me. Or so it would seem.

I continue to have many unanswered questions, but all roads lead back to my baby brother, who must be held to account for upending all of our lives so. And as soon as I can get a shave and some proper clothes, I'm going to visit with him and see to it that he is properly reprimanded. For what will be the last time.

199

But… I also consider that Christine came looking for me. Christine did. Not Danny. Not anyone else. Christine. And in so seeking, she conscripted the service of the one person on the planet I know she would least wish to ask help of. And she succeeded. She got me free.

And then I met my daughter for the first time. A tiny, female, 3-D printing of myself. Well, not only myself, of course. But in the brief moment I had with the child, there could be no mistake that she is a van den Berg. There is something resolute in her even now and even on just a brief glance.

Eish. It's been a fokken day, man.

And all those tumbling, rumbling thoughts lead me to one logical realization:

It's my fault.

It's not Lars'. Or Christine's. Or Eliza's. Or Danny's. Or anyone else's culpability that has created this mess. It is my own set of defects that has caused this to be. It is my passel of imperfections that has resulted in the woman I love sitting in the back of a car, being held by the man I love, and mourning the loss of something so much greater than the sum of its parts.

I am responsible.

Responsibility is the burden of power. I have worked hard to possess power my whole life, and it is fitting that I must now bear the burden. Pride and ego are not in short supply for me, but neither is the tug I feel in my heart when I look at them. And that tug is strong enough to rip the pride and ego that would otherwise prevent me from speaking, right out of my chest.

"Christine…"

She buries her face into Danny and shakes her head. A muffled, "Leave me alone," makes its way to my ear.

Danny looks at me with a *be fucking careful* look. I will be, Danny. I am.

"I will. I will leave you alone, if that's what you want. But as long as we're in this car together, I feel like I should say a couple of things. And then, when we get where we're headed, I can disappear and be gone for good. If that's what you want."

"I don't know if that's what I want," she mumbles out. "I don't fucking know."

"I understand. I very much understand not knowing what you want. You know... when I woke up this last time—in that place—I actually did think I was dead. You know how I feel about death—"

"Like you can't be killed because you are death or some stupid bullshit." Her head remains buried in Danny's chest.

I smile. I can't help it. "That's right. It *is* stupid bullshit. But I know that. You know I know that, right?" She pulls her face up just enough to regard me. I raise my brows and nod. "I do. I know it's something I tell myself so that I won't have to feel... whatever it is people feel. Because, believe it or not, I am also aware that I am a person."

"I don't believe it. People don't act like you do."

"No, *good* people don't act like I do. But that's not the point. The point is that I know that a lot of what I do and say is affect. But it serves a purpose. And for most of the last decade, that purpose has been to make sure that you... that both of you... are protected."

That seems to have gathered their attention. I hope I can keep it.

I go on.

"And the simple truth is that I failed in that. I failed you. Not only did I not protect you, I am responsible for just about the worst thing a person can do to another person in their time of need... I thought about myself instead."

They don't look shocked or anything as common as that. But they certainly appear perplexed. I can only imagine what this must sound like to them, coming out of my mouth. Eish, man. I can barely understand it and I'm the one speaking.

I go on.

"I don't know if you can recall, but after... what happened, I started doing more work without you."

"Of course, I remember."

"Yes, well... at the time, I sort of told myself that what I was doing was giving you time to rest. Allowing you time to grieve. And continuing on with life as usual because that would be the best way to help you move past."

"That's fucking bullshit."

"Indeed it is. It is. One hundred percent bull kak. Yes. Because what I was doing was avoiding the fact that not only was I impotent to do anything to help you—because I couldn't protect you from what happened—but that I had my own feelings about the matter. And I just couldn't allow myself to feel them."

"But—"

"Yes?"

"But you *could* have. You could have helped me. You could have been there for me. You could have done a million things. But instead you fucked someone else. And, honestly, I don't really give a shit about that. Jealousy is for girls." Again, I can't suppress a tiny smile. "But you got someone *else* pregnant. Someone *else* got to carry your baby. The baby you made with *them*. The baby that should have been ours…" She spins her finger around to indicate all three of us. "And that only even happened because of what happened with me. Is that not true?"

She looks at me, imploringly. Danny stares a hole right through me.

"Perhaps. Probably. I mean, the arrangement I had with Eliza always had certain parameters. One of them involved seeing to it that nothing like a child could ever happen."

"So why did it? Was it to…?"

She chokes off. Presses her lips together.

"What? Was it to what?"

She closes her eyes, shakes her head, and says, "To punish me somehow?"

I can't stay seated any longer. I kneel forward and go to take her hand. She pulls away. Retreats into Danny. There is a greater volume of vulnerability currently in the back of this car than could be held inside Ellis Park Stadium, and the air is thick.

"Nunu… no. The last thing I would ever want—*ever*—would be to hurt you."

"But you did."

"I fokken know I did. I know. What I started to say is that when I woke up back there in that house, I assumed that I *must* be dead. I must be. Because I know that if there is a Hell, that's where I'll be spending my eternity. And for me, the truest definition of Hell would be to spend all of time in the one place where I most hurt the only person on the planet that I would never want to hurt." Danny shoots me a look. "Fine," I add. "One of only two people I would never want to hurt."

She looks as though she remains unconvinced. I go on.

"Look. Christine. Christine Keene. My whole life, I never wanted a child. Never. I couldn't even imagine it. I mean, my childhood, while having the appearance of being all one could want, was far from it, to say the least. You and Danny? Your childhoods? Well… I couldn't even begin to think what a wretched cunt of a father I would be. But then… finding out you were pregnant. You. With our baby… All I wanted, *all* I wanted, in the blink of an eye, was to be that baby's father. And to love it. And protect *it*. And give it a picture-book life. Even if that picture book was drawn using extraordinarily garish colors that spilled well outside the lines. But still. One thing that child would never have had to question is that it was loved."

She is no longer sobbing, but a single tear does drop down her cheek.

"And," I continue, "when that was unable to happen… When not only did I fail you, but I failed that baby that was to be ours—because I couldn't protect it either—I could see no reason to go on. So I got into situations that I knew might very well kill me. I wanted, desperately, to test Death. To see why she comes for some but not for others. To see how far I could push the boundaries. And that extended to Eliza. I think… I think I wanted to see how far I could push the boundaries there before I broke everything into an irreparable deconstruction. And I think it's very possible I found my answer. It didn't come as swiftly as I might have thought. But it certainly seems to have arrived. So…"

I trail off. Because words are words are words and can only accomplish so much. Apologies are generally worthless. An apology is almost always for the one offering, not the recipient. People do not want apologies. They want penance. They want to know that the person who has wronged them is going to pay. Is going to suffer. At the least, they want to know that the person who has wronged them is going to change.

There is an argument to be made that I have paid my penance. What has happened between us would be, for most, enough. But the cost to her has been greater than any cost to me. She was robbed once. Then she was robbed again. Then she was robbed of her memories and fooled into believing that there was a happy ending to be had. And when her memories returned, she was robbed of that illusory happiness yet again.

No. Whatever I have suffered is a pittance compared to what Christine has endured. And so... I don't bother to say, "I'm sorry." I don't ask for a forgiveness that I very likely do not deserve. I just let my explanation for my role in the whole, miserable failure of fortitude stand on its own and wait to see if there's any chance that Humpty fokken Dumpty can be put back together again. Someday.

She tried to kill me. She took up with my little brother, and for God knows how long, plotted to bring my world to an end. I should be pissed.

No, Alec van den Berg. You shouldn't be.

That sounds about fair.

CHAPTER THIRTY

Danny

I can't look at him.

It's not fair, it's not gonna help anything, it's not gonna make anything right. But I can't look at him.

So in the ensuing silence, I look at my phone. I contact the new hotel we'll be staying at and text the information to the driver, even though he's on the other side of the glass right behind my head. I can't be bothered to speak about mundane details right now.

Christine is pressed up against me, Alec is so far away in this moment he might as well not be here, and I don't know where I'm at.

No clue where I'm at.

So for lack any idea of what to do next, I pet Christine's hair, lean my face down, right next to her forehead, and say, "I'm sorry I wasn't there."

It's no good saying 'I'm sorry you lost the baby' because sorry will never be enough and it wasn't my fault anyway. I had nothing to do with it.

But not being there—that was my fault. That's something I caused. Something I could've fixed. Something that mattered.

I would not have made her happy or made her forget the shit deal she was handed, but being there would've made a difference. Even if it was just to run interference between the two of them or keep Alec at home more.

There's no way he would've taken back up with Eliza if I was there.

Maybe that's giving myself more credit than I deserve or maybe it's just the truth.

I wouldn't let him walk out. I wouldn't have allowed him to distance himself. And I wouldn't have let Christine's anger and resentment fester into... betrayal.

"You have nothing to be sorry for," Christine replies.

I catch Alec's response to that out of the corner of my eye. He takes a deep breath and holds it. Like he's trying to prevent the tired sigh that wants to escape.

He hasn't earned that sigh and he knows it.

It occurs to me that Old Danny would take advantage of this situation. Old Danny would say something like, "Let me take you home, Christine." And Old Danny would take her home. Back to the dirty city we grew up in. Back to the old life we lived. Back to a time when there was no Alec.

Because that's what I wanted, right? That's all I wanted before Christine got hurt and Alec called me to go take care of her.

But that's not what I want now.

I'm not sure where this is going. I'm not sure the three of us are as tight or as strong as we thought. I'm not sure of anything except I don't want to go backwards.

So I say, "We're gonna take a day."

"A day for what?" Christine asks.

"To process," I say, finally turning my head to meet Alec's gaze. He lets out that breath and it is a sigh, but not the exasperated one he thought it'd be. It's one of relief.

I'm in charge now. I might not be in charge later, but right now I call the shots because these two can't.

That's what makes us strong, I realize. When there are only two people in a relationship and it begins to fall apart there's no one to step outside the situation and be objective. But when you have three, and two of you are having trouble, that third person can hold it all together. That third person can be the glue.

For a little bit, anyway.

So that's what I do. I become the glue.

"We're gonna get a room and relax. Alec…" I look at him. He looks like shit. "Alec needs some rest."

"Rest." He laughs, averting his gaze to look out the window at the passing countryside. "I've been resting for months, man."

"No," I say. Because he's wrong and besides, he doesn't get to decide. "You've been held captive for months. And before that you "—I almost say 'fell over a goddamn waterfall and somehow survived'. But I don't. I just say—"were hurt."

He looks at me, his eyes not teary, I don't think, but very sad. He was hurt and not just from the fall.

He was hurt by Christine's betrayal.

By Lars' betrayal.

Hell, I'm the only one he cares about who didn't fuck him over.

Which is so ironic, I half chuckle out a laugh.

Christine lifts her head slightly. Just enough so her eyes can find mine. *What's funny?* she's asking with that look.

I shake my head in reply. Nothing's funny. It's just… ironic.

She forces a smile of understanding and goes back to hiding her face in my chest.

I pet her hair again. Because I love her and her hurt is hurting me in this moment. I know it's years late. I know there's no way to take back my mistakes. Time doesn't ever go backwards.

But the cool thing about time is that it allows for change.

That hurt she feels over losing their baby can't be erased. The hurt Alec feels over being betrayed can't either. But with time... with time we can replace those feelings with new ones.

The rest of the ride back into London is quiet.

We're thinking, I guess.

I know I am.

I'm thinking about the past, mostly. Those days and weeks on the beach in the Cook Islands. Not the ones that just happened, but the ones that came before that.

The good ones.

It's gonna be a rough climb back up the mountain. It's gonna take a while. But we can find that place again.

We can find that... *peace.*

And when we pull up to the London Ritz-Carlton I make a decision.

We start looking for it again today.

I untangle Christine from my body and open the door just as the driver is getting out. "Meet me inside," I say, looking from her face to his.

They stare back at me blankly, but I don't add anything else. Just grab my backpack and get out of the car.

My ambassador meets me at the door.

How she knows who I am, I don't know. But they always know who their guest is. I assume, since the three of us have stayed at the Ritz more times than I can count, they have my picture in their database. At any rate, she greets me.

"Good afternoon Mr. Night. I'm Jessica, your ambassador. Your room is ready for you." Mr. Night is my old alias from back in the peaceful days. Funny, or maybe just continuing irony, that I'm now referring to those times as the peaceful days.

"Good afternoon," I say. "My friends are coming," I say, nodding to the revolving door where Christine and Alec appear, coming through separately. "We're going to need clothes for Mr. Berger Can you do some shopping for me?"

"Certainly. What can I get for him?"

"I'll give you a list."

"Absolutely," she says, beaming her luxury-hotel customer-service smile. "Would you like to see your room now?" she asks, just as Christine walks up and slips her arm into mine. Alec stands next to her, looking uncomfortable in his ill-fitting clothes, and pretending to smile.

There is a private elevator for all ambassador-level guests, and that's the route we take up to the Prince of Wales penthouse in the adjoining mansion. It is opulence on a grotesque level, but that's what we need right now.

We need to be reminded of just who and what we are.

That is my job in the triangle today.

Ironic, yet again. Because historically it has always been Alec who wore this hat. I don't look the part, I don't act the part, and I don't want the part.

But sometimes we all gotta take one for the team.

CHAPTER THIRTY-ONE

Christine

It's not that I haven't been drowning in luxury for half my life and it's not like I haven't been to the Ritz in half a dozen cities around the world, or even that I haven't stayed in this particular part of the Ritz London before.

It's just... I haven't been in a place like this with *them* in a very long time.

Four years. A little over four now. It doesn't seem like a long time and in the grand scheme of things, it's a blip and nothing more.

But it feels like lifetimes since we did this. Many, *many* lifetimes.

And even though it's somewhat childish that this kind of pampering can make me smile after all the things that have happened over the past few months, I do smile.

I hold tightly to Danny's arm all the way up to the room, and keep hold of it even after we enter and he's digging through his jeans for some cash to hand out a tip to the talkative ambassador in charge of us.

She thanks him and leaves.

We have no luggage to speak of. Danny has his backpack and I have a bag leftover from shopping that I left in the car... this morning. Jesus. Was that just this morning that we arrived?

213

"OK," Danny says, prying my arm off his. "This is home for now. Alec, I need you to jot down your measurements. Jessica is going shopping for you. Christine, if you need anything, put it on the list. I'm gonna have her get me some sweatpants."

I smile. I can't help it.

"What?" Danny says. "I want to cut them off into shorts so I can feel comfortable."

Alec walks over to the desk and takes a seat. He looks tired. No. Weary. Tired implies you're working too hard and maybe just need a nap to recharge. The look he's wearing implies he's been through hell.

I feel bad for unloading on him in the limo but then again, when I catch sight of myself in a hallway mirror, I realize I look weary as well, so the guilt fades.

Danny looks... resigned. He's fucking with the switches that control the drapes in the living room. He flicks all the wrong ones, opening the inside curtains first. Then they close and the outer ones open. Which he decides is not what he's after, so he flicks all the switches again.

There's a symphony of whirring motors as the two sets of curtains do the exact opposite of what he intends.

It's so him, I smile again. He never could figure out how to work the curtains in hotel rooms.

Alec gets up, drops the pad and pen on the desk, and walks over to him. "Jesus, man. I've explained this a million times. The outer curtains are on the inside and the inside curtains are on the outside."

"Because that makes sense," Danny quips, heading for the minibar. Which is actually not mini at all, but a whole slew of top-shelf liquor behind an actual bar.

214

He chooses a bourbon, something with a green label that I don't recognize, gets three glasses, and pours us all drinks.

I'm watching him do this. As is Alec. And he's just about to start handing them out when he looks at us, holds up a finger, then fishes two ice cubes out of a bucket and plops them both into one glass.

Mine.

Smile number three. Because he remembers.

"I don't want one," Alec says, putting up a hand as Danny approaches.

"It's not optional." He says it with a snide, sideways smile. "You need it. So drink it."

I don't bother protesting, even though I don't want one either. I guess he thinks we need this to soften up, and I'm not up to making my own decisions at the moment, so I accept the glass and begin to sip.

It goes down smooth, the burn coming whole seconds later once the drink is in my gut.

Alec downs his whole glass in one gulp. Which has Danny raising his eyebrows behind the bar. But he just shrugs and drains his as well.

"Let's have another," Danny says, once again pouring. He takes the bottle and his new drink over to the coffee table in the middle of the room, and then refills Alec's glass.

Alec considers objecting again, but he's too weary. So he just downs it as well.

"Sit," Danny says to both of us. "We're gonna figure this shit out."

I sit on one couch, Alec takes the one across from me, and we stare at each other for a second before averting our eyes.

Danny places the list Alec made into the butler's cubby, then presses a button on the wall near the door, indicating we have needs that require attention.

Gotta love five-star hotels. You never have to see anyone if you don't want to.

Danny takes the chair to my right, props one ankle up on one knee, and sets his glass down on his thigh. "OK. Have one question for you both." He stares at me, then Alec. Neither of us say anything. "Do we love each other or not?"

This morning I would've said, *Of course we do.*

But now?

I don't know.

I love them, I know that. Even after Alec's betrayal and Danny's abandonment, I can't imagine loving anyone else.

But I hurt Alec. I did this to him. I am the reason he's… *weary.*

So I can't get the word out.

Alec averts his eyes and pours himself another drink. Sips it this time. Then looks at me and says, "Of course I love you. But…"

But.

That's all I hear.

"But can you ever forgive me, Christine? Can you ever love me? The way you used to?"

My eyes tear up. Because that's not the 'but' I was expecting.

I nod my head and croak out, "I can. I do. I never stopped. I'm so sorry."

I look at Danny. He's blurry. But then a tear falls and he's clear again.

And he's smiling at me.

"Good start," Danny says. "But this is way bigger than one *I still love you*. This is some deep, deep betrayal, friends. And we can't move forward until we go back." He looks at Alec again. "So tell me... Alec. When, exactly, did you fall in love with me?"

CHAPTER THIRTY-TWO

"Did you happen to go off and get a psychology degree when I wasn't looking, Daniel?"

"When?" he repeats. "When did you fall in love?"

"What are you doing, Danny?" Christine asks.

"Fixing it," he says.

He smiles at her. She smiles back, her cheeks still wet from her tears. An inside joke. One that I wasn't privy to and, right now, don't feel I should ask about.

"When, Alec? When was it that you decided you loved me? Loved us? When was the moment you knew?"

I stop sipping my drink and go ahead and down it whole. The muscles in my jaw spasm a bit when the flash of liquor passes over my tongue. I wipe my bearded lips with the back of my hand and place the tumbler on a side table. I trace the rim with my finger.

"I've always known," I say.

"Not good enough," he replies. "Be specific."

"Why?"

"Why?"

"Why?"

"Because. Because… a lot of reasons. Because you're always so fuckin' witty. You're always so goddamn charming. But right now, I just want you to be honest. I

JA HUSS & J McCLAIN

want all of us to be honest. I know honesty is in short supply in this bunch, but I wanna give it a try. Because there's a lot—a whole fuckin' lot—that suggests we should go our separate ways again, but only one thing that suggests we should stay here together."

"Love," I offer, quite on impulse.

Danny points his finger at me and nods his head. "Gold star for Alec."

I feel itchy to leave. On the surface that's because I'm eager to go back to my estate. I want to get to Lars before he disappears. I want to know why he brought me here. How he saved me. How he survived himself. And what his goddamn plan is. Maybe, *maybe* there's a chance that he'll say something that keeps me from killing him where he stands. Because if not, I have to protect these people here and one little girl I only just met. I have to. Because I'm the one who can, and something tells me that if I don't then it might not happen.

But, as I say, that's on the surface. Below the surface is the fact that I feel itchy to leave because opening up a vein and bleeding my truth all over this suite is not something I'm eager to do. I've already bared just about as much of my soul as I can tolerate. But he's right. It's either get clean, get bare, right here, right now, or pretty much accept that I never will and say goodbye to them both. So that don't leave me a choice I can stomach. I have to live in this discomfort. And thus...

"Do you remember Misty?"

"Misty?" Danny asks.

"A girl that I was distracted by for a bit."

"I do," says Christine. "The one in Alabama. The one we stole the necklace from."

"Was it Alabama?" I ask. "I can never remember. Regardless... yes. That one."

Danny squints his eyes, thinks, then says, "The one you threw off the bridge?"

"In fairness, I didn't *throw* her. I was attempting to keep Christine from killing her and she was lighter than I had anticipated."

"What about her?" Christine asks.

"Then," I say. "That was when."

"That was when what?" she says.

"That was when I knew."

"You knew you loved us when you tossed some chick off a bridge?" Danny says.

"Yes, Danny, that's exactly it. You get it completely." The sarcasm in my voice should be sufficient, but to be sure, I emphasize it with a small golf clap and then continue tracing the rim of my tumbler. "To be clear: I *wanted* to throw her off the bridge. I did. Of course, I did. She laid her hands on you." I nod to Christine, who blinks. She sniffs a bit. "I can't describe the feeling—"

"Try," Danny says. I twist my neck and clear my throat.

"Yeah, well, it felt like... it felt as though she was striking me. And not just with her fists. Her words. The wretched venom she was spitting out at you both, I could feel it in my gut as real as any punch. I'd never felt anything like that before. That type of emotional reaction to something that wasn't aimed directly at me was altogether new. I didn't know what the feeling was at the time."

"And you think that was love?" Christine asks.

"No, no," I answer, carefully. "No, I think that was... passion. Maybe even com-passion, if the idea that I can feel compassion isn't too radical a concept to consider." I

221

don't know if it's the bourbon or all the truth, but I'm actually starting to get just a wee bit lightheaded. At least I don't feel any discomfort in my ribs anymore. "Hearing her call you those things, and knowing what you two had both had to fight through just to be where you were—which is to say, alive—caused me to become hurt for you. Because she had never known pain. Had never known suffering. She was just a spoiled brat who was angry because she couldn't have what she wanted and was taking it out on those who she saw as inferior. The entitlement sickened me."

"Wow. Well, that's fuckin' funny, ain't it?" Danny says.

"Yes, Danny, my bru. I reckon it is. But when Christine fought back... Christine, when I pulled that car over and saw that you weren't about to back down... that you weren't going to be marginalized... that you weren't about to let anyone else define you or play second fiddle to anyone... well. I think it's possible that that's the moment I fell in love with you. When I saw that you were a person who will not be broken. That you will always fight back. How could I not love that?"

"I was, like, thirteen," Christine says.

"Yes. You were."

"You think you've loved me since I was thirteen?"

"No, nunu. I know I have. The essence of who you are. The parts of you that make you you. They've always been there. And I've always loved them. And Danny..." He's dropped his leg and slumped down into his seat now. He has his hands folded by his chin. "Danny, my boet." I smile. "I thought you were so fokken cool from the first time I saw you. I've told you before the whole reason I beat that oke in the boxing gym that day was to impress you. I wanted you to think…"

"Think what?"

"That we were the same."

"We're not," he says, with a small laugh.

"No, I know. But I wanted you to *think* we were." He laughs louder. "But just as with Christine, it was the night that Misty fell that I discovered that I loved you. Truly loved."

"How come? What about it?"

"When she went over the side and Christine cried—"

"I didn't cry," Christine interrupts.

I don't want to correct her because I don't want to start an unnecessary fight but… "You did, luv." She's wrong.

"I so did not."

"Christine"—Danny wanders in—"you did."

"Fuck you both. I don't remember that."

I start to say, *You don't remember a lot of things*, but good-natured joshing seems like it's still a fair distance from being earned.

"Well," I say, "regardless, you were upset. Understandable. We had just watched a girl go flying over the edge of a fifty-foot drop. But you were upset, and I saw the way Danny raced in to comfort you. He wrapped himself around you like a protective cloak. And that immediate care for you. That honest, human goodness. That love for you. It made me love him." I look up at Danny as I finish saying it. He's staring at me. Expressionless. "I fell in love with you, Danny, because I knew then that no matter what happened between us… you'd always be there."

"Yeah?" he says. "But I wasn't. Eventually, I wasn't."

"I beg to differ. But no matter either way. You're here now." My eyes smile at them both. It doesn't land on my lips, but my eyes beam at them. "But... and I want to be very, very clear about this... even if you were not here, I would love you just as much. The very same way. I have loved you both since that night. I have loved you when I've been near you and when I've been apart from you. I have loved you fully and without reservation. I have loved you without qualification or caution. And while I love the joys you bring to my life, that is not why I love you. I am the most selfish person you will ever know. I want what I want, how I want, when I want. But when it comes to you two, I only want for you to be safe and for you to be happy. I've done a fokken wretched poor job of showing that always, but it is always how I've loved you. Underneath it all... I would trade my life for either of yours any time. Always."

I pick up my glass and regard a small, swirling amount of liquor left in the bottom. I reflect for a moment on all the words I just said, examining them to make sure I didn't leave anything out and that it's all completely honest. I feel certain I didn't and that it is, but I want to be sure, so I add...

"I mean, look, I'm not much of an expert in matters of the heart. I'm not certain that what I described is even love in any traditional sense. I don't know. I have no idea what other people feel. But to me, that's what love is, and I mean every syllable of it."

I take in the tiny trickle of remaining bourbon and feel the hint of a sting.

When I finish swallowing, I conclude with...

"And I hope that answers the question, Danny. I really, really hope it does. Because honestly, my sweet,

sweet bru, for a worthless bastard like me, it's the best I can do."

CHAPTER THIRTY-THREE

Danny

I stare at him for a second then look over at Christine to make sure this is acceptable to her. Her lips are making a pursed pout, like she's considering things. Then she nods, closes her eyes, and lets her head fall back into the couch.

For a few moments I just stare at her throat. The way it's stretched taut from the position of her head. How easily someone could hurt her. The many ways one could end things using a throat.

It's sick.

Kinda.

But it reminds me of something I'd forgotten. The way one throat could change the lives of dozens of people. "Remember that time we took the polar bear trip?"

Christine lets out a chuckle.

Alec says, "Eish, man. Why do you have to bring that up?"

"Because Christine got sick, remember?" I turn to her and find her nodding. "Your throat was a mess, you were coughing so hard you bruised your ribs, and you lost your voice."

"But she still made us stay in that god-forsaken cabin for six more days," Alec says.

"Long enough for all of us to get sick," I add. "By the last day, the entire camp had strep throat and the whole place was on lockdown. They wouldn't let anyone leave until we'd all been on antibiotics for forty-eight hours, so we ended up staying two extra days."

"And by that time the three of us were better." Christine smiles. Then laughs. Because we made the most of those last two days.

"My mad, crazy girl," Alec says, remembering how the trip ended.

"Hey," Christine says. "I wanted to see some fucking bears, OK? And we paid a lot of money for that trip. It wasn't my fault I got sick on the plane ride out there. So..." She shrugs.

"So you stole a fokken truck in the middle of the night, came and got us out of bed, and we went out alone."

"Hey, I stole their rifles too," Christine adds. Like this makes it so much less insane.

There were so many bears out that night. Dozens of them. And I'm pretty sure they thought the three of us were a tasty late-night snack.

"You were fearless," Alec says. Now he's got his eyes closed too. Head propped back against the couch. But he's smiling as he remembers.

"You were always fearless," I add. "No fucks to give about anything or anyone."

"Not true. I gave all the fucks."

"For us," I say. "Sure. But not anything else."

"Remember those three bears we saw going back?" Alec says.

And of course we do. Because it was two big ones bloody from fighting and a smaller one, pacing back and forth, watching them like it was upset.

"They were us," Christine says.

I nod. Because they were. I don't know jack shit about polar bears except you can't trust them. Which pretty much makes them like most people, I guess.

But these three looked like they were up to something. Some secret plot was concocted, and it didn't end well, so they were hashing it out.

"And we came up with that story about them," I say.

"*They* stole the Crown Jewels." Alec laughs, eyes still closed. Head still back. "And almost got caught because someone else didn't do their job."

"Fucking Eliza," Christine says.

I'd forgotten that part. That Christine's story about the fighting bears was about her and Eliza's elaborate plan to steal the Crown Jewels.

"You liked her back then," I say.

Which makes Christine open her eyes to stare at me. "Yeah, well, that was before…"

But she doesn't finish.

Doesn't need to. Everybody knows everything now.

"Anyway," I say. "That's when I fell in love in with you, Christine."

She makes a face. "I was seventeen. It took you all those years to fall in love with me?"

"I mean, I loved you before that. But that night, out there in that truck, watching those bears. The way all of us just… played along with your silly game. And how it was you who did that. It was you who got Alec to laugh and have a good time even though he never wanted to take that trip in the first place. Not me. Wasn't me who did that. You were the glue. You were the center of my universe. There was no version of Danny who existed

229

without Christine and that night I realized it. I wanted you."

By now Alec has his eyes open too and he's staring at me. "Why didn't you take her?"

"Because she wasn't mine, she was ours. Our world was held together by very thin lines of varying degrees of love. Yours was always strong. Mine was new, and only for her, and hell, I have no idea what Christine was thinking that night. I just knew that if I tried to take her away from you we'd end up like those bears. Fighting until we were bloody. Christine pacing back and forth with worry."

He closes his eyes again. Drops his head back. Weary look on his face. But then he smiles. "You always were a selfless bastard."

"Not always," I say, looking at Christine. "You made me this way."

She gets up, walks over to me, plops down in my lap, wraps her arms around my neck, and sinks against my chest. "You made me this way too."

Alec is watching us. Pained expression on his face. Jealousy? Maybe. But I think he's just sad. I think he's sad because he thought, for all these years, that Christine loved him just as much as she loved me. And right now, I think he has doubts about that.

Doubt. That's what that expression says. Doubt that the sharing we've been doing with Christine was ever equal. Doubt that we will ever work out the way he wants us to.

He has always thought that I was the one who wouldn't go along and now he's starting to realize that it was never really me holding things up.

It was her.

"So," Alec says. He swallows hard, staring at me. "When did you start loving me?"

"The moment Christine shot you out in the woods."

He sighs. Long. Loud. Resigned. "Pretty recent then, eh?"

I nod. "Yup. Took me a while, I guess. But I knew in that moment that there was no us without you."

CHAPTER THIRTY-FOUR

Christine

It's true, what he's saying.

There is no us without Alec. I think that's the part that scared me after I lost the baby. I always knew Danny was there. Even when he was thousands of miles away, we were tied together somehow. And one tug from me, or one tug from him, would rewind that link and we'd be back to who and what we were.

Christine and Danny.

But that's not how it felt with Alec.

I turn a little in Danny's lap so I can look him in the eyes. "I fell in love with you the moment you came up to me in that foster-home back yard. You were this incredible older man—"

He laughs. And everything inside me gets hot with pleasure at this laugh. "I was fourteen."

"Like I said, older man." We take a moment to smile at each other. I'm acutely aware that this must be uncomfortable for Alec, since he was not in our world back then. But I don't know that I care. "Anyway. I fell in love with your looks first. You were wearing those faded jeans and that white t-shirt. And you had boots on." I look down and find his boots. "Not like those. These were brown."

"You remember the color of his boots when you were ten?"

"I only had the one pair," Danny says by way of explanation. "And I wore them every day for almost two years."

It's true. But it's not why I remember them. I remember the leather bracelet he wore on his wrist too. And the rip in the hem of his t-shirt. And the flavor of ice cream he ordered when he dragged me out of that back yard and took me under his protection.

"I remember everything about that first day with Danny because I loved him instantly." He smiles at me. He knew this but I suppose it's nice to hear all the same. I smile back and then lift my head so I can stare at Alec.

"So when did you fall in love with me?" he asks.

"Which time?" I ask.

That earns me a confused look.

"Because I've fallen in and out of love with you, Alec van den Berg, several times already in this life."

Danny holds his breath. Alec says, "Fair enough."

And I feel like telling him everything.

So I do.

"There used to be a time when I was infatuated with you. That came early. Like the night we first stole our first diamond." I look down at Danny, smile at him and say, "But it wasn't love." Danny tilts his head. I continue. "I didn't fall in love with you for real until after Danny left."

Alec nods and says. "Go on."

"By that time we were sleeping together. Not sex. I mean we were *sleeping* together. In the same bed."

Danny is tense beneath me. He'll relax once he sees where I'm going.

"And I used to think to myself… *God. I cannot wait for it to be night again so I can crawl under those covers and slip my body up next to his.* And he would put his arms around me or slip his fingers between my legs. But I didn't really care what he did next because I knew we had hours and hours alone together in that bed before he'd leave me again."

When I glance at Alec he's leaning forward, elbows on knees, staring down at his feet.

"I was in love with you back then," I say.

"And when did that end?" Alec asks. He looks over at me. Eyes bloodshot and tired. "The first time?"

"When I lost the baby."

He nods and resumes looking at his feet.

"When I lost the baby," I say again, this time with the intention of going on. "I lost everything. I lost my joy, I lost my hope, I lost my love. And I don't understand why. Well, I understand parts of it. But I don't understand why, all of a sudden, the thought of climbing into bed with you at night suddenly felt… well. It felt like nothing. I had no feelings about it at all. And that scared me. Because just a few months before it was all I thought about. I craved the night. I craved our connection."

I look down at Danny, who is frowning up at me.

"I lost my love, Danny. It just disappeared one day."

He swallows hard now. Nodding.

"But then I noticed Alec wasn't coming home as much and I started to miss him. I started calling him during the day. I started thinking I'd go out. Go do things. Get back to work."

Alec sighs. He knows where this is headed. Because he was there.

"And there was one night when Alec came back and took my hand, and took me to bed, much the same way he'd done many times before—and I felt it again. That old excitement. That flutter in my stomach. And I thought… *OK. I'm getting better now.* So for one night I fell back in love with you, Alec."

"And then you found out about Eliza," he says.

"And I fell out."

Alec looks at me with those same bloodshot and tired eyes and asks, "Do you love me now?"

I nod. Because it's true. I do. "But it was Danny who caused that love to come back."

"Of course it was," Alec murmurs.

"It was watching Danny fall in love with you, for the first time, I realize now, back on the yacht as we made our way to the Cook Islands that made me see what we had, and what I was missing, and what we could be again."

I look down at Danny. "You were so sad, and it wasn't because you loved me or the idea of us. It was because you thought Alec was dead. It was because you thought you were too late. You thought you'd never get another chance to see him and tell him how you felt."

Danny just nods.

"And I realized that there's no time for regrets. There's no time for grudges. Because life is short, and it could end instantly, at any moment. And I didn't want to die feeling like Danny. Like I had love to give and I lost my chance. So yes, Alec van den Berg. I love you again. And I'm sorry for my betrayal. I'm sorry I hurt you. And if you can't forgive me, I'll understand. But either way, I want you to know… that I forgive *you.*"

I want to say more. Poetic things like… this triangle we've been making was always precarious. Always skewed in one awkward direction one moment, then another the next.

And it wasn't until now that we had the chance to make all the sides equal. Make all the love equal.

But only if we let it.

I want to say... *We control the shape of our love. We decide what it looks like. We can put all this back together again if we really want to.*

But I can't say that. Because I'm not the glue. Danny isn't the glue. Alec isn't the glue.

Our shape can't pull itself together until we're all on the same page.

It's a mutual decision that we must all make together, and I don't know how that could possibly happen after all we've been through and everything that's left to be considered.

So I don't say anything.

Watching my hand grip the rim of the tumbler and rotate the base like a gyroscope on the side table, I make a small 'O' with my lips and puff out several small expulsions of air. I nod. I chew the inside of my mouth, involuntarily. There is a massive world outside this room, spinning in disorder.

My brother is alive. My child can speak and walk and spill tea. My child's mother and I have had eyes on each other again. Something that I thought would never again happen. Hearing the word "diamond," I think of the diamond—*the* diamond—that started our journey, and it causes me to realize that I don't know where it is. It may still be back in that destroyed house of glass in the woods. And on and on and on and on the list of untended items goes. The dangling threads that, once pulled, could unravel whatever fabric we have managed to stitch together.

And I don't care.

I don't have one moment's worth of concern for any of it.

And *that* is the most compelling evidence I have that I love them both. For someone who is obsessed with control, as I am, to allow so much probable bedlam to build and swirl without forcing my way out into the world to manacle it all down, in favor of sitting here with these two people discussing my undying commitment to them… that is the most profound declaration of love I can make.

But I will not say that out loud. Because, in this moment, I relish the quiet. I relish the love in this place. And I don't want to risk compromising it by giving voice to the jumble of thoughts in my head. Ach, man. I don't know when I stopped being a cynic. This vulnerability makes it hard to not care about anything.

"I think I may have a shower," I say. I'd like to reach out and touch them both. Seeing them sitting there so close, I just want my hands on them. But I can't. I don't have control, and everyone here knows it. So I can't just do as I like. I'm hoping a shower and a shave will restore some sense of myself to myself.

"OK," Danny says, stroking Christine's hair. Something happened while I've been away. Danny and Christine have become each other's. For lo these many years, I had believed that Christine and I were the duet who would survive if everything otherwise fell totally apart. How naïve.

I am not the anchoring force in our love. They are.

Christine and Danny are the alpha and the omega. Not me.

I push myself out of my seat and watch them watch me. This sudden break in our action to profess our feelings for each other had been intended to bring us closer. I know this. And while it's no one's fault, somehow, I'm left feeling more unsure. Hayibo, man. How it's possible that talking about my love for them both aloud, with no posturing or arrogance, would cause me to feel less secure about my standing than being shot off the side of a fokken mountain, I don't know. But here we are.

I nod to them and excuse myself to the loo. It's gotten quite dark out. A sudden, quilted blackness has fallen over this part of the earth. I've never understood why nighttime in London feels so much more night-like to me than other places, but it does. I flip on the light in the toilet and, squinting, say aloud, "Ach, man. Fokken strive for ambience, you naaiers." I don't know who I'm talking to. I suppose whoever designed the lights. They're far too bright. I don't need to see everything quite so vividly now. It would be preferable for things to remain a bit hidden just yet.

Turning off the switch, I make my way to the sink and find the toggle for the small vanity lights around the mirror. I flip it on. Much better. It creates an almost halo-like effect. Which is laughable, but I don't laugh.

Opening a drawer or two, I discover razor, shaving soap, and brush. As I swirl the badger hair into the bowl, watching it lather, I think about the recurring dream. The one I've been having these last… however long it's been. Finding out Eliza was pregnant and Christine arriving at the house. Discovering us. Confronting us both.

That's not at all how it happened.

It's all very dramatic and romanticized, but it sure as fok ain't reality.

I apply the brush to my jaw and start lathering my stubbled chin.

I remember it now as Christine just reminded me. Coming back to us, Christine and me, after my time away with Eliza. After recovering from the scrape I had been in. After finding out that Eliza was pregnant and that she wanted me to have nothing to do with her or the yet unknown and unnamed Alexandria.

Not being shocked or sad, but somehow relieved in an odd way, knowing that she could see what I knew in my heart as well... I'm no parent. No parent anyone would want anyway. There are plenty of examples of terrible parents. One only need look around this suite to observe that. But I don't think I'd want to add my name to a list as ignominious as that. I'm on enough ignominious lists already.

I lift the razor and draw it down my cheek. Watching myself return, millimeter by millimeter.

So I came back to Christine and I chose not to say anything. Nothing about Eliza or pregnancies, or anything. And I dropped back into something resembling normalcy.

I shift sides with the razor and begin to expose the other cheek.

And the night that Christine just mentioned—the night I drew her into the bed, and I held her close—I felt it. I felt her love for me. I felt a connection and felt that everything would be as it used to be.

And then I woke up the next morning and told her that Eliza was going to have our child. And then I felt her love flee. I knew it was gone again.

The razor glides down my throat.

These last couple of years I have believed that I did that because I simply can't let things be. I must disrupt that which is placid. It's the only way I know how to exist. Occasionally, if I thought back on it at all, I considered that I told her because I wanted to test the strength of our bond. That sounds very much like something I might do. Oh so very 'Alec,' if you will.

But those were not the real reasons. The real reason I told her was because I didn't want to lie to her.

I didn't want to withhold a truth. I didn't want her to find out some other way. Lies and deception had already driven Danny away. Greed of spirit had already fractured our lines. And I thought... *Ach, man, I've lived my life telling untruths and manipulating reality. Let's see what happens if I just, as they say, 'come clean.'*

I watch the soapy water wash the hair from my face down the drain.

And now I allow the comically undersized clothing to fall from my body onto the bathroom floor and I stare at my naked form in the mirror. I touch gently at my ribs. Not bad. Sensitive, but not impossibly so. There is no more bruising of note on my flesh. Not really. No damage that one can see on the surface. But underneath, the pain still lingers.

I step into the elaborately tiled glass enclosure behind me and turn on the rainfall showerhead. I step back and remain standing on the outside until it reaches peak temperature. I want to feel the water scalding when it touches my skin.

You know, back when I told her the truth, I wish Christine had made her anger known to me rather than plotting with Lars to try to murder me and take over my entire world...

But then again... eh. I can't really blame her. I helped mold her into who she is.

'Water under the bridge,' as they also say.

Such an odd expression. I suppose it implies that once something is washed away, it's gone and should be let go. But now, here, the expression causes me to think of Misty going over the side of that railing and that being the moment I knew my love for these two people was real.

The glass inside the shower begins to fog with steam.

It also causes me to think of what Danny said. That my going over the side of the falls was the moment he decided he truly loves me. Spawned of Christine's hurt, and lost love, came new love. From Danny.

Water under the bridge. Water over the falls. *Water, water everywhere*, I allow the words of Coleridge to play along in my thoughts as I step into the steaming, scorching rainfall. Perhaps, if I'm very lucky indeed, it will wash away everything now.

That is a lot to expect from a shower in a suite at the Ritz-Carlton, but then again it is a very nice hotel, so—

A tap on the glass snaps me back to the present. I wipe at the steam-frosted window to find both of them there. They look… I don't know. Mischievous, maybe.

Also… naked. Or, at least… she is.

"Hey," Christine says.

"Hi," I respond.

"Hey, dude," Danny says. "Better." He indicates my shaved face by placing his hand along his own jawline and pointing at me.

"Thanks." I say.

Then no one says anything for a moment. We all just stare at each other. I have to wipe clean the glass once more so that I can continue to see them. Finally, after I wipe it a third time, Christine is the one who asks…

"Can we come in?"

CHAPTER THIRTY-SIX

Neither of us turn our heads to watch Alec disappear into the bathroom. We just sit. Holding each other. It's everything I never knew I wanted from Christine, but these new feelings for Alec—the ones I've started to accept but haven't had the chance to fully embrace yet— feel unfinished.

For both of us.

"We need to do something," I say, still playing with Christine's hair.

"Yeah." She sighs. "We do."

"We should go in there. Join him."

But she shakes her head. "I don't feel like it."

"Why not?"

"Because this feels good."

Yeah, that's the problem. But I don't say that. Christine has been through a lot these past few years. Hell, her whole life has just been one fucked-up misadventure after another.

"We have to make a decision. Are we three? Or are we two?"

"Three," she says softly. "We are three, for sure. But it all feels so impossible. He's never going to forget that I took up with Lars. That I was the cause of all the bad things that have happened to him these past few months."

I kinda laugh. Not because it's funny, just because it happens to be... ironic. Fucking irony.

"Why are you laughing?"

"You forgot," I say.

"Yeah, but..." She huffs out something that might be a laugh too. "That was a head injury."

I turn her in my lap so she has to look me in the eyes. "Look," I say. "We've built something here and it's about to fall apart. And this moment, right now, is the time to put it all back together."

"I know that. Don't you think I know that?"

"Then what's the problem?"

"It just feels... unimaginable. Everything feels very unimaginable right now."

Which makes total sense. I get it, I do. This is one fucked-up situation. But then again, the answer is so easy.

So I make a decision. I stand up, forcing her to stand as well.

"What are you doing?"

I don't answer. Just drag her jacket down her arms and toss it on to the couch.

She smiles. Again asks, "What are you doing?"

But she knows what I'm doing. That's why she's smiling.

"Danny?" she says, her smile turning into one of those playful smirks.

"Shhh," I say, lifting her t-shirt up over her head. "Stop talking."

She giggles a little but doesn't object or speak again.

I drop the shirt on the floor and take a moment to appreciate her body and the black, lacy bra she was hiding underneath the plain black t-shirt. Her stomach muscles are cut like diamonds. Hard and edgy. She has always been a diamond. Unbreakable, brilliant, and beautiful.

And I have not had enough moments with her like this. All to myself. A quiet one between the two of us where we both know where we stand, and how we feel, and what comes next. Maybe... Maybe on our way here. On the boat. But that was something else. Fueled by something else. From somewhere else.

Up until now it's been adrenaline, and passion, and maybe lust.

But that's not how I want this night to go. So I don't rush when I let my fingers drop to the button of her dark jeans and pop it open. I take my time dragging down the zipper. Looking into her brown-green eyes as she looks up into my blue ones.

Then I bend down, still looking up, and pick up her foot. She places a hand on my shoulder to steady herself, still smiling as I pull off her sneaker and toss it behind me. I tap her other leg and she presents her foot. That sneaker goes behind me too. Then I grab the waistband on her jeans and drag them down her legs, getting hard as her matching black panties present themselves right in front of my face.

She smells like the sun, and the wind, and there's still the scent of saltwater swirling around her too. She steps out of her jeans and kicks them aside.

I press my face up against her bare belly. My lips kiss their way up her body as I stand and place both my palms flat against her face.

"I love you," I say, looking down at her now.

She gives me a sad smile but says nothing. Perhaps waiting for my kiss.

247

But I don't kiss her. I reach around her back and unclasp her bra. It falls loose in the front and when I drag it down, she brings her arms in front of her, pushing her breasts together as we let the bra slip away and fall to the floor.

I smile and she smiles back. And then I reach for her panties and bend down again, taking them with me.

The whole process is slow, and seductive, and a little bit unnerving if I'm being honest.

I have never seduced Christine. The sex we had before, with Alec and without, was never about seduction.

And she is far too important, too beautiful, too loved—to not have a night of seduction.

It's probably naïve of me to think that sex can fix us, but I'll take my chances.

I press my face up against her belly again, dragging my tongue up her body as I stand. Stopping midway to squeeze her breasts and playfully bite her nipple.

I place my hands on her face, just the way I did a few seconds ago, and we stare into each other's eyes like a moment on repeat.

Only this time she's the one who says, "I love you."

And I say, "You smell like the ocean. You smell like salt, and yachts, and tropical paradise."

She smiles and starts to say something else, but I place a finger over her mouth to stop her words. Because I'm not done. I have had her to myself for months. And even though I liked it—definitely enjoyed it—we were never really meant to be together. Just us. Not like that. So I say, "And that's something we need to wash off you."

"What?" she asks. The hum of her question filtering past my hushing finger.

"Because that smell belongs to us." I nod my head toward the bathroom. "And we belong to him."

CHAPTER THIRTY-SEVEN

Christine

We belong to him.

Those words repeat over and over in my head a million times as Danny takes my hand and walks me across the suite toward the master bedroom.

Ten minutes ago, I'd have argued with him over that statement. Because even though I was hopeful we'd all find our way back to each other, I was overflowing with doubts.

I saw no way in which Alec and I got past our mutual betrayal. I saw sex, sure. I saw us together. Mostly because it's a habit now. We are Alec, Christine, and Danny. The team. I saw us doing more jobs. Killing more people. Perhaps we'd even find a way to have fun again.

I never, ever let myself hope that we'd be something more than that. Not truly. It was just an endless stream of hotel rooms, and yachts, and private-jet trips to exotic places to wait out the heat after we stole something.

But I never thought we'd find something new. Something better.

And now I do.

Maybe?

I bite my lip as Danny opens the door without knocking, feeling unusually nervous.

We find the whole room filled with steam. Hot, misty air that swirls around my chilled body and then parts as Danny and I enter holding hands.

I look up at him.

He shoots me a smile that says so much.

Things like, *Don't worry. I've got this.* And, *We'll be fine. Better than fine.*

And because if there's one person on this planet I trust, it's Danny... I believe him.

Alec is standing under a rainfall of water in the glass-enclosed shower, his body blurry through the semi-opaque steam. But I can tell he's looking upward, letting the water rush over his face like he needs a good cleansing.

Danny taps on the glass and Alec steps out from under the water and wipes the glass clean.

I smile at him. Because he's clean-shaven. The way I know him. The old version of Alec. It makes him look young. Like the boy we met way back when.

God. We've made several lifetimes of memories in the span of ten years, haven't we?

And while all of those years were filled with good and bad things—killing, and stealing, and wondering if we were gonna make it through the day—even the dangerous times were good.

We were happy together, I realize. It's only when we split apart that things went bad.

So I make a decision right then and say, "Hi." Like we're meeting again for the first time. Because maybe we are.

And Danny says, "Hey, dude. Better." Indicating his lack of facial hair.

"Thanks," Alec says.

After which comes a moment of hesitation as Alec wipes at the glass again so he can see us.

He looks at me. My naked body. And wipes the glass a third time so he can see more.

And I realize it's up to me now. Danny has done all he can do and it's my turn.

So I say, "Can we come in?"

I think Alec was holding his breath because it rushes out, audible even over the sound of the water falling behind him. He pushes on the door, opens it, and extends his invitation.

Danny has already dropped his leather jacket on the floor and is dragging his t-shirt up over his head. For a brief moment I wonder if I should undress him the way he did me.

Slowly. Methodically.

But Alec is already reaching for my hand, gently urging me to join him.

I give Danny a last look over my shoulder as I take that first step, and he finds my gaze and meets it with a smile as he finishes tugging off his boots and begins taking off his pants.

I step into the mist of hot steam and look up to Alec. He looks better, yes. But still… unsure. And I hate that. I hate it because I did that to him. I'm the one who ripped his world apart, so I have to be the one who puts it back together.

I just don't know *how*.

Danny joins us, closing the door behind him. He slides a hand around my waist, which is now wet, and tugs me close to him. And for a second, I think it's a possessive gesture, but then I realize it's just a comforting one.

He takes a step forward, toward Alec, bringing me with him until our bodies are so close we're all touching in one way or another. My stomach pressed up to Alec's hip. Our hands still holding each other's. Danny's thigh bumps up against Alec's, which makes Alec look down, then up to meet his eyes.

That erases all the distance between us. Because he leans in, arm still around me so that my upper thighs straddle Alec's leg, and he kisses him.

It's hesitant at first. But then it's not. And Alec kisses him back. I stare up in wonder, and feel the heat rise inside me. The longing. The want. The lust coming back.

And I hope this will be enough, I really do.

But those doubts are still there. Lingering around my head like spiderwebs.

Then they break apart and I'm the one holding my breath. Because I don't know what to do. I don't know how to make this better. I will never be able to—

"Get on your knees, Christine," Danny says.

I snap out of it and look at him. "What?"

But he doesn't respond or repeat himself. Just places his hand on my shoulder and presses until my knees buckle and I drop to the floor. I look up at them as Danny guides my head towards Alec's cock. He's not quite hard when I grab him with my hands, our eyes locked. But one pump and I feel him grow and thicken in my palm.

"Don't do it because he's telling you to," Alec says.

But I just say, "Shut the fuck up, Alec. Since when do I do anything Danny tells me?"

And even though it's stupid, and it's not even true... it helps. It's the old me, and the old Alec, and the old Danny. Because we all break the silence with a laugh.

I gladly wrap my lips around the tip of his cock, sucking on him as I swirl my tongue. And then I close my eyes and take him all the way to the back of my throat.

Danny grabs my hair, urging me. But when I open my eyes again, they're kissing. And it's not the tentative, uncertain kiss of before.

Danny kisses him the way I do. He kisses him the way he kisses me.

I reach for Danny's cock with my other hand and begin to pump him too. They moan into each other. Enjoying me, and each other, and this new shape we make.

That's when I know we're going to be OK.

CHAPTER THIRTY-EIGHT

I haven't touched anyone since I last saw Christine and Danny. Almost quite literally. Apart from smashing down dear old Liam earlier, I don't think I've had my hands on another soul before now. To have my reintroduction to physical contact come in this way, with these people, is more than I could have hoped for. Had I attempted to hope for anything at all.

I don't know that before this very moment I could have understood that a kiss can be both passionate and tender simultaneously. But that's what this kiss with Danny is. It is filled with lifetimes of familiarity and want and yet it is as fragile as new love. Which, in so many ways, is exactly what it is.

When I last 'left'... which isn't the right word, but I'll choose it nonetheless... Danny and Christine, we had only just begun to understand this new version of us. And after my departure, I have to assume we all believed that was as far as it would ever go. So to now be rejoined, reborn, reimagined, is something none of us could have predicted and despite the heat of the moment, it feels essential that we go slow.

However, Danny's mouth on mine and Christine's lips on my cock are making it difficult.

The clenching in my stomach smarts just a tiny bit and I moan in discomfort. Christine can't hear, I don't think, with the sound of the water splashing down about her ears, but Danny senses it. He stops kissing me but leaves his mouth close to mine. He takes me by the back of the neck with one of his rugged hands, slides his lips along my cheek, and lands at my ear, whispering, "You OK?"

He rolls his forehead around to mine and presses us together, staring into my eyes with a probing look. Christine is still absorbing my cock entirely and stroking at Danny. Both Danny and I are heaving breaths, drinking in the shower as we gasp. I make sure I keep my eyes open so that he can see I'm telling the truth when I nod and whisper back, "Yes," before I force my mouth back on his and bite at his lip as I kiss him with the exigency of a long-lost lover. Which is exactly what I am.

It's been so long since I've had my cock in anyone's mouth that I'm worried I'm going come too quickly. Especially with the power of Danny's kiss intersecting with mine. So I pull back—both from Danny and Christine—and shudder as my body lands against the wall of the great, massive shower box.

Christine stands, a worried look on her face. It is matched by Danny's worried look as he reaches out for me. "Are you OK?" they both ask now.

"Yes. Yes," I assure them. "I'm very well indeed. Possibly too good, in fact."

Danny chuckles a bit and steps toward me. There is a look in his eyes that I may have seen once. Maybe twice. But I've never seen it directed toward me. It is a look of power and seduction. Of anger and love simultaneously coexisting. It is frightening and electrifying. Competing emotions abound.

"C'mere," he says. Rhetorically. I'm not going anywhere.

I take a step toward him and he takes my wrist and forces my hand onto his cock. I wrap my fingers around it, tightly, and I begin to pull. The burning heat from the water stings my back and chest. Danny throws his head back and with lips closed, he moans long and slow.

"Don't stop," he says as he now takes Christine's hand and places it around my own cock. She smiles at Danny. He smiles back. They kiss as I jerk on him and she jerks on me. And now, Danny takes my other hand and places it at the entrance to Christine's pussy. They are still kissing, but he guides me there with his eyes closed. Then he wraps his palm around the back of my hand and forces both my fingers and his up inside her at the same time. I feel the firm muscles of her stomach contract as he does this, and her thighs shiver as we finger her, slowly.

We are a perfect simulacrum of a triangle. Forced into being once again. Only this time by Danny. If I was proud and filled with glee at the idea that I caused us to be the last time we found our way to each other—and I was—in this moment, in this place, in this time... Danny is in charge. He is the one who is dictating the terms. Again, this is a Danny I have seen. But never this close and never with this level of command. It is magnificent.

Our slow, methodical fingering of Christine's pussy is turning more urgent. And the harder we stroke inside of her, the harder she pulls on my cock. And the harder she pulls on my cock, the harder I pull on Danny's. And now we all lean into one another and strive valiantly to have our mouths on each other's at the same time. Three tongues darting and piercing. Each fighting for communion with the other two. We are drinking in as much water as we are each other.

And suddenly, Danny pulls away, spins me around, and pushes me face first against the glass. He presses his body against my back, and I feel his throbbing cock against my ass. He grabs my hair, pulls my neck back, and places his mouth by my ear once more. "Tell me you love me," he whispers.

"What?" I say, feigning that I didn't understand him. I don't know why I do it. I think, more than anything, I'm just a bit shocked. For so long, Danny refused this journey. Refused every attempt I made to get him to come along. Even back before the evening of... the unpleasantness... while he was there, while he was willing, he wasn't fully present. He was the reticent figure. The ambivalent one. The one who seemed as though he could run away at any moment.

Here, now, he is as demanding of me as I have ever been of him. Something happened in this intervening time. Something inside him has been unleashed. Something, perhaps, between him and Christine. I don't know, but I'm going to be very curious to learn how far this part of Danny is ready to push things.

"I said, tell me you love me," he says again.

"I love you," I say. "I love you. I love you. I do, Danny. I love you." I make no attempt to free his hand from my head or push his cock away from my ass. Whatever it is he wants to do to me, it shall be at his pleasure.

He reaches behind him, grabs Christine, and pulls her to join us. He slides to one side, places her on the other, and now they effectively straddle me, his hard, throbbing cock on one hip, and her pulsing, wet pussy on the other. They have their hands on my ass. I can feel them both starting to finger my asshole, from both sides. Just as Danny and I split Christine, they are now finding their way inside me. He leans in yet again and says, "Tell Christine."

I turn to look at him. He nods, indicating that I look over at our nunu. As he does, he forces his fingers into me deeper. I tense and smile and turn my head to face Christine. She looks nervous. Her fingers are still working their way inside along with Danny's, but she appears anxious. Anxious and wet and beautiful. And I tell her how beautiful she is to me, in so many words.

"I love you," I offer. "I love you, Christine. I love you with all my heart. I love you both. This is where I want to be and I will do what it takes, all it takes, forever and always, to see to it that we are never apart again." It's such a profoundly eager proclamation that I fear I may come over as fulsome, but I don't care. It is not only how I feel, it is imperative that she hear it.

And suddenly, she calls to mind my dream. The one in which she arrives in the rain and I cannot tell if the water on her face is from the weather or from tears. I see the streaks on her delicate face now, and I don't know from what source the water is streaming. Her eyes or the cascading shower. But I suppose it's likely both. Because she says, almost inaudibly over the sound of the beating water and three frantic lovers finding one another again, "I'm sorry."

I grab her face, force my mouth onto her—as I do, both she and Danny finger my ass harder and faster—and kiss her with the intention of swallowing her whole. Of consuming every last bit of her. And when I finally break the kiss, I tell her, "I am too, my love. I'm sorry too."

And though I'm sure it's just the heat of the shower landing against my back, I could very nearly swear that my tattoo—the triangle—pulses with energy along all three lines.

CHAPTER THIRTY-NINE

When I first saw Alec in that gym back when we were teenagers, I had no idea that ten years later we'd be this... this perfect threesome. It took a long time. It took a lot of shared danger, and adventures, and fear to get here. It took a lot of arguing, and fist fights, and blood too. Hell, it even took a couple of betrayals and a lot of time apart.

But we made it, I realize.

We're still here, we're still committed, we're still friends.

Anyone can be lovers. It's not that hard to let things go and give in to sex. And most people can even find a way to fall in love. But it's an altogether other thing to find one person you love, like to fuck, and are friends with at the same time.

So finding two is like winning that billion-dollar Powerball.

That's how lucky I feel right now.

I ease my finger out of Alec's ass. He groans, turning his head to look at me. Questions in his eyes. Simple ones. Like, *What's next?*

I glance at Christine, who's asking the same thing. It's only then that I realize I'm in charge tonight. But that's

263

OK. I have a pretty good idea of how I want this night to go. So I bring Christine over to me, forcing her to remove her finger too, and place her between us. She's facing me, and Alec has turned slightly so that his chest is pressing into her back. I look at him and a sly grin creeps up my face.

Christine mutters, "Yes. Yes," as I smile.

I don't even have to say what comes next. It's like Alec is reading my mind. Because he reaches down, grabs his thick, hard cock, and parts Christine's ass cheeks. And just as he does that I reach down, hands clasping the underside of her knees, and lift her up.

She automatically wraps her arms around my neck and her legs around my waist. We are all wet from the shower. We are hot and flushed from the steam and the water. But I can feel *her* wetness as she begins to rub her pussy against the shaft of my cock. Pressing it up against the length of my stomach.

Alec maneuvers behind her and she gasps, the muscles in her face tightening as her fingernails dig into the back of her neck when he enters her ass. Her shoulders tighten and come inward, forcing her perfect round breasts together. Her nipples are tight and erect, and water is dripping down her face, droplets catching on the edge of her upper lip and then silently melding together and streaming down the corners of her mouth.

I lean forward and kiss them. Licking her lip, then biting it with the edges of my front teeth. She sucks in a breath of air just as Alec's mouth finds a place to nibble on her ear.

"Oh, God," she says, letting her head fall back onto his shoulder.

He's looking at me, smiling as he whispers, "Put yourself inside her now."

I might like to drag this out a little longer. Bide my time and go slow.

But I can't. I can't wait to follow his command.

Alec's grip on the underside of Christine's ass holds her in place as I let go of one thigh, reach for my cock, and force it downward. The head drags along Christine's belly, the pressure almost too much to bear, but then, just as I think I can't stand it, my cock is between her legs and I'm pushing my way inside her wet pussy, slick with her desire.

Alec moans as I do this. And when I glance up at him, his eyes are closed, but fluttering. His jaw is clenched. The muscles of his face contracting, then relaxing.

I can feel him. Such a soft, thin piece of flesh separating us we move in opposite directions inside her. He thrusts forward as I pull back. Then we switch and do the opposite. Each of us understanding our part.

We fuck Christine like we're playing instruments. The two of us take her and make a song. We turn sex into a symphony.

Christine kisses me relentlessly. Her fingers wrapped up in my mostly wet hair. Tugging and pulling until my scalp feels the burn of her demanding urgency.

Fuck, I like that. I like that a lot. So I kiss her back with desperation. A driving need to push my tongue inside her mouth the way Alec and I have pushed ourselves inside her ass and her pussy.

We are totally connected in this moment. I don't think it can get any better than this.

But when Christine turns her head and Alec leans forward, and all three of our mouths collide—it does get better.

I can't even describe how good this feels.

Alec lets go of one of Christine's legs and she drops a foot to the tiled floor. I glance down at the shape of her, the muscles straining as she stands on one tiptoe.

But Alec's hand in my hair, squeezing tight as Christine's grip pulls in the opposite direction, refocuses me on him. Our eyes meet. His amber ones. My blue ones. And Christine knows what to do. She moves her head to the side, just a little. Just enough. So that he and I can kiss.

He draws blood with his first bite, and I laugh through the stinging pain. Because it feels good. Too good to care.

I reach around him, my large hand flat on the small of his back, my fingers splayed wide, and force him closer. Closer. Until we are nothing more than a mass of hard muscles and soft breasts. I allow my hand to fall, letting my fingers slip into his ass.

"Yes," he groans. And then his hand is on my back. Falling along the lines of muscle that define my hip until his fingers are inside me too.

"Holy shit," Christine says. Because we are pumping faster now. Our rhythm still perfect, but our motion more urgent.

We fuck each other like that for several seconds. Breathing hard. And moaning. Alec's hips bang into Christine's ass with such force the water begins to splatter off her body with each slap of skin.

I think I lose control then. I can't stop myself. I pump fast, trying to force my cock deeper. I grip Alec harder, my fingers desperately trying to be deeper inside him too.

Christine throws her head back, mouth open and eyes closed. She is moaning, "Oh. Oh. Oh," over and over again as her legs begin to tremble and then suddenly go limp.

I have to stop fucking Alec with my finger to catch her before she falls, and she laughs. Softly moaning, "Sorry, sorry…"

And Alec laughs too. Just a small chuckle into my mouth as he kisses me softer now.

Because we all know what's coming…

Christine's pussy grips around the shaft of my cock and Alec and I have to stop kissing. I know she's gripping his cock with her ass and this… it's just…

She comes. Moaning turns into a litany of "Oh, shit, oh, shit… oh…"

I can't hold it in. I come too. I release everything I have inside her. I grab her hair the way she was grabbing mine and press our faces together. Her eyes open and we stare at each other. Breathing too hard and loving each other too much.

Alec pushes me, forcing me backwards until I bump up against the tiled bench on the far side of the shower and automatically sit.

His cock withdraws from Christine's ass and I stare at it. Hanging long and hard between his legs. He reaches for my hand as Christine slumps against my chest. Bringing it towards him. I look him in the eyes as I grip his cock and he steps forward.

And then I force Christine's head down with my other hand and say, "Open your mouth, Christine."

And she does. With eyes closed.

I pull on Alec until he reaches out for the wall, trying to steady himself. And then I aim his come into her mouth.

CHAPTER FORTY

Christine

My eyes open just as Alec's salty come hits my tongue. And then, just when I think it's over, Danny's fingers slide along my cheek, collecting the parts that missed their mark, and he drags even more sweet, salty climax over my lips.

I lick his finger, then wrap my mouth around it as he pushes it back and forth, in and out between my lips. Fucking me one more time, in one more way, before Alec collapses onto the bench seat next to Danny.

We sigh together. And that sigh tells me that we are back.

We are one, and all the sides to our triangle are equal for the first time ever.

"I don't want to move," I say.

"I don't think I could move, even if I wanted to." Danny laughs.

We both turn our heads to glance at Alec. His clean-shaven jaw just another sign that things are normal again. His head is resting against the wall. Slight smile of contentment on his face. Eyes closed.

Normal.

Probably a bad choice of words because none of this is normal. Hell, we're not the least bit normal even when we're not fucking each other in a perfect threesome. Our lives are chaos, and danger, and daring missions. We are thieves, and killers, and liars.

But fuck it. I feel lucky to be a part of this abnormal family. And maybe, for the first time in my life, I'm not jealous of those who have it different.

Good for Eliza and her perfect, thatched roof. She and her fairy-tale back yard can go fuck itself.

But then the little mini-Alec pops into my head and I reconsider.

Because even though it would be easier to pretend that I didn't want a little me, Danny, or Alec, I do. I desperately do.

"I'm not on birth control."

It takes me a second to realize those words just came out of my mouth and then all I want to do is take them back.

But Alec leans over and says, "Good," as he kisses my mouth.

I glance up at Danny and find him in the same position Alec just pulled himself out of. Head resting against the wall, mouth slightly smiling, eyes closed.

Content.

"Yeah," he mumbles, not bothering to opens eyes. "I could maybe dig a kid."

Which makes me chuckle and Alec sigh.

"Your kid's not bad," Danny continues. "But I'm not playing hopscotch with her."

This makes Alec laugh and scoot just a little closer to us. His hand finds my thigh and he twirls the pad of this thumb along the outside of my leg. "I can't imagine you would," he replies.

"I sorta promised her."

"When?" Alec laughs.

"Earlier today. God, how is this still the same day?"

"I don't know," I say, nestling deeper into Danny's chest. "But I think we've done enough for one day. It needs to end."

"Then let's end it properly," Alec says, standing up and walking under the rain shower. "Come here."

He extends his hand. And even though I'm perfectly comfortable ending this day in this shower, I know we have to get out eventually. So I take his hand and let him pull me to my feet. My legs are still trembling from the exertion of clamping them around Danny's waist as they fucked me from both directions. So Danny stands too, reaching for the bottle of shampoo Alec is handing him.

I lean against Alec now and let him hold me.

It's kind of a sad hold because I know we're both thinking about the baby we didn't have.

But I'm distracted by Danny's hands on my scalp as he massages the luxurious tropical-scented shampoo bubbles into my hair.

"That feels nice," I say.

"That's the point."

Which makes me smile and close my eyes.

Alec comes up behind me and begins rubbing liquid soap along the curve of my waist. He reaches up and fondles my breasts until large soapy bubbles cover my nipples.

I sink back into him as he places his mouth against my ear and whispers, "We'll have our baby one day. I promise. Maybe it's mine, maybe it's Danny's. It doesn't matter. We will have that life you want. We can let go of the past."

I nod my head and keep my eyes closed. No words necessary.

We wash each other like that for a while, slow and easy, taking turns standing under the rain shower. Not saying much. Just kinda enjoying the calm silence.

That's why I loved the Cook Islands so much. There was a lot of stillness there and stillness is hard to find in our world.

But eventually the washing is over and I think the entirety of the day hits us all in the same moment.

Danny turns the water off and Alec gets out first, holding a towel open so he can wrap me up as I step out.

I don't bother with clothes, just hold the towel against my body as I walk to the huge master bed, and then drop it to the floor and climb under the covers, naked.

Danny and Alec both join me, dropping their towels too.

We are a tangle of arms and legs. Danny behind me, his hands around my belly like maybe... maybe he's thinking about that baby we'll have some day.

Alec lies flat on the bed. My head on his shoulder, his hands behind his neck as he gazes up at the ceiling.

I sigh and they echo it.

All of us relax and drift into our own dreams.

Happy.

CHAPTER FORTY-ONE

The yellow windbreaker *she has on feels in contrast to the darkness in her eyes. She and Eliza continue talking and I step closer to hear them. But no matter how close I get, I can discern nothing. Their mouths are moving, but no sound is coming out.*

Christine is growing increasingly animated and Eliza, as is her natural state, remains inscrutable and unmoving. Then, finally, Eliza reaches out and places her hands onto Christine's shoulders. I brace myself, waiting for the punch to the jaw Eliza is surely about to receive. But it doesn't happen. Instead, Christine's shoulders drop, and her expression softens. She looks over to me. Then Eliza turns her head toward me as well and they are both staring. I wish I could hear them.

Eliza turns, stands next to Christine, and they look at me for a very long time indeed. The sun goes down, the sun comes up, the sun goes down, the sun comes up. Over and over and over again. It's like one of those sped-up nature documentaries where they show the deterioration of a rose petal over days or weeks.

But nothing here deteriorates. In fact, everything stays the same. We are captured in amber, it seems. I try not to blink. I have this suspicion that if I do, when I open my eyes, it will all be gone. But eventually, I can no longer keep my lids lifted and I do. I blink. And when I do, and my eyes open again, I find Eliza walking away, holding the hand of a tiny person carrying a battered teddy bear. And where Eliza stood, Danny now waits.

It all happened in the blink of an eye.

And I fall to my knees and cry.

I have never cried in front of anyone other than my father. I cried in front of him once, when I was a boy, and the slap he delivered on that day warned me off crying in front of anyone ever again. But here, in front of these two people, I kneel and weep.

They rush over now, and as they approach, the sound of the world suddenly warps back into my ears. Like a tornado in reverse.

"Hey, hey. Hey, dude, why so sad?" Danny asks.

"What?" I respond, looking up at him through a veil of tears.

"He asked what you're crying about," Christine says. "Is it Eliza? Is it Andra? Do you want us to go after them for you?"

There's no heat in her voice. No anger or jealousy. Nothing but kindness, compassion, and love. Danny's face is the same. Pure love. Pure care. Unquestioning devotion. I shake my head at them.

"No, no, it's not that," I say.

"Then what?" Danny asks. "What's wrong?"

I pause to consider the answer. I realize I have none. "Nothing, I don't think. Nothing's wrong. I... I just... I think I felt like crying."

And then Danny laughs. And Christine laughs. And I laugh, even though sobs still emanate from within. And Danny smothers me in a hug. And I hug him back. And Christine wraps herself around both of us, opening her windbreaker wide, and enveloping us in the bright warmth of the sun that is she.

And the yellow sun around us grows bigger and bigger, and it glows ever more intensely, filling the room, and then bleeding free from inside the house and covering the walls and the grounds beyond. And rising and rising and rising up to touch the sky itself and compete with the rays coming down to earth from the vastness of space.

And like some type of nuclear reaction that blinds the world, we explode as one into that cloud of love and light, and we shower down on everything we touch.

And as I'm falling through the air, drifting throughout the universe, now transported and turned into pure energy, I see in front of me a face. A face growing larger and larger, careening into view.

It's Lars.

Lars is there. Waiting. He opens his mouth as if he means to consume me, and I try to stop my trajectory. I try to slow my collision course with him. But I can't. I can't slow and I can't stop. And all the light and beauty that I feel and that I am is in danger of being swallowed up whole.

And, with my heart racing and my breaths ragged and frantic...

I sit up in bed.

It's just starting to become light outside. The curtains are of the blackout variety, but there is a crack in one of them and I can see sunshine just peeking through. To my left is Christine. Still asleep. The covers of the bed have been all but kicked off and her naked body is visible in the dim light of the room. Her hand is resting on my thigh. She moans slightly as I wake.

Danny is to her left. Also still asleep. His arm is draped across her stomach, the fingers of his hand also just grazing along my thigh. He doesn't move. He is as still as a mountain. Strong, powerful, eternal.

My breathing slows as I look around and realize that we are alone. I roll my neck back and cast my eyes at the ceiling. I laugh—almost—at my dream. At the completion of a dream I've been having for weeks. At least. I laugh because I'm not a terribly deep thinker. I'm truly not. People mistake me for someone who possesses some sort of philosophical acumen simply because I attended some

275

lekker schools in my day and I have a fair facility with language. But I'm not actually all that bright. I just know how to present for the situation in front of me.

When all is said and done though, deductive logic ain't really my strong suit. I follow my impulses and operate from instinct. However, even I, as shallow and petty as I know myself to be, don't have to work terribly hard to figure out what the fok the dream is all about.

Lars was working all this time to take from me, and I never even saw it. Never even thought to consider it. Never took steps to mitigate the damage until it was too late.

As I say, deductive logic ain't really my strong suit.

But fokken taking control back when control needs to be taken is.

I work to extract myself quietly from their shared touch without waking them. My ribs, they argue with me, owing to the workout they got last night. But I ask them, politely, to kindly fokof as I slide free and stand at the edge of the bed.

I look at them. I look at us.

Alec, Christine, and Danny.

This is how you say our names.

It has been ever thus, and if I have anything to say about it, it is how it ever shall be.

This will not be the last time the three of us hold each other throughout the night. And the next time, the dreams I have will not be violated by uninvited guests.

I need answers. I need to know how Lars and I survived. I need to know why he brought me to that place and why he kept me in the dark. I am supposing it was to draw Christine and Danny out. To me. Or perhaps it was to draw Eliza and her brothers out and to me. But that presumes that he somehow knew Christine and Danny would seek them. And, to be quite honest, I don't even know if Lars ever knew about the Watsons. He wasn't around during that time. I don't know if we ever talked about them in front of him. I...

Ach. Again... deductive logic is not where I excel.

All I do know is that he is alive and if he tried to kill me once, he will try again. That requires no deduction on my part. I know it's what he'll do, because it is what I would do. I don't know my baby bru well, but I do know his heart. If there's any part of it left that isn't blackened beyond repair, maybe there's a chance we can work through whatever it is between us that maddens him so and avoid more bloodshed.

And maybe Eliza and Christine will become best friends and we'll all go on trips to fokken Disneyland together, and perhaps someone will anoint me father of the year.

Onosel fokken etter you are, van den Berg. Face reality.

I make my way quietly to the valet closet and open it. In the night, little elves have procured some new finery for me. The garment bag with my new suit hangs next to a clear plastic drapery, underneath which is a pair of brand-new sweatpants. I cannot help but smile. I take the garment bag out, unzip it, and feel the fabric. While not made explicitly for me, it has come from Savile Row, and there is still magic woven into its form. If one has never had the good fortune to adorn oneself in a handmade, fully canvassed suit jacket, one cannot understand why it matters. But once one has worn such a piece, one will never be content to wear anything less than.

Unless one's name is Danny Fortnight. In which case one could give a flying fok.

And, as if summoned by the thought… "What're you doing?" comes from behind.

I turn to find Danny standing there in the semi-illuminated entryway to the suite. Still naked. I'm also still naked, of course, so I don't feel in any way self-conscious about staring at his cock. Because he's doing the same thing to me. It's a lovely way to wake up, frankly.

"Go back to sleep, bru."

"Where are you going?"

"I'm just—"

"Or, actually, where do you *think* you're going?"

"Daniel Fortnight, are you getting all alpha on me, man?"

"Dude," he says, with a hushed intensity, taking a step in, "things are super fucking chill right now. We're all good. Everybody's good. So maybe it would be best if you don't tip the fucking apple cart right the fuck now by doing whatever you think you're about to do."

"The apples have already tipped, man. I'm just—"

"I don't care. It's fucking selfish. Read me? You're here. You're with us. It's *us* now. So it's not just about *you* anymore. You feel me? This shit is not negotiable."

He's so close to me now, our cocks are almost touching. I have to be honest, I find it terribly distracting.

"Listen, man," I say, putting my hand on his shoulder. He looks at it. "There's an incredibly good chance that he's gone. I certainly would be. But Lars is still alive, Lars brought me here for a reason, and only Lars can answer what that reason is. I have to go talk with him."

"No fucking way."

"It's not a request, Danny."

"Good, *Alec*," he says my name with a sneer, "because if it was, you still wouldn't have permission."

278

My mind riffles through the various responses I can give. Some of them involve words, some involve striking, and a couple involve me wrestling him to the floor and having someone's dick wind up in someone's mouth. But before I can implement any of these responses, a whirring sound and a sudden explosion of light into the room—an all-encompassing light that seems to swallow us whole—breaks my concentration.

I squint in the direction of daybreak streaming through the windows. The rich, tufted burgundy fabric in which much of the furnishings are covered springs into vivid color, also waking from its muted slumber. The light shines off the Thames, bounces across St. James' Park, and lands right in my pupils. Danny turns to look in the direction of the sudden sunburst as well.

Standing, facing us, is the inconceivably sexy silhouette of a naked Christine Keene. She is backlit and shows herself as a seductive and deadly shadow. She has one knee bent and her hip thrust out, further emphasizing the effect. I must say, if Danny doesn't want me to leave for whatever reason, he and Christine are offering nakedly seductive reasons to stay. Quite literally.

"What's up?" she asks, raising her fist to her mouth to stifle a yawn.

"Alec," Danny replies. "Alec is up. And he's trying to sneak the fuck out."

"What? Why?" she asks. "Where?"

I feel I must state the obvious. "Bru. Nunu. I love you both. That has been made abundantly clear, yes?" Neither one responds, so I continue speaking. "And it is precisely because I love you that I feel a responsibility to pay a visit to my little brother, see if he's still about, and make at least an attempt at containing the situation."

"What situation?" Christine asks.

"Precisely," I say. "That is exactly what I aim to find out. Why did he conspire with you to try to kill me only to save me and keep me hostage when it didn't play through as he expected?" Again, no one responds. Again, I continue. "Nunu. Love," I say, passing by Danny and taking Christine close to me, my hands on her ass. I can feel blood pumping to my cock, but I want to be close to her, even if it proves a distraction. "What was the plan? Do you remember? Do you have any recollection of what was supposed to happen after you and he did me in?"

She looks down, shame radiating from her.

"Hey," I say, lifting her chin, "it's fine. We're past that. And who amongst us hasn't tried to murder someone they love and plan to spend their lives growing old with?" I fake a yawn. "I mean, if I had a nickel..."

She laughs. It makes my heart smile and my dick jump. I glance over my shoulder. To my great relief, Danny is smiling too. Good. Normalcy. Or our version of it.

She shakes her head. "It's still... honestly, I never had a complete picture of what was what. I was kept in the dark about a lot of things. I do know he was working with someone else."

Well, that certainly gets my attention. "Someone else? What do you mean? Who?"

She shrugs. "I don't really know. It's all so..."

I stroke her cheek. Run my hand down her hair. "It's all right. Just tell me anything you think you can recall."

She sighs a bit. "The whole thing was supposed to be made to look like you and Brasil Lynch"—she looks at Danny, sheepishly—"were in some kind of war with each other."

"Why?" Danny asks.

She shakes her head. "Because… I dunno. I think Lars was trying to find a way to take over Alec's business…" She pauses. Corrects herself. "*Our* business, and Brasil's. I guess—and I don't have the details, but I guess—Brasil has something going on that Lars wants part of? Or something?"

Now Danny says, slightly louder than is required, "Fucker."

"What?" Christine asks.

Danny shakes his head. Blows out through his lips as he steps to the valet closet, rips the plastic off the sweatpants and puts them on, saying, "Brasil told me that some of our shipments were being stolen and our trucks were being used to smuggle diamonds. I thought it was you," he says to me. "But it was Lars."

Christine shrugs. "Yeah. I guess so."

"Are you fokken kidding me, man?"

"Why?" Danny asks. "What?"

"Remember when I told you that I had sent Christine to take care of an oke called Jimmy Sotoro?"

"No." He shakes his head.

"When we was escaping from your warehouse? I told you that she was on a job to take care of an oke called Jimmy Sotoro. You don't remember that at all?"

"No," he says more decisively.

"Eish. Fokken looi n plooi, man. Well, I did. And I truly thought that it was Jimmy what had stolen some diamond shipments from me. I did. That's why Christine was sent to handle him."

"Why did you think it was this Jimmy fucker?" Danny asks.

I hang my head. "Lars told me." Deductive logic. Not at all my forte. Fokken kak, man. Well... Jimmy Sotoro's the lucky one in all this, I reckon...

"But..." Danny says. "But Christine killed David. Brasil's guy. And then... fuck. And then your guys... or, I guess, Lars' guys... came in and took the shipment." Then a look that I don't know comes over Danny and he says, "Goddamn it," slamming his fist into the wall.

"What?" I ask. "Fokken what, man?"

"Brasil told me, just after all this went down, that for the past couple of years he'd been trafficking in people."

A silence falls on the space that Christine finally breaks with, "Say that again."

"Yeah. Women. I found out that he'd been trafficking women. Which Lars clearly knew about. So, when Lars was talking about trying to take over Brasil's business too, *that's* the business he was trying to take over."

I close my eyes. Because what I'm hearing right now is difficult to process. I am a violent, unrepentant, horrible cunt of a human being, as was my father, and probably his father before him. But never, in my most unrepentant cunty-ness, would I ever have imagined doing something as morally bankrupt as trading human life. I know that things I've done have cost people their lives. I'm under no illusions about that. But it was always flesh as the cost for something else. Never flesh as the something else itself.

Jesus. Lars.

What the fok happened to you, my bru?

For the first time since I can remember—maybe the first time ever—I don't have money to tip a delivery boy. The laaitie who brings us our breakfast regards me in my suit, Danny in his sweats, and Christine back in her sneak assassin regalia with a completely understandable amount of curiosity as he wheels the cart into the suite. And as he's placing the food on the dining room table and taking the cart away, I reach into my pocket only to realize... I have no money. Not a single note. Nothing.

Danny is the one who says, "Hold up," runs to retrieve his backpack, and pulls out a crumpled wad of twenties. He hands them to the laaitie, who actually says, "Oh! Much obliged, guv'nor." There's something about the insulting way that I think the kid must be taking the piss with what he perceives to be stupid Americans that makes me decide I like the lad. Regardless, now that the food is here, perhaps we can get down to discussing what happens next. Danny has refused to talk plans of action until he has his coffee.

I've said it before. He is the only one like himself in the world.

"Okay," he says, pouring a cup of black, steaming brew and biting into a piece of toast. "So here's what's going to happen..."

I don't know how my plan has somehow turned into Danny's, but I don't argue. Just pour some juice from a carafe and listen to him talk.

"If we're actually going to get back to that place to find out if he's still there, we need a better fucking plan of action than the one we had before."

Christine butters a scone and says, "Well, I mean, first things first, we should probably just get close enough to see if all those guards are still there."

"Yep, yep," Danny says, biting down on a slice of well-cooked bacon.

I find this entire enterprise irrepressibly quaint. Alec, Christine, and Danny waking up and chatting about the day's affairs over a hearty breakfast. It's so remarkably conventional as to be almost domestic.

"Maybe we should try to get hands on a sniper rifle and position you at a safe distance, just in case."

Almost.

"Safe distance?" Christine asks. "Why?"

"Well," Danny says, downing his coffee and pouring another cup, "you and Lars… you did also try to kill *him*. I don't know if he's going to be happy to see you."

She shrugs as she bites her scone. "Yeah. I guess."

"I have a thought," I volunteer. They both look at me, mouths full. "Why don't I just walk up to the front gate and ask to speak with him?"

They chew more slowly. Danny says, "Fuck are you talking about?"

"I'm suggesting that for whatever reason I was being held, I was being *held*. Not tortured or killed. Just not allowed to leave. And when they spotted us—or, I presume, *me*—they stopped firing. Clearly, whatever the intention is in keeping me alive, it's to… you know… keep me alive. Perhaps he's not finished with this Brasil Lynch business yet. Perhaps he still needs me alive to pin it on. I don't know. I'm not particularly good at knowing why people do things, just that there's always a reason."

They both consider this. Then Danny turns to Christine and says, "I hate to say it, but I think we may need the Watsons again."

Not only was I ignored, but the casual suggestion, by Danny, that we employ the Watson clan again suggests that I have entered some parallel dimension where the laws that govern the known universe no longer exist.

What follows is a spirited debate between the two of them about the merits and demerits of this idea and whether or not we should just try to get out of the country altogether and forget about everything. At some point, Danny emphasizes Andra, my daughter, and wonders if we don't at least owe it to the child to ensure that she's safe.

Christine just bites into her scone and stares at me.

I decide to offer my expert assessment. "Forget the Watsons. They'll be fine. I might think we will never hear from them again."

And because in parallel universes things like this happen... the room phone suddenly rings.

We all stare at each other before I finally wrench myself from where I stand and answer it, cautiously, as if it was dipped in poison

"Hello?"

"Mr. Night?" comes a cheery voice from the other end.

"Uh, no. No, this is Mr. Berger."

"Ah, yes, Mr. Berger. I have a Ms. Stetson for you, sir."

And now, as is also the case in parallel universes, time stops. I turn and look to Danny and Christine, who wait, expectantly, for me to speak. Finally, Danny whispers (for some reason), "Who is it?"

"It's Eliza," I say.

CHAPTER FORTY-TWO

Christine

How dare she.

How dare that bitch call my boyfriend at my fucking hotel room and interrupt my morning.

"What the hell does she want?" I ask.

I realize my rage is slightly unjustified because Eliza did help us get Alec back. *However.* I still hate that bitch and I was assuming I'd never have to see her face again after yesterday.

Naïve, perhaps. On my part. Since she and Alec have a child together. Which means that if Alec decides to take an active role in little mini-Alec's life, she will be part of my life as well.

But it's been *one day.* One goddamn day since all these feelings from the past came bubbling back up to the surface and you know what?

I think I deserve more than a fucking day to adjust.

I'm pissed that she's calling. So what. Sue me.

Alec pauses to listen to something Eliza is saying, his eyes darting to mine. Then he sighs, lowers the phone from his ear, and presses the button for speaker.

"Good morning, Christine," Eliza says.

My rage is not in check. "What do you want?"

"I'm fine, thanks. Yes, you're welcome for yesterday. I know that you know that I didn't have to help you, and yet I did. But let's not dwell on who owes whom favors."

I make that sound people make when they're feeling amused and incredulous in the same moment. She has balls, I'll give her that. But so do I. "Charlie told me he called in a favor. For me," I add. Just to rub it in. "So let's not pretend you did this for any other reason than you were forced, OK? Good."

Danny sighs. Rubs a hand down his unshaven face. Closes his eyes. Then sighs again. "Hey, Eliza. Thanks for the help yesterday. We really appreciate it."

"Oh, I can tell," Eliza says.

I look at Alec, realize I'm glaring, and force myself to stop. I say, for the third time, through gritted teeth, "What. Do you. Want?"

There's a brief pause as Mini-Alec says something in her sweet little-girl voice on the other end of the phone. Something about Danny. It might be about hopscotch. I stop my eye roll because I'm looking at Alec when all this happens, and he's got an expression on his face I can only assume is… longing.

He has feelings for the child.

Of course he has feelings for the child. It's his fucking child, Christine.

Danny gets up and walks over to me, pulling me into a hug. I lean against his chest and crumple. Let my rage fade, just a little.

I hate this. I can't even describe how much I hate this. But I have to deal with it because like it or not, Alec and Eliza have a little girl called Andra. And even though, for all these years, I've been the child in this relationship, I'm not that kid anymore.

I have not been that kid for a very long time. Much longer than the six years it's been since I turned eighteen.

It's what I've always wanted, wasn't it? To be taken seriously. To be seen as an adult. To be a *woman* in their eyes.

So I ravel all my unraveled parts back up and make a decision to grow in this moment.

And in that same moment Eliza says, "I know I'm disrupting things. I know"—she takes a deep breath— "that I'm just an additional line in the triangle called Alec, Christine, and Danny. And there's no room for extra lines. There can only ever be three sides to a triangle. So I'm going to do my best not to remake this shape into something else... but I'm worried. And if I didn't call, and something happened—"

"What happened?" Alec says.

"—then I'd hate myself after."

"What happened?" Alec repeats. "Is everything OK?"

"Someone was here last night," she says.

"What do you mean?" Danny asks. He's still hugging me. Which I appreciate more than he'll ever know.

"The perimeter alarm went off this morning. And while I admit the alarm goes off on occasion because of squirrels and the odd overzealous crow pecking at motion sensors, it was three AM and there's no reality in which rodents and birds are responsible for this one."

"Explain," Alec says.

"I saw a shadow lurking in the back garden."

"What kind of shadow?"

"The usual creepy, lurking shadow," Eliza says, almost out of patience. "I don't know exactly. But we did break into, and extract you, from a heavily guarded mansion yesterday. And all my brothers seem to think that we have a problem."

"We do have a problem," Russell says, butting in. "I don't like this one bit. Eliza and Andra have been safe for more than two years. No thanks to you, van den Berg. And then you come back into their lives and suddenly we have alarms going off at three in the AM and no way to account for it."

Alec, Danny, and I trade looks.

"In other words," Russell continues, "there are loose ends that need to be tied up. And you need to tie 'em."

Well. There you have it. Russell Watson is calling to cash in his favor.

Didn't take him long, did it?

"What do you propose we do?" Alec asks.

"We all saw your brother," Charlie says.

"And we weren't there to extract *him*," Brenden adds.

"So what's the fucking deal, Alec, mate?" Theo asks. "What the hell is going on?"

Apparently, the whole family is gathered round for this conversation.

Alec looks at me because I am the only one who can answer this question. Except I don't really remember and that's a lame excuse the Watson crew won't accept the way Danny and Alec did.

Danny comes to my rescue. "We have a problem with Lars."

"What kind of problem?" Russell asks.

"He tried to kill me," Alec says. "Actually, he destroyed my house several months back. Came in with a tactical assault and then things got messy—"

"*Then* things got messy?" Russell says.

"—and we wound up tumbling over a waterfall. Then... I don't know. I woke up some time later—maybe weeks later, maybe months, I'm not really sure—and I was at the estate. Being held... not quite prisoner, but unable to leave, either. So, that's a bit of what's that. If it helps, I was already planning to handle it. *We* were planning to."

Silence from all eight of us. We make an octagon now, I realize. Then, like she planned it this way just to remind me that the shape of us has changed, Eliza says, "Andra, dear. Please stop jumping around. Mummy is having an important conversation."

"But I want to talk to that man Danny..."

I think someone physically removes her from the room because her voice fades away.

I glance at Alec and find that same, pained expression on his face. It's not simply *feelings*.

It's love.

We so far away from the triangle right now, I might be sick.

We aren't even a square.

We are... whatever the fuck it is you call a shape with nine sides. I have no idea, I just know... it's complicated.

CHAPTER FORTY-THREE

"Why would Lars try to kill you, then?" Russell asks.

Christine goes stiff in my arms.

This shit is getting complicated. More complicated.

"Well," Alec says, threading his fingers into his already mussed-up hair.

I like him like this, I realize. Messy and disheveled. Probably not the best time to reflect on how goddamn sexy Alec is, but there you have it.

"Well, what?" Charlie asks. "Fucking spit it out, mate. There's no room for heavily guarded secrets. We helped you, now you need to tell us exactly what's what."

"It was me," Christine says.

"Christine," Alec interjects.

"No," she continues, disconnecting herself from my embrace. "They need to know. It's not fair. There's a little girl involved now... and it's just not fair."

I know this is hard for her. Hell, just seeing her in that back garden yesterday told me everything. The look of longing on her face was unmistakable. She was jealous. That's the life she never had. That's the child she never had. And whether she wants to admit it or not, she won't be able to live with herself if she's the reason it all gets ripped away from Andra.

Oh, I have no illusions about Eliza. Christine and Eliza, that's never going to resolve into anything more than hate and anger.

But Andra is another story.

Christine is, and always has been, one of the most ruthless people I've ever met. I've known that since she admitted, without a second thought, that she wanted to poke the pretty out of an innocent blue beetle when she was ten years old.

I've come to terms with who she is because it fits with who I am. Who Alec is too. She's damaged and hard. I'd even go so far as to call her cruel. Maybe even savage. At least to her enemies and targets.

She has come to terms with who she is too, I'm sure of it.

But she would not wish her life on anyone, especially a child.

And she proves me right when she says, "This is all my fault," and proceeds to catch the Watsons up—completely—on what happened.

She explains, and Alec and I let her. We remain quiet as she recounts waking up in that apartment. The ambush at my garage—did I really have a custom bike business? I can barely remember that life back in the city with Brasil. Can barely recall the four years of separation.

She tells them about the ambush at the glass house next and how Lars and she were presumably working together. How she was confused and had to make a decision on who to trust.

How she chose me.

How Alec and Lars ended up going over that waterfall.

Eliza huffs out a sigh of disgust at this point.

But Alec says, "Don't," in a harsh enough voice that Eliza shuts her trap and lets Christine continue.

But there's not much to say after that. Christine throws up her hands. "I don't remember much more. I think that concussion I got after falling off the roof was worse than I figured. I just don't know why I would do all that. And why, for fuck's sake, I'd take up with Lars to bring Alec down."

"I do," Eliza snarls. "You were jealous—"

"That's enough," Charlie interjects. "Shut up, Eliza."

"We taking her side now, luv?"

"I was there, remember?" Charlie says. "I was with her after she lost the baby."

And this is, I suppose, where gaps get filled in.

"Oh, shit," I say.

So does Alec.

Apparently, he had no clue either.

And suddenly a few pieces of this puzzle make more sense. Charlie and Christine, at least, make sense.

He was there when the two of us weren't.

Everyone takes a moment to let this solidify.

We weren't there.

Finally, Russell takes over. "So... we're in agreement, then, mates? Because I don't want to step on any toes but seems to me that Lars is a loose end who requires tying off."

More silence as Alec considers what his answer will be.

On the surface it's easy. Hell, just an hour ago he was going to sneak out and take care of business with Lars himself.

But now there's a bigger plan of action in play. Now the Watsons are involved. If they go in with us—to make sure, to see that it's done—there's no room for second-guessing. There's no last-minute, *Let's make up and be brothers again.*

There is only one way this ends and that's with Lars dead.

Everyone knows that this is Alec's call. Even Russell. Because he gives him whole seconds to decide, and object, before he says, "Good. Then it's settled. I'm sending Brenden and Charlie to pick you all up. Danny will get a text when they arrive. Change your mind before you get in the car… we're still cool as long as you understand that we'll take care of business on our end and there will be no further contact with anyone in our crew."

He pauses. Just so we're all clear that Andra's last name is Watson and this decision includes her.

"But get in that car and we're working together. You cross us, in any way, van den Berg, and we'll hunt you all down after we're done with Lars. Not even Charlie could save you then."

Alec opens his mouth to say something. I know him well enough to predict it's gonna start an argument about who's in charge and who'll be hunting down whom, so I interject and say, "We got it," then walk over to the phone and end the call.

"Alec," Christine says.

He looks at her, squinting his eyes.

"You don't have to—"

"Yes," he says, cutting her off. "I do. I choose you, Christine. I choose Danny. I choose…" He lets out a long breath of air. I don't hold it against him. This is his brother we're talking about. And with this final declaration, his brother is dead to him. "I choose us."

CHAPTER FORTY-FOUR

Alec

Once upon a time, Christine said something to me. It was a private moment. We were sitting on a dock somewhere... Antigua? Anguilla? Angola? Don't recall.

All I remember is that we had done something. Something typically dangerous and dramatic and altogether impossible, in the course of which an item was probably stolen and someone was maybe killed. It's better than fifty-fifty odds that was the case. And in this quiet moment after the fact, Christine admitted to me that sometimes she dreamed of a different life.

I asked her, "What kind of life, nunu?"

She said, "I don't know. One where I go to a cubicle, or maybe a small office, and am, like, a personal assistant or something."

I laughed. I laughed so hard. She slapped me on the shoulder, telling me to stop. But it just seemed ludicrous to me. Because there is no way that Christine would ever be satisfied with a life like that. Something as boring and tedious as the kind of lives that others have. But I also laughed because I couldn't imagine why, of all the dreams a person might dream, *that* is the one she chose for herself.

I can now.

297

Sitting in the back of the SUV, staring out the window as the city streets of London become country roads to… wherever, I understand. Perhaps it's the pastoral placidity of it all, but something docile and domesticated doesn't seem like the worst thing in the world at present. I'm sure that paying bills and showing up at some office on time, lest one be reprimanded for tardiness, would get wearisome. But I'm also sure that in a scenario like that, the chances of having to formulate a plan to kill your baby brother before he tries to kill you and possibly the people you love—for the second time—is greatly diminished.

We're not heading to Eliza's, it would appear. We're being shuttled in the opposite direction to Theo's house. This is where the Watsons have convened to work out, with the three of us, exactly what happens next.

No one has spoken since the car pulled up and we got inside. Not a word. Danny looked at Charlie with a bit of a scowl. Christine looked at me with something akin to longing. And Brenden looked at his phone, playing some type of escape room game.

And now we find ourselves pulling up to the cottage. It's quaint and sweet. Just like Eliza's. The Watson brood have always been somewhat frugal with their money. I know they earn a fair amount of it, doing what they do, but for them, it has always seemed that just somewhat better than where they're from has been good enough. That placid, docile life that Christine once mused about… the Watsons seem to have discovered it.

The SUV rolls to a stop and we all step out. There is the slightest chill in the air, but it is an otherwise lovely day. In some respects. In other respects, it is a horribly ominous one. I don't imagine the two are separable.

Entering through the main door, I hear the sound of tiny feet galumphing down the stairs. The child called Andra sees the five of us and immediately runs over to...

Danny.

She tugs at his hand and says, "Hopscotch," as she jumps up and down. She has quite a great deal of energy, this one. A restless and demanding spirit.

She probably gets it from her mother.

In any case...

Theo descends the stairs after her, and Russell and Eliza enter from another room. Eight of us stand looking at each other somewhat awkwardly while one of us continues to enjoin that hopscotch be commenced directly. Danny appears both distracted and flattered. It is a charming look on him that I can't help but smile at.

"Andra, come here," Eliza commands, and the little girl obliges. She joins her mother, as do Brenden and Charlie. And the tableau is now made unmistakably manifest. On one side of an imaginary dividing line are me, Christine, and Danny. An unlikely trio that, at a glance, would not be easily recognized as a family. And other the other side, five Watsons who it would be impossible not to observe as one. In the middle: A small Watson-Berg. Or possibly van der Watson. Whatever one might call her, she is the lone, unifying element that causes us all to be here now.

Eliza's eyes drift across the three of us. I see no judgement, exactly, but there is an unmissable assessing. "You look rested," she says to me. "Got a shave, did you?"

"So it would seem."

"And you all had a good evening? Comfy? Happily reunited?"

"Lize," Russell interrupts, but she goes on.

"Nobody creeping around *your* place in the middle of the night, were they?"

"Lize, come on," he says again.

"Mummy, this is boring," the child says, looking up at her mother.

"Why don't you go practice in Uncle Theo's foam pit, love?"

The child's eyes go wide. "Really, really, really?"

Her mother nods her head. "Just don't jump from too high."

The little one doesn't respond, just goes tearing off to the rear of the house somewhere.

"You're letting her fuck around in a foam pit without supervision? OK..." Christine says, nodding her head after Andra is away from earshot. Eliza's jaw tightens in a way I have seen many times before and she bites at her bottom lip.

Russell, as is his role, steps around to the front of the brood and says, "Here's where we're at: Nobody wants to be here, but here we be, so let's just discuss what needs to happen so we can never speak again, shall we?"

I internalize a laugh because it is now painfully obvious to me that the probability of us never speaking again is slim indeed. It would seem that some vengeful god plans to keep thrusting us into each other's paths until whatever cosmic debt we all owe is paid. But, perhaps, just maybe, what's going to happen next will be the thing that pays it off once and for all. I fokken doubt it, but I'm a goddamn optimist.

"Right," I say, stepping forward. "Before anyone says anything else, I just want to offer this: All of you"—I point my finger at the Watsons, en masse—"don't have to be part of anything. You came along to help retrieve me, and

I appreciate it, and if you like, your work with this is done. This is our concern. Christine's, Danny's, and mine. It has nothing to do with you. So I am right now offering you the chance to step away. You offered the same to us, an opportunity to step away and let you handle whatever this perceived threat is. But it's not yours to handle. So I'm suggesting that all six of you get on a plane—I'll arrange one—and have it take you anywhere in the world. Anywhere you want to go. Perhaps Nara would be a good place to lie low for a while…" I look at Eliza, who glares at me. "And once we have seen to it that all concerns related to me, or us, or you have been dealt with, you can return. Or stay. Or do whatever you like. The point is, I'm offering. I encourage you to consider seriously."

I don't know what I expect. Eliza wouldn't take me up on this exact offer once before, so I have no idea why I think she might now. Except I do. It's the same reason they all might.

The child.

Before, the child was just an idea. Something as yet not fully formed. Not a walking, talking person who also has to share in the burden of being part of a world in which this type of thing is what passes for normal. Now, seeing the way they clearly love her—and seeing that she is a curious, special, odd, and wonderful little being—perhaps they will all think differently.

I think they must be mulling it over sincerely, because the looks on their faces suggest that it's at least worth their proper consideration. Or that's what I think their looks convey. I realize that what their looks actually convey is disbelief because after about three seconds they all burst into laughter simultaneously.

"Fuckin' hell, mate!" Russell says. "Are you taking the piss? Is he taking the piss?" He turns around and presents his rhetorical question to the group. "Mate, let's be clear about something…" He steps in closer than I would encourage him to. I have a history with his sister and his niece is my child, but if he violates my personal space, I may not be responsible for what happens after.

He continues talking. "I ain't never liked you, mate. I ain't never trusted you. And you're off your fuckin' trolley if you think I'm going to trust your poncy South African arse now. The only reason you're even here is because she asked for you to be." He points at Eliza, who looks away. I can feel heat behind my neck. Palpable heat. And I turn to see that it's coming from Christine's glare.

Regular little *Days of Our fokken Lives* we've got happening here. Eish, man.

"Look, bruv," he goes on, pointing a finger at me, which I do everything in my power not to snap in half, "I woke up yesterday morning, drank my tea, and set about having a normal day. Me and the lads were planning to go over the details of a job at a jeweler's in Oxford, maybe play some footie, and visit with me mum for an hour or two, when you lot showed up." The finger passes across Danny and Christine as well. "And suddenly, we's been thrust into a scenario where men with guns shot at us, and me sister and niece don't feel safe in their own home at night. And if you think for a moment that we's the type of people who'd just hand over the resolution to a situation like this to the very wanker who put us in said situation, then mate, you don't fuckin' remember us terribly well."

I can feel his breath on my face. His tension. His anger. His fear. That's what anger is, after all. It's just a reconfiguring of fear. Or sadness. Or some other vulnerable emotion that one doesn't want to feel. Anger is the mind's brilliant way of interceding and overpowering the weaker feelings.

Ironically, of course, anger can also make you weak because it shows you for who you are. A person. Like other people. As my father once told me, if you are unfrightened, the other oke will be forced to take up that fear in compensation and you will be made powerful by his absorption of what you cast off.

When the world is off its axis and others fear losing control... that is when I am at my most powerful. Because I breathe into myself and become greater than I am.

Death thrives on fear. Death is not welcome here.

And just like that, I remember this, and I feel like myself again. All it took was to look in the eyes of someone who believes they have something to lose and counter that look with the belief that I do not. There is nothing that can be taken from me. I will not allow it. And so, Russell's anger has brought me back into balance.

I'll have to remember to do something nice for him.

"Aces," I say, and smile.

He scowls at me, furrows his brow, and says, "Let's go work out a proper fuckin' plan." And he marches off into the house, his brothers in tow. I step to watch him leave, and when I turn back, I see that Eliza is still here, standing by the stairs. She is to my right, Christine is to my left, and Danny stands across from me.

That this quadrilateral formation is the one we inadvertently find ourselves in should be observably absurd, but I am beyond the point of surprise anymore.

"How did you know where to find us?" Christine asks her after a moment.

"I assumed you'd still be in London, and if you're in London there's only one place you'd be."

"Why?" Christine asks.

It's unclear what the 'why' refers to, but Eliza chooses a very particular answer. One designed to achieve some type of objective. I'm just not clear exactly what.

She responds, "Because, whether I like it or not, in this particular instance, Alec is the one person in the world best situated to protect *his daughter.*"

And now, Christine's breathing is all I can hear.

I glance at Danny. He tilts his head at me.

How does life get so complicated so easily, man? How does it happen?

I don't know. But I do know it doesn't have to be.

I step over and stand beside Christine. Danny steps to the other side and joins us. I allow my finger to graze her hand.

And as we reconnect, Eliza regards us with an unknowable expression. Then she takes in a deep breath, pulls her shoulders back, exhales, and after a moment, says, "Indeed," before she walks away, leaving the three of us alone.

CHAPTER FORTY-FIVE

Christine

So here we stand. Just the three of us. And that's just fine with me.

"OK then," Danny says, following the Watsons into the other room.

And now it is two.

"Christine—"

"I know," I say, more anger and resentment in my voice than I'd like. So I take a deep breath and turn to face him. "I got it."

I turn to follow Danny but Alec grabs my hand. "Wait."

"What?"

"Are you angry with me?"

"No," I say, exasperated. Because I kinda am. And I kinda have reason to be. But I do understand I don't have reason to be as well. So I say… "It's just our new reality, that's all."

He nods. Continues to hold my hand but says nothing. This is all me.

"I'll get used to the idea, OK?" And in this moment, I feel that is a very generous offer.

But Alec shakes his head.

"Fine, I like her, is that good enough?"

He offers me a smile. Like I'm close, but not there yet.

So I huff out a resigned sigh and say, "She's perfect. Is that what you want to hear? She will be very easy to love. Hell, I'm already in love with her. It's not Andra's fault I have... issues. And I know better. I would never, *ever* take it out on her."

The smile grows. "I know that," he says. "I never had any doubts and neither did you. I just think it's good to say things like this out loud so they become our truth. Our team got a little bigger while we weren't looking. I'm sorry you weren't consulted—"

"Alec—"

"—I'm more sorry than you'll ever know that you weren't the one who gave us our addition—"

"Alec, please—"

"But we're here now and I need you to know... nothing has changed."

Everything has changed.

"Not between us," he says, shaking his head like he's reading my mind. "We are stronger, better, and more in love than ever. She is ours, Christine. *Ours.*"

"I don't think Eliza will see it that way."

"Eliza will have to find her own way forward. She is not our concern. You," he says, his thumb stroking my hand. "And Danny. And me. We are the ones who count."

"OK, so let's stop fucking talking about it and go make a plan to kill your brother."

He just stares at me and I wilt.

God, what is wrong with me? Why do I let Eliza Watson turn me into this... this... petty, sad little girl? Why do I give her power like that? Surely I can adult my way through this? Right? I can be the better person. Not stoop and all that nonsense?

But Eliza has always made me feel small. And I am small next to her. I am young, and small, and weak and...

Alec reaches out with his other hand and places his palm against my cheek. He gazes down at me like I'm the most important thing in the world.

Not Eliza. Not even Andra, though we're probably tied for first place at this point and she will most likely overtake me soon. She will overtake everything. Because that's what children do. They upend your life. They pull it apart until there's nothing left but little pieces. But then you put all those pieces back together in a new way and you move on with a new center of light.

That's how it *should* be. That's all I ever wanted from the people who brought me into this world. That's all I wanted to give our child and never got the chance.

But I do have the chance to do that for someone else.

So I owe it to Andra to grow up and deal.

I am not that little girl anymore. I am strong, and bold, and capable. And Alec helped make me that way.

I owe him too. So much. But that's not why I give it one more try.

"I'm sorry," I whisper. "I'm being a childish bitch."

"I'm not looking for another apology. We both said them. We both accepted them. Now we rise above it and get the job done. And you're not being a childish bitch. You're acting like any normal person forced into this situation. I just want you to understand you were my first choice then and you're my first choice now. And I'm sorry as well. I'm sorry that our painful past has to be part of our present. I'm on your side. I truly am."

And that, for whatever reason, feels like what I needed to hear. It feels like enough.

It shouldn't be good enough. Not after I took up with Lars and helped him. After I betrayed Alec in such a nefarious, backstabbing way. Not after the hurt I felt after losing the baby and discovering I—*we*—had been replaced.

But it is.

Because I didn't mean to betray him, and he didn't mean to betray me.

And even if I did mean to betray him, and him to betray me, we *still* didn't mean it. Our choices were unconscious actions that grew out of pain, and guilt, and past experiences that were never dealt with.

So I say, "I'm on your side too. Forever."

Alec strokes my cheek and squeezes my hand. "Good. Then let's go take care of business."

CHAPTER FORTY-SIX

The Watsons lead me into the back room of the cottage, which is a large eat-in kitchen with a cozy living room. There's even a fireplace and large floor-to-ceiling windows spanning the entire back wall that look out into yet another perfect backyard.

This one isn't a garden. It's a lawn coming to life in the spring. And in the center is a pavilion that covers a playground.

Only this playground is a foam pit and little Andra is climbing up a stack of large foam blocks. She spies me through the window and waves, shouting, "Come play jumps with me, Danny!" in her weird, little-kid accent that still makes her sound like she's from Brooklyn.

"Does she need speech therapy?" I wonder aloud.

"The fuck you on about?" Charlie says.

"She talks weird."

"She's two," Eliza snaps.

"Yeah," I say, still watching Andra as she jumps down into the pit filled with bits of cut-up foam. "Makes sense I guess."

"You ready to focus?" Russell asks, bringing up a satellite view of the estate we broke Alec out of... yesterday. Jesus. Life sure can turn on a dime, can't it?

I nod and pretend to pay attention. Christine and Alec are still in the other room and I can hear them murmuring quietly. Having some kind of personal discussion.

They need that discussion and I knew it was coming, so that's why I gave them some alone time. But when I glance at Eliza, she's chewing her thumb, nervously glancing in the direction of the murmuring.

They're talking about her and she knows this. Probably Andra too.

Does Eliza love him?

Yes. For sure. And every one of her brothers knows this. Which is why they made a big deal with all the alpha-male posturing.

They hate Alec. And half of them probably hate me too. But Russell doesn't. I don't know why Russell and I get along like long-lost cousins, we just do.

Russell slaps me upside the head. "You here with us, mate?"

"Standing right here," I say.

"Yeah?" he says. "Cause you look about a million kilometers away."

I am a million kilometers away. For good reason. These Watsons can make all the plans they want and I'm happy to pretend I'm cool with it. But Alec is calling the shots for this little operation. So I give no shits what Russell is going on about.

"No, I'm listening," I say, looking at the satellite map, then snap my attention back at the door when Alec and Christine appear holding hands.

I glance at Eliza out of instinct. She lets out a long breath. Then I glance at Alec and Christine, both of whom are watching Andra play outside.

I nod my head at Christine and without even looking in my direction she nods back.

That's our little secret language for:

Me: *You OK with it?*

Her: *We worked it out.*

Me: *Good, because you know this kid is cool as fuck, right?*

Her: *Shut up, Danny.*

Just like that. Goes exactly like that.

"Do you three mind if we stop all these secret looks and mental fuckin' conversations and get back to the job at hand?" Russell asks, directing that comment to Alec.

And now we can. Because Alec is here.

There's the usual production of going over the perimeter of the map. We collect all the intel we got from yesterday's venture and collate it into something cohesive. And there's a lot of talk about sneaking and stealth. We'll have weapons, of course. But this time there'll be no distraction. We are going in quietly, completing the mission now called Kill Lars, and exiting without fanfare.

"And then Bob's your uncle," says Russell, "that'll be that."

Of course, it'll never happen that way. Too many variables, too many people, too much acreage on that fucking plot of land.

But we all feel better once it's decided.

Two teams. There's a fair bit of loud protests and arguing over this part but in the end it will be me, Charlie, and Brenden on Team Danny and Eliza, Russell, Alec, and Christine on Team Alec.

Russell tried to stick Christine with me but Alec squashed that idea before it even fully materialized.

"I need Christine with me," Alec said. And his tone left no more room for discussion.

And for a split second I wonder… does he want to confront them both together? Get some answers from Lars and Christine before he takes his brother's life for betraying him?

Because that would be counterproductive in my opinion.

But Alec hears my question, even though I never said it out loud, and looks at Christine to shake his head.

That's our little secret language for:

Alec: *It's over now, Christine. I just need you by my side when the shit goes down.*

Christine: *I know that, asshole. It was Danny's stupid question, not mine.*

Eliza sighs in the wake of this and Russell says, "Stop fuckin' doing that."

And then everyone, including us, looks at him like he's lost his mind.

I think that's why Russell and I get along. He hears my secret language. Not Alec's or Christine's. Just mine, for some reason.

This is what links us. Like it or not, the Watsons are here to stay. It just took us all the better part of five years to understand that point.

We spend the next several hours preparing and then, just a few minutes past midnight, we get in two separate vehicles and make the long drive up to complete Mission: Kill Lars.

CHAPTER FORTY-SEVEN

Alec

In private moments, I have sometimes mused over what it might be like to be the type of person who doesn't think so much. The type of oke who doesn't spend half of his day considering angles and wondering how to manipulate circumstances. Would it be nice, I wonder? Would it make my life easier? Would it, at the least, cause it to *feel* easier?

I don't know. I do know that it would probably cause me to be less suspicious. Which could be a good thing or a bad thing. Bad, of course, insofar as my suspicious nature has kept me alive. Good, less obviously, in that right now I likely wouldn't be wondering over the particulars of this engagement with the Watsons.

I have multiple thoughts, colliding in no real order.

- Somehow the Watsons are involved. Somehow this excursion we're on is in some way orchestrated to wipe me, Christine, and Danny off the face of the earth.

Which is ridiculous and even in a world of senselessness makes no sense.

- Eliza is in the process of cultivating some plot to bring me back into her life. Because now that she's seen me again, she is desperate for my love.

That idea is even more senseless than my previous one.

... In private moments, I have sometimes mused over what it might be like to be the type of person who doesn't think so much ...

I'd probably not miss the obvious truths staring me right in the face. Like Lars. Like, I neglected to care for Lars, to see after Lars, to notice Lars, for years. And the one person I *should* have been considering got overlooked. And now this, here, is the price I have to pay.

I've no clue what is going to happen when we get there, but I won't have to wait much longer to find out because we are here. We've arrived.

Danny, Brenden and Charlie should be in place on one side of the grounds. Russell, Eliza, Christine and I are making our approach from the other side. There had been some discussion about possibly trying to gain access from within the tunnels out of which I emerged yesterday, but it was deemed ill-advised as those are now likely guarded more strenuously, and we would be cut off from radio and satellite contact.

We're operating under the presumption that, assuming the force that was here previously is still here, they'll not be expecting us to return. Or, alternatively, that they're one hundred percent expecting us to return and we're about to enter into a woefully mismatched battle that we really shouldn't even be considering taking on.

There is a not insignificant part of my mind that wonders if perhaps we all missed this. By "this," I mean this one-upmanship. This continuing game of "who can steal it better." I wonder if we are all just addicts. Addicted to the thrill. Addicted to the intrigue. Addicted to the risk. Addicted to each other in one way or another.

No matter how one examines it, and as much as any of us may wish it not to be so, the Watson clan and the triangle that is me and my family are now bound. Inexorably linked. It could be ignored before, but now that we have all seen each other again and seen the child called Andra, I wonder if we are going to be a unit for more of our lives than we previously planned.

I wonder.

"Theo?" Russell whispers into his microphone from where we're crouched in the woods. "How we looking, mate?" He nods. Then his eyes narrow and he says, "What?"

"What? What is it?" Eliza asks.

"He says there's no movement."

"What do you mean, there's no movement?"

"He says there are no heat signatures, no images on the satty, nothing."

"No guards?" Christine asks.

"Not so far as he can see," Russell says.

Again, my mind starts riffling through the possibilities.

- They've gone to find us before we can find them. If I know what Lars might do, he must know what I might consider.

- They are, in fact, hiding in the underground tunnels. They know we're coming and they're waiting to ambush us.

- None of any of this has happened, it is all still a dream, and I'm going to wake up in bed with Danny and Christine again, and won't that be fokken better?

"Is the gate up, Theo? The electrified fence?" Russell looks us all in the eyes and shakes his head 'no.'

"This suddenly seems like a bad idea," Christine says. "Nobody's here? The fence is down? What the fuck?"

"Well," I offer, "perhaps it's as simple as... if the Crown Jewels have already been stolen, there's no longer any need to protect the tower."

"So, in this scenario, that makes you the Crown Jewels?" Eliza asks.

"In all scenarios, I am the Crown Jewels, love." I wink. I do it just to be cheeky and to try to gin myself up the way a fighter will do before a bout when he wonders if he is outmatched, but looking at Christine's reaction, I realize that cheek is perhaps best stored elsewhere when Eliza is involved.

"Well, what the fuck do we want to do?" Christine asks

"What do you mean?"

"I mean, we drew up a plan based on a certain situation and that situation looks quite a bit different than we prepared for." She *is* right. And as I think about that, I can't help but smile. "Why are you smiling?" I don't answer, directly, just continue grinning. "No," she says. "Alec, no. We already—"

"Danny, bru?" I say into my radio.

"Yeah?"

"Are you all in position?"

"Yep. Charlie and Brenden are playing rock, paper, scissors for who gets to fire the .50 cal if it comes to that, but we're here."

"Hundreds. But listen, man, turns out that apparently there may be nothing to do here and no one to do it to."

"What? What are you saying?"

316

"I'm saying that the plans, all the scenarios we considered, were predicated around the manor being occupied, and… it may no longer be."

"What? Are you serious?"

"As cancer, my bru."

"Fuck. Do you think that's true?"

"That no one is here?"

"Yeah."

"Not one bit."

"Me either," he says. "So, well… OK. What do you want to do?"

Still smiling, I say, "I think we may have to improvise."

There's a pause, and sure as I'm grinning like a Cheshire Cat, I'm certain I also hear a smile in his voice when he responds with, "Copy that."

Emerging from the wooded surrounding area, past the not-currently-electrified fence, and stepping into the open grassiness of the estate itself, I do have a bracing moment of stiffness. That hitch one gets when one is certain they've emptied their pockets of all metal but still aren't sure if the metal detector is going to go off or not. If a spotlight were to suddenly illuminate all of us and our bodies were to be riddled with bullets, I would be less than shocked.

But that does not happen. No light. No bullets. No riddling. Something does catch my attention out of the corner of my eye. A rabbit. A tiny, white bunny with what appears to be a handful or more of bunny children. I didn't know rabbits were nocturnal. I certainly don't think baby rabbits should be out this late. It must be well past their bedtime.

Ach, look at that, I sound like a parent. A parent wearing a five-thousand-pound suit and carrying a T91 assault rifle, stalking the grounds of an eerily deserted-seeming mansion with the intent of finding and murdering his own brother.

Well… at least I'm not some type of bosbefok circus acrobat like Andra's mother. That's just strange.

"It really does look empty," Christine says, regarding the darkened, monolithic colossus of a structure here in the midst of nowhere.

"It does *look* that way," Eliza offers.

"You think it's a trap?" Russell asks.

"I always think everything's a trap," Eliza says. "Which is why I'm still alive."

"Are you fucking quoting *The Princess Bride*?" That's Christine. Eliza smirks. "Just… fucking don't. I love that movie. I want to still be able to."

"Brilliant," Russell chimes in. "Let's be careful, shall we?"

"I don't like this at all," Christine says. "It doesn't feel right."

Before I lead our way, I give her a kiss on the head and assure her that no matter what, we'll all come away from this intact. Every one of us. And while I have made a vow to no longer lie to her… or Danny… in this one instance, I'll make an exception.

Where did you go, Lars?

Where are you now?

CHAPTER FORTY-EIGHT

Christine

There is an air of competitiveness between Eliza and me and I hate it. I used to enjoy it. A little. Back when I first met her. I used to think she was so cool. So smooth. So in control. So slick. I thought she was the mistress of thieves. She might even have been my role model.

Which now makes me want to gag.

But that was before I found out she was falling in love with my Alec.

He is mine.

There is no doubt.

I know this, she knows this, he knows this.

So why do I let her get to me?

Jealousy, I suppose.

Which is why, when Alec leads the way across the lawn, she and I power-walk, silently competing with each other to be directly behind him.

I can practically feel Russell rolling his eyes because he hangs back a few yards, stalking forward alone.

"I'm sorry," Eliza whispers into the night.

"What?" I hiss back.

"I said I'm sorry. I didn't know about you and... well... I didn't know. I thought we had an agreement."

I huff out some air, shaking my head. "About?"

"Alec. I thought… you knew. As long as we were in England it was fine. I thought you knew."

"Are we really having this talk right now?"

"I'm just trying to make peace before… whatever happens, happens."

What does she think is happening? "Fine. Whatever," I whisper.

"You knew about us, right?"

"Yes," I hiss. "It wasn't about you, Eliza. Don't flatter yourself."

"I know that now," she says, turning her head to find my gaze. We continue to power-walk but the air of competitiveness has dissipated a little. "But I had no idea that you—"

"Just shut up, OK?"

"I have always liked you, Christine. Have always respected you. We were friends."

"Just… *later*, for fuck's sake."

"I know he's yours. I understand that. Accepted it long ago. Before Andra came along. Before any of that. He has always been yours. He has always belonged to you and Danny. I never had any illusions otherwise. I just want you to know I'm not a threat. OK?"

I don't know what to say. I want to hate her with every fiber of my being. I want to give in to the loathing and the blame. Make her my archenemy for life.

But the truth is… it's no one's fault. No one did this to me. No one made me into this person, or forced me into this life, or took anything away from me.

It just happened.

And if I really take a good hard look at things… every one of these people here gave me something more than what I had. Alec and Danny are my family. We are married

320

to each other. We are in love. We are a team. It's us three against the world.

But the Watsons are like family too. They have been around us for several years now. We've done jobs together and we played the game of who can steal it better. Sometimes we won, sometimes they won, but the fact is… they're here. Right now, with us, doing *this*.

And we're all here for the same reason.

Some might say we're all here for Andra. And I guess that's true. No one wants her to be collateral damage in the shit we do. But that's not the only reason we're here. We're here for each other.

We might never admit it. We might even hate it. But it's the truth.

So I say, "OK," and leave it at that. Because we've made our way across the lawn and are now on the walkway that leads around the house.

There truly is no one here. No lights on in the mansion, no outside lights on the walkways, no cars in the driveway. No one and nothing moves except us.

I spot Danny, Charlie, and Brenden on the other side, coming in from their neck of the woods.

Charlie and Brenden are clowning around like twin brothers. Jabbing each other, smacking each other, and generally being fucking idiots. They aren't loud. Not in any real sense of the word. But they are loud in this world of thieves we're in right now.

They chuckle and joke as we make our way down the dark pathway toward the front of the house. Danny probably wants to murder them. He catches my eye and shakes his head.

Why do you like this asshole? that shake says.

He's fun, my silent look back replies. *And he was there for me.*

Which makes Danny sigh as our two groups meet up at the front door.

The front door.

Which is ridiculous.

"*Dun. Dunt, dunt, dunt, dun. Dunt. Dun. Dunt. Dun,*" sings Brenden as they close the last few yards between us.

"*Neener neeer. Neener neer. Neeener neer. Nit net,*" adds Charlie.

We all just look at them like... *Mission: Impossible* song? Really?

Danny's look says: *How the fuck these two idiots are still alive, I'll never understand.*

My look says: *I got nothing for that.*

Russell slaps them both upside the head and says out loud, "Shut the fuck up."

Charlie and Brenden try for a look of professional gravity but fail miserably. Charlie says, "Ain't no one home, mates."

To which Brenden replies, "Look, the arseholes didn't even bother locking up."

We all turn to stare at the door, which is slightly ajar.

"What the hell is happening?" Eliza asks.

"It's a trap," Russell says.

"Or," Charlie adds, "blokes have up and left," and pushes past us to give the door a shove. "And there ain't no fucks left to give about security because there ain't no one here."

The door opens wide with a creak that seems oddly out of place and creepy as fuck at the same time. Beyond is just a hazy darkness. The outline of a grand staircase.

The faint moonlight passing through a long hallway coming from a window on the far side of the house.
     And silence.

CHAPTER FORTY-NINE

Everything about this plan is wrong and every one of us knows it.

Even Charlie and Brenden have gone quiet. Alec steps forward, crossing the threshold, and it takes all my self-control not to pull him back by the sleeve of his suit coat and tell him it's not worth it. Whatever it is he's looking for, that's not what we're gonna find here. We should just back up and leave.

But of course, that's not what happens.

Russell pushes past me and follows him in and then, as if we're connected by some invisible tether, we all step inside.

I hold my breath. Waiting for it. Waiting for the bullets to come streaming from the rooms on either side of the foyer. Waiting for the hot sting of death, and the inevitable collapse to the ground to bleed out.

But it never happens.

And then there's a rush of air as we all exhale and look at each other.

For some reason I find Eliza's gaze and she finds mine. We lock eyes and I read her.

She's scared.

As she should be. I think we're all scared even though there is no apparent reason for it.

Something happened here. Something is *still* happening here.

"Well," Russell whispers, respecting the silence. "Now what?"

Alec tilts his head, looking up the staircase. And then without speaking he walks towards it.

This time I do reach out and grab his sleeve. "Let's just leave," I say.

"No," Alec says, shrugging me off. "I have to go up there. I need to see."

"See what, mate?" Charlie asks. "There's nothing to see."

"Shhh," Alec snaps, still looking up the stairs. "Do you hear that?"

"Hear what?" Christine says. "Alec, I don't—"

"Shhh," Alec says again. "Listen." He points a finger up the stairs. "Do you hear that? Sounds like... clicking. Like a pattern of clicking."

"Oh, shit," Eliza says.

"What?" Christine asks, moving in closer to her.

Eliza looks down at Christine and says, "It's code. Can't you hear it?"

"Oh, shit," Christine says.

"What?" I ask. I want to shake them both and make them talk.

"It's Morse code," Russell says. "Listen."

We all crane our necks. Let the silence wash over us.

And then... in the stillness comes a tapping.

S. O. S.

Alec starts up the stairs. I reach for him again but he's practically running and the chance to go back disappears with him as he enters the darkness ahead.

The rest of us have no choice but to follow.

There's a collective drawing of weapons. Someone beside me, maybe Brenden, maybe Christine, loads a round into a chamber.

At the top of the stairs Alec hesitates, arm out in front of us, telling us to stop.

He looks up towards the third floor and we all follow his gaze.

S. O. S.

He starts running again. His long legs taking the stairs three at a time. I do the same and overtake Russell, then bound up past Alec because I see now that he is not holding his weapon. He's being drawn upward by some spell and he's forgotten to arm himself.

"It's a trap!" Russell yells. "Alec! Alec, stop, it's a trap, mate!"

But Alec doesn't stop and neither do I. I reach the top of the stairs first, gun panning back and forth as I move forward, checking the empty rooms, finding nothing.

The tapping is coming from the end of the hallway to the right, and I move forward quickly, jostling with Alec to enter the last room at the end.

But I get there first. Gun drawn, high ready, finger about to squeeze the trigger…

And I stop.

Because I have no idea what I'm looking at.

CHAPTER FIFTY

"Stop!" That is my voice. I know it is mine because I can hear it ringing out into the world as the word leaves my mouth. Simultaneously, I see my hand striking at Danny's weapon, knocking it from its position of readiness. My voice, my movements, my thoughts are happening, I know it, but they are all occurring in some type of fugue state. And though I am no seer and cannot presume to predict what this moment might augur, I do know that in the years to come I will look back on this scene and wonder if I was really there.

As I guessed might be the case, Lars did not leave. Whether he stayed with the intention of confronting me, as he surely knew I would return, or whether he never even really had awareness that I was gone in the first place, I shall likely never know. I would ask him. I would query him and hold him to account for his betrayal of me and his manipulation of Christine in such a state as she was in at the time. I would seek to know the answers to these and so many more questions. I would, if it appeared he could provide any type of response.

But he cannot, it would seem. Because sitting, as he is, in a wheelchair, wearing silk pyjamas identical to the ones in which I was outfitted for the last four or almost

JA HUSS & J McCLAIN

five months, he appears in no state to provide anyone with anything.

"What the fuck?" Danny whispers. Or possibly says at full volume but lands on my ear as a susurration after traveling down a long, smoky corridor of confusion and—if I am interpreting my emotions correctly—regret.

The other members of our collective arrive now at our stern and they all stop short. Danny holds them back with his arm. I think. The only thing I can make out for certain is a gasp that sounds like one of Christine's and an, "Alec?" which is definitely Christine's. I turn my head to note her expression and I speculate that it is a mirror of my own.

I turn back to see my brother—my baby brother who I never knew that well, who I was charged with caring for after our parents died, and who many years later would attempt to kill me—in a near catatonia, his arms and legs strapped to the wheeled, metallic perch on which he sits. He appears to have been beaten. Badly. His eyes are swollen, and his lips are bloodied. He struggles to take in air. He is a marooned guppy.

"Alec...?" I hear again. Again, it is Christine's voice. Looking back once more, she appears in need. The Watsons all stand in stock-still silence. I fear that none of us know what to do exactly. We wildly, and some might say foolishly, concocted a plan to come here tonight for our own various reasons. All of us bound by whatever it is that binds people. All of us with our own set of expectations for what we might find when we arrived. We planned for myriad scenarios. And when we materialized here, it looked like nothing we anticipated. And now what's before us looks like nothing anyone could have anticipated even if you had drawn an explicit diagram of what we would find.

The clicking we heard stops. Placed under the fingertips of Lars' bound left hand is a pistol, the barrel striking the arm of the chair as it pecked out an anemic call for help, the sound that drew us here. S.O.S. For over a century, the universal code for maritime distress. A nonverbal cry for aid from sailors at sea. How violently poetic.

Christine summons herself forward, passing Danny who tries to take her arm, but she pulls free and stands next to me. After a moment, Danny draws ahead as well and joins us. One of the Watson okes starts, "Do you—?" But I put up my hand and whatever question he was about to ask is stopped short. Now that the tapping has ceased, it is almost aggressively quiet in the house, save for the strained rattle coming from Lars as he tries with only marginal success to breathe.

"Watch behind us." I don't turn around to address Eliza and her brothers directly, but I will assume they know I'm talking at them. I take a tentative first step. Christine and Danny step with me. A second step. They follow in kind. A third step and I now see Lars attempting to open a tumescent eyelid. Four, five, six steps in quick succession and we are now knelt in front of and beside him.

"Lars. Lars, man. What the fok, bru? What happened? Bru? Bru?"

His head swivels a bit, his chin tracing his chest like a ghoulish metronome. He makes the suggestion of a sound. It is indescribable and possibly an attempt at words.

"Lars?" Christine. "Lars? Where is everyone? The men who were here? Your men?"

His metronomic head swivel manages five percent more energy, and through a clenched jaw he mumbles out what sounds like, "Aaaawaaaay..." Then a breath in through his nose and, "Nnnnot... nnnnnot..."

"Not what, bru?"

"Nnnnnnnot... mine."

And it is now all I can do to wrestle down the lightning strike of energy that wants to overtake me. I do. I breathe. I expand. I need to become bigger than I am. I need to consume all the space around me. Danny, spying something that I missed, reaches up to the pocket of the pyjama shirt and withdraws what appears to be a hastily scribbled note.

"What is that?" I ask. He doesn't respond, just unfolds the note and reads, his brow furrowing as he whispers, "What the fuck...?" Then his entire face contorts into a mask of rage. "Motherfucker!"

The sound of his shout echoing around the emptiness of this place is jarring. Eliza darts into the room. Christine startles and says, "What? What is it?"

Danny thrusts the note at me. I take it. Look down at the slapdash penmanship.

This was David's gun. He should have had the chance himself. If ye find this and if ye give a shite about this one, you'll put him out of his fuckin misery. The girl's a good enough shot from distance. Point blank should be easy. Wish I could see ye now Fortnight but had someplace else to be. Don't worry brother. Soon.

"Fok is this, man?" I ask, shoving the paper back at him.

He hangs his head. Says nothing. Christine reaches across me and grabs it from my hand. Reads it as well. Whispers, "Brasil."

"Fuck!" Danny shouts again, standing, looking for something to punch.

None of this makes sense. None of it. Not a fokken thing.

Lars. Lars knows something. Lars has answers.

"Lars," I say, reaching up for his chin. Weakly, he tries to retract from me. "Lars, man, let us help you. Look, bru, we've got some shit to work out, obviously." I smile a wee bit and try for a laugh. Not successfully, but I try. "But let's just get you some attention right now and then let's unpack some of this nonsense, yeah? Bru?"

Again, I try to tilt his chin to get him to look at me and again he tries, with strained effort, to avoid my touch. When I finally manage to take him with both hands and lift his head up, I understand why he resists. Sort of. I don't know what happened exactly, but his jaw appears somehow glued or wired shut, and the movement of his neck compels him to swallow. Forces him to. I see his Adam's apple bob, its laryngeal musculature tighten then loosen.

And suddenly, he begins convulsing. His body, strapped to the chair, spasms uncontrollably. Froth begins spilling from his still-clenched teeth and though clearly beaten, ruptured, and without strength of his own, he is now adrenalized into agonizing motion against his will.

… if ye give a shite about this one, you'll put him out of his fuckin misery.

"What the fuck is happening?" Christine shouts.

I cannot tell if the wrist and ankle guards that hold him in place are creating new lacerations as he struggles or

333

if they were already there, but the brutality of watching him strive and fail to flail free is almost too much to bear. Even for me.

The gun that had been placed under his hand—David's gun, I reckon—falls to the floor. But only for a moment. Only for less than a second. Because almost before it even lands, I snatch it up.

And I place the barrel against my poor, dear baby bru's temple and pull the trigger.

CHAPTER FIFTY-ONE

Christine

There is no such thing as silence in the moments after a gun goes off. Especially indoors. So that's not what I hear in the wake of Lars' brains being splattered against a wall.

It's an echo of silence. Some facsimile of silence. Laced with ringing and scented with blood.

"I don't understand," Eliza says. "What's going on?"

"What the fuck just happened?" Brenden adds.

I turn away from the remains of Lars and don't know who to look at first. I don't have any answers for them. I don't really understand it myself. But I choose Charlie to focus on. And for some reason I say, "Payback." Because it's the only thing that makes sense.

"Who in bloody hell is David?" Russell says, having stepped forward and grabbed up the note.

Danny opens his mouth to say something but ends up just giving his head a slight shake.

Which means: *Leave us now. We don't need you.*

And somehow Russell hears our secret language. Understands it immediately. Because he says, "Right then. Let's go." And turns away.

Eliza follows immediately. Like she can't get out of this room fast enough. Brenden turns too. But Charlie and

I are still locked together with our eyes. He holds out his hand and says, "Come with me, Christine."

And I hear *his* secret language in that moment. His hidden words. But even if I couldn't read him, it wouldn't matter. I can see it all in his eyes.

What the fuck have they gotten you into, Christine?

I don't want to go with him. I can't go with him. Because it's me who's gotten us all into this, not them.

"Go with your family," I say. "We need—"

I stop because Russell is talking out in the hallway. On the phone, I realize. Has to be with Theo. Talking quickly in ruptured sentences that make no sense. Telling him—or trying to tell him—exactly where we stand.

Then he says, "Theo, brother. What's that noise? What's going on?"

And it's the tone of his voice, not even words, that makes the rest of us in this room turn to look at the door leading out into the hallway.

"Theo?" Russell says again. "Theo!" he yells.

He panics. I can only see half of his face through the doorway, but I don't need to see more. Because he puts the phone on speaker and we hear it all go down in real time.

More gunshots ring through the echo of silence after Lars.

Theo yelling and then...

... and then Andra screams.

CHAPTER FIFTY-TWO

There is no discussion after Andra's scream. No silent conversations necessary either. We leave Lars up in that room. Feet pounding down the stairs in a rush. Running as a group across the lawn, back into the woods to the vehicles. I stay with Alec and Christine this time and Brenden and Charlie go alone.

Inside the car there is true, true silence. The drive is long and Christine is sitting between Alec and me in the back seat as Russell takes curves at breakneck speeds. He flies through roundabouts like a maniac and Eliza jostles back and forth next to him with one hand braced on the door and the other flat on the dashboard.

We have all come to the same conclusion.

This is no rescue mission.

Whatever happened at the cottage is over. Finished. Can't be undone.

All we are doing now is making our way back to see the fallout.

The repercussions of all the things we've done, all the people we've crossed, all the debts we owe.

By the time we pull into the cottage driveway all the adrenaline has drained away. Our collective rush into the house is just a facade.

We know it's over.

The front door is open and it feels like winter has returned for one last ferocious hurrah because the wind bangs it against the doorjamb like a very bad omen.

Eliza pushes Russell out of her way and enters first. Stops in the small foyer, mouth open as she takes in the scene.

The rest of us enter behind her, Alec pushing his way past me and Christine to stand next to the mother of his child.

Tables and chairs are overturned.

Windows are broken and the wind whips in from outside, blowing the once-quaint curtains.

"Andra!" Eliza yells. "Baby! Where are you?"

"Theo?" the brothers call.

But silence is our only answer.

They are gone.

There is nothing in life that cannot be conquered.

Not even Death.

Except that is not true. Death, as it turns out, is unconquerable.

She remains undefeated.

I am still glad it was me who took Lars' life. As opposed to someone else. For all I could not do for him in life, I owed him that much in death.

But watching him die by my hand was not as I had expected it to be. Because my hand was forced. The choice was not entirely mine. And seeing his candle snuffed out felt very much like glancing into a crystal ball and seeing my own fate. He looked like me. He sounded like me. He was _of_ me. The same spring that produced his lifeblood also produced mine.

The one thing I must strive to remember—now more than ever—is while the fortunate man will say, "Fate is kind," and the unfortunate man, "Fate is cruel," the truth is it is neither.

It is fate.

It is not personal.

To take on the turns of events in my life as somehow particular to me is to endow them with dominion over my mind. And right now, I cannot allow that to happen. Because so many questions remain unanswered.

Is there a version of my story in which I reflect back and consider that if I had shown a greater interest in Lars, none of this would have happened? Of course. Is there a version that traces even further back in which I do not steal my father's irreplaceable diamond and none of the events that led to today are set in motion? Certainly. But the more meaningful question is: If none of those things had happened as they did, would I be with Danny and Christine right now? In the way that we are together? Would we have bonded as we have? Survived as we have? Loved as we do?

I may never know.

But it is a wasteful expenditure of energy to consider, because I cannot change the past. The past is, by definition, past. I can only learn from it and prepare. And so, as I look out the window of the suite, I consider what education I have now gained.

As a child, Lars, my baby brother, was not given a chance. I did not see that, just like Danny and Christine, he was born into chaos. Simply because his chaotic childhood was not marked by hunger and physical abuse does not make it any less chaotic.

And so, while I took care of Christine and Danny, protected them, because I could see they needed it and I needed them—it was mutually necessary, our relationship—Lars... Lars needed me too. And I needed to be there for him. I couldn't see that at the time because I hadn't yet learned as much, but it makes it no less true. And I know it now.

I am grateful it was me.

It should have been me in the end.

It was the least I could do.

And what of the future? I have a chance to have an impact on a new life. A new life that I learned I played a role in creating in the same environment where I ended another life.

It is a new life that I only just met. A new life whose lifeblood is drawn from the very same spring. Just as my blood pumped through Lars, my blood pumps through the veins of the child called Andra. I couldn't save Lars. I was too late. I can save Andra. And I will.

I must forget the past now. Wholly. Entirely. There is no place for it here. I must forget the things I've done and the mistakes I've made. I believe I can. I have held onto it all long enough. It served its purpose. It brought me here. But now it is time to put it to rest.

I can tell that Danny has already done this. He seems like the best of the Danny he once was and the promise of a Danny I don't yet know. Whatever he and Christine shared between them in these last months has seemed to strengthen him. To empower him. His energy is palpable and resolute. The uncertainty about 'us' is gone and the sturdy, sexy, unshakeable Danny that I fell in love with is all I see. His resolve to punish this Brasil Lynch oke is like nothing I've watched him showcase before. Though I blame him for none of what's happened, he's taking it personally. I understand. In his situation, I might too.

Christine, conversely, is not quite there yet. Not in the present. Still in the past. Not quite looking to the future. She wants to be. I can feel how much she wants to let go of the pain of everything and move on. But it will take more time. I don't wish to compel her. I don't want to force her hand or manipulate her. I've done enough of that, I decide. But I do want to encourage her. With Danny, I believe we'll get there. We have to. We must.

There is just the one last thing we have to do. This one last thing. And then… and then we can rest. We can sleep and make love and hold each other close and feel safe in our shared embrace.

We can find a place where the sun shines every day.

A place that's in stark contrast to where we are right now.

The rainy, foggy Belfast morning hangs heavy in the sky outside the hotel. Eliza, Russell, and the twins went mad, but I somehow managed to persuade everyone that the only chance we would have of retrieving Theo and Andra is to remain calm. It's not a guarantee that we'll succeed, but it can't hurt to not become too emotional.

I feel their emotion though. Myself. I do. I have a sense of what it is. I barely know the child, but I feel the tug. Partially because she is innocent and I know very few innocents any longer, and partially because she is mine.

So many questions still to be asked. So many questions still to be answered. And if we have to set fire to the world and let it burn until the truth is all that's left to be seen amidst the ashes, so be it.

I hear the door open behind me. I don't turn around. "Well?" I ask, still facing the window.

"I couldn't get inside, but I saw a couple of guys I recognize. It's still his place."

"Still whose place?" Christine asks, coming from out of the shower. She smells of hotel soap and shampoo. Grapefruit and bergamot or some such.

"Declan's. Brasil's uncle."

"Why are we going there again?" she asks.

"We have to start someplace. I'm not waiting around for him to dictate what happens next."

"No," I say. "No, indeed. We will decide that."

I hear him toss his leather jacket onto a chair behind me. I glance toward Christine, who wanders over in her towel. She lands by my side, puts her arm around me and I wrap mine around her in kind. I'm clad only in my trousers. Her damp hair drips water down my ribs. I give her a kiss on the head.

"Alec?" she asks.

"Hmmm?"

"Do you think—?"

"I have no idea, nunu."

She cocks her head. "You don't even know what I was going ask."

"It doesn't matter."

She considers this and then lets her cheek drop against my chest.

Danny comes and stands on the other side of me. He places his hand on my back as well and stares out the window with us. I can feel the placement of their fingers. They are each resting on their lines. Their individual places in the ink.

We all look out. Forward. Ahead.

It's silent for a long, long moment. Which is nice. Because I have a feeling it won't be this way again for quite some time.

Finally, Danny breaks the quiet, asking me, "What are you thinking about?"

I let the question linger just enough to contemplate the many answers I could give, and then, before I let myself drift too deep into thought, I tell them both...

"What happens next."

Welcome to the End of Book Shit where we get to say anything we want about the book. Sometimes they're long and wordy, sometimes they're short and pithy. You never know. But they are never edited, so excuse our typos. And they are always last minute. Like... right before we upload. So don't mind us if we ramble.

Johnathan

On a couple of different occasions in this book, characters comment that there's "a lot to unpack." That's true for them as characters inside the story and that's also true for the story itself. There is a lot to unpack. An *amazing* amount, if you will. And not just in terms of the plot and its complexities and revelations, but also in terms of the ideas we are finding ourselves examining as we write.

The word "complicated" appears repeatedly in this book. This is not an accident.

We are exploring betrayal, trust, hope, despair, forgiveness...

We delve into how one processes loss and moves on from the past while taking a look at how one prepares for the future.

What does it mean to be alive and how does one face death? The perpetual cycle of new life emerging while — sometimes simultaneously — other life is ending. For, indeed, right now, at the very moment you are reading this, someone is dying.

And someone else is being born.

Someone is celebrating and someone is suffering.

It is all happening now.

And now.

... And now.

So, yes, there's a lot to unpack within the pages of these books. An amazing amount. Because, quite simply, there's an amazing amount to unpack in every single moment of our lives. If we choose to unpack it.

And so... What I'd like to talk about here is one of the less obvious but, I think, related and possibly more important ideas presented in this particular installment.

At a certain point in this book Alec makes the observation that anger is essentially a substitute emotion. Which is to say it is a secondary one. It is the emotion that springs up to cover the true, prevailing emotion that gets masked underneath when the anger emerges.

It is a shield.

I'm not saying that it's insincere. Or unnecessary. It can be very sincere and most often it is very, very necessary for survival. I'm just suggesting that it is, in fact, secondary. And frequently it only surfaces to protect us from feeling something more ... authentic. Usually because that authentic feeling is painful, or at least uncomfortable, and the anger takes what was an emotion we felt victimized by and transforms it into something we feel gives us power and energy.

It seems like it's active and not passive. It seems like it puts the ball in our hands and re-forms the vicissitudes of life into something that gives us the illusion of having control.

And I would like to suggest that our anger is, in fact, just the opposite. It is not the powerful weapon that spares us hurt. It is actually the thing that keeps us in a perpetual cycle of pain and disallows us the chance to heal and grow.

When anger overtakes whatever our hearts genuinely want to feel, we are suffocating that instinctive, gut-level reaction to the thing it is that we convince ourselves is "making us" angry. If it's fear (fear of loss, fear of heartache, fear of pain, whatever), then we are denying ourselves the chance to confront that fear, inventory it, and learn how to deal with it so that in the future whatever it was that caused us to become afraid no longer holds its sway over us.

If it's sorrow, the anger rises up to block the sadness, once again denying us the privilege of learning to sit in our melancholy until we make friends with our heartbreak and it no longer feels burdensome. Because it's not a burden to feel sorrow. Or to feel fear. It *is* a privilege. It means that we are alive. Not just breathing and walking and talking, but actually living a fully realized existence.

We cannot presume to wall ourselves off from the things that cause us anxiety, indulging our anger and denying our purer emotions, and expect to ever grow into anything more than we are now.

And, y'know, hey... That's fine. There's no rule that says you *have* to grow or learn or advance in any way at all while you're here on this planet. But it's no coincidence that the people I've met who are most resistant to the idea of growth and take the greatest precautions to keep their personal risk at a minimum, are also the ones who are most afraid of dying. Perhaps it's a chicken/egg conversation, but I might want to suggest that it's not always fearless people who take risks and go on adventures. Sometimes it's that through the process of adventuring you become less afraid.

I'm not talking, necessarily, about life-risking adventures like squirrel suiting or shark wrestling. I'm talking about adventuring into your own psyche. Your own individual worldview. Challenging yourself to look at the things that make you feel angry or resentful and take a

349

look under the hood of that feeling to see what's actually making the engine turn. Ninety-nine times out of a hundred, I'd be willing to bet that what you'll find is just a withering set of feelings that you've never dealt with.

This is not pontification, by the way. This is coming from someone who spent much of his life angry at everything all the time. I've talked about this before in another EOBS, but I grew up with a mentally ill parent. Something I haven't talked about is that I also grew up with addictions. Drugs. Alcohol. The usual. I have always presumed that the two things are related. Largely because, with one parent in and out of the hospital all the time, and the other parent so distracted by that that they couldn't possibly be expected to notice everything going on with their kid at every moment, it provided the ideal opportunity for me to do whatever the hell I wanted.

Which, at fourteen, was excellent. Talk about adventures? I had some goddamn adventures, that's for certain. I don't know that I really *enjoyed* them or appreciated them, usually because I was too fucked up, but it gave me a chance to do some shit that was — to say the least — educational.

And I never once, at all, felt angry. Because between the distractions of my misadventures and the chemically induced haze I maintained, all my feelings were muted. The state I stayed in was what the anger would later become for me: A substitute for having to feel anything I didn't want to engage with.

And then, at twenty-one, I got sober.

And that's when the wheels fell the fuck off.

With nothing to mask the more vulnerable emotions I found myself feeling all the time, I had to find a new way to cover them. It seemed like a matter of survival. So, I got really, really angry. All the time. I don't even know that I understood how angry I was.

A few years back (maybe fifteen or so now), I made contact with someone I had known during that time in my life and had then lost touch with. I forget how or why she and I reconnected, but I just remember that in an email she wrote something like, "It's so great to hear that you're doing so well. I always recalled you as that angry young man with so much misplaced emotion, your fists would shake with the energy of your impuissant frustration." (Or something like that. I may be embellishing. I just recall it being fairly elegiac and also a little bit like, "Really? Why the fuck didn't anybody say something at the time??)

The reason, of course, that no one said anything at the time is that you cannot coach someone into an evolved state of being. They must find it on their own.

Which brings me back to my point: The only way personal evolution can occur is via a path of discovery that is illuminated by a willingness to get comfortable with your discomfort.

In other words: Sit in your sorrow. Make friends with your fear. Celebrate your sadness.

Whatever the thing is that's *pissing you off*, don't get pissed off by it. Allow it to exist on its own terms, in its own way, and run its course in its own time.

There will be one more book in this trilogy. One more set of adventures for our heroes to face that will challenge their ability to best their anger, adventure into the unknown, and find what for them will be a happily ever after.

As the authors, we know where we intend for the story to go. But we must face the reality that as we get into it, the characters, the story, the reality of these people may carry us somewhere we're not comfortable with. Like all our characters, Alec, Christine, and Danny tell us where *they* want to go. And sometimes... Sometimes those assholes take us to places we don't want to travel. So, there's no guarantee that won't happen in the final book in this story.

And, if it happens, it will be on us not to get angry and not to try and rend the story back into a place that causes us to feel more comfortable. As storytellers, we have to sit in our own discomfort with that fact that sometimes a story will tell itself and, eventually, a story must end in whatever way it wants to end.

We can fear it, we can be saddened by it, we can even resent it, but we will ultimately have to accept it if we are to learn from it.

And if we engage with it correctly and honestly, we emerge as better storytellers and better people.

The world is a scary fucking place. We are living in a frightening time in the history of the human experience. And yes, someday we are all going to die.

But rather than raging at those truths, I would encourage all of us, every single one, to take a breath, take a look around, observe our feelings without judgement, and see how long it takes before, instead of being mad as hell about it all, we look at the complications we have to unpack in these big, messy, finite-so-live-it-while-you-can lives of ours and think...

"Goddamn. Isn't it all just ... *amazing?*"

JM
24 January 2019

Julie

Welcome to my first End of Book Shit for 2019!

Like most people I like to take stock of my year when the new one starts. Look back and think about what I was doing five or ten years ago. But this New Year I've been thinking about seven years ago because that's when this whole fiction author thing started.

Almost exactly seven years ago I made a decision to write a fiction book. I didn't really know what I was doing. I take that back—I had no idea what I was doing. I just kinda had this weird science fiction story in my head and back then I was working as a hog farm inspector for the state of Colorado.

This was a part-time gig and I mostly worked from home. But about every two weeks I had to drive in to Denver, pick up a state car, and then drive back out to the Eastern Plains of Colorado where all these hog farms lived. My territory was literally from Julesburg, CO (which is on the border of Nebraska) to some random number of miles south of Holly, CO (which is pretty close to Oklahoma and right up against the state line of Kansas.)

So I had a lot of time on my hands. The actual inspections took anywhere from thirty minutes to three days, depending on the number of farms I had to look at. So some days—those days I went south of Holly—I would literally drive for about six hours, do my thirty-minute inspection on their two farms, then turn around and drive home.

I did a lot of thinking in that state car. So I came up with this story about a girl name Junco and built a whole world based off the Eastern Plains.

When people think of Colorado they think of the mountains but half of the state is prairie. Most of that is farm and ranch land and it's very rural. All these farms were on dirt roads and there were never any street signs that made any sense. It was CR CC or CR ZZ or CR 157. Like, I never really knew where I was. I just knew where I needed to be and figured it out along the way. I can remember someone calling me from the office asking me where I was. And I was like, "Hell I don't know. Somewhere between Limon and La Junta, bitches. What do you want?"

Going down to Holly I literally based my direction off a flag pole and a lama. (Turn left at the flag pole, turn right at the lama... drive south until I see the farm.)

And I remember being in one of my farm manager's trucks as we were looking at farms south of Burlington, and he and I were talking about getting out of this fucking hog farm business.

He wanted to sell his house, put his kids and wife in an RV, and go travel. Maybe write a travel blog. And I was telling him how I was writing too. I had my whole science textbook business but I really wanted to write fiction.

I think about him a lot because I liked that guy. He was a very good guy. All the hog farm people were. Just honest people who worked in agriculture and did a job no one ever wants to think about. The state regulation I was in charge of enforcing was an environmental one and I'd say 95% of the time every single hog farm in Colorado (and I had about 120 of them) passed their bi-annual inspection. Every once in a while I'd have to write someone up, usually for a torn water liner edge because we get wicked winds out here and if the edge of something is flapping, it's definitely gonna rip. But most of the time it was just me and these farm guys riding around in a dirty white pick-up truck shootin' the shit.

So this Burlington guy had a dream to go do something cool. And I did too. I lost touch with him after I left the hog farms so I never did find out if he sold his house and went traveling. But I did write that book. I wrote three of them that year and have written more than 50 since then.

So I've been thinking about that decision a lot lately for some reason. Probably because it's January and it's the anniversary of when I quit the hog farms and became a fiction author. But mostly because I often wonder what my life would've look like if I hadn't taken that chance. And then I feel so grateful that I did.

2018 was INSANE for me. So much has changed, and so much happened, and so many things are still in the works, it's just crazy.

And I don't really have anything to relate back to this story, The Square. But the EOBS is all mine. You can read it, or not. Appreciate it, or not. I just get to say whatever I want. So that's what I'm doing. Just sharing my random thoughts with you.

I also want to wish you a very happy new year and say… if you're thinking about making a change this year—whatever it is—*do it.*

The perfect time will never come. Believe me. There is no perfect time.

Just believe in yourself and take that chance. Because

you never know what will happen. And if you had asked me seven years ago if I'd be here now, writing this for you, I'd have called you crazy.

But here I am.

Thank you for reading, thank you for reviewing, and I'll see you in the next book.

Julie
JA Huss
1-23-19

www.JAHuss.com
www.HussMcClain

Johnathan McClain's career as a writer and actor spans 25 years and covers the worlds of theatre, film, and television. At the age of 21, Johnathan moved to Chicago where he wrote and began performing his critically acclaimed one-man show, Like It Is. The Chicago Reader proclaimed, "If we're ever to return to a day when theatre matters, we'll need a few hundred more artists with McClain's vision and courage." On the heels of its critical and commercial success, the show subsequently moved to New York where Johnathan was compared favorably to solo performance visionaries such as Eric Bogosian, John Leguizamo, and Anna Deavere Smith.

Johnathan lived for many years in New York, and his work there includes appearing Off-Broadway in the original cast of Jonathan Tolins' The Last Sunday In June at The Century Center, as well as at Lincoln Center Theatre and with the Lincoln Center Director's Lab. Around the country, he has been seen on stage at South Coast Repertory, The American Conservatory Theatre, Florida Stage, Paper Mill Playhouse, and the National Jewish Theatre. Los Angeles stage credits are numerous and include the LA Weekly Award nominated world premiere of Cold/Tender at The Theatre @ Boston Court and the LA Times' Critic's Choice production of The Glass Menagerie at The Colony Theatre for which Johnathan received a Garland Award for his portrayal of Jim O'Connor.

On television, he appeared in a notable turn as Megan Draper's LA agent, Alan Silver, on the final season of AMC's critically acclaimed drama Mad Men, and as the lead of the TV Land comedy series, Retired at 35, starring alongside Hollywood icons George Segal and Jessica Walter. He has also had Series Regular roles on The Bad Girl's Guide starring Jenny McCarthy and Jessica Simpson's sitcom pilot for ABC. Additional TV work includes recurring roles on the Netflix comedy PRINCE OF PEORIA, the CBS drama SEAL TEAM and Fox's long-running 24, as well as appearances on Grey's Anatomy, NCIS: Los Angeles, Trial and Error, The Exorcist, Major Crimes, The Glades, Scoundrels, Medium, CSI, Law & Order: SVU, Without a Trace, and CSI: Miami, amongst others. On film, he appeared in the Academy Award nominated Far from Heaven and will soon be seen in his first leading role on the big screen in the upcoming WALKING WITH HERB, starring alongside George Lopez and Academy Award nominees Edward James Olmos and Kathleen Quinlan.

As an audiobook narrator, he has recorded over 100 titles, iincluding the Audie Award winning Illuminae by Amie Kaufman and Jay Kristoff and The Last Days of Night, by Academy Award Winning Screenwriter Graham Moore (who is also Johnathan's friend and occasional collaborator). As well as multiple titles by his dear friend and writing partner, JA Huss, with whom he is hard at work making the world a little more romantic.

He lives in Los Angeles with his wife Laura.

JA Huss never wanted to be a writer and she still dreams of that elusive career as an astronaut. She originally went to school to become an equine veterinarian but soon figured out they keep horrible hours and decided to go to grad school instead. That Ph.D wasn't all it was cracked up to be (and she really sucked at the whole scientist thing), so she dropped out and got a M.S. in forensic toxicology just to get the whole thing over with as soon as possible.

After graduation she got a job with the state of Colorado as their one and only hog farm inspector and spent her days wandering the Eastern Plains shooting the shit with farmers.

After a few years of that, she got bored. And since she was a homeschool mom and actually does love science, she decided to write science textbooks and make online classes for other homeschool moms.

She wrote more than two hundred of those workbooks and was the number one publisher at the online homeschool store many times, but eventually she covered every science topic she could think of and ran out of shit to say.

So in 2012 she decided to write fiction instead. That year she released her first three books and started a career that would make her a New York Times bestseller and land her on the USA Today Bestseller's List eighteen times in the next three years.

Her books have sold millions of copies all over the world, the audio version of her semi-autobiographical book, Eighteen, was nominated for a Voice Arts Award and an Audie Award in 2016 and 2017 respectively, her audiobook, Mr. Perfect, was nominated for a Voice Arts

Award in 2017, and her audiobook, Taking Turns, was nominated for an Audie Award in 2018.

Johnathan McClain is her first (and only) writing partner and even though they are worlds apart in just about every way imaginable, it works.

She lives on a ranch in Central Colorado with her family.

Made in the USA
Monee, IL
01 December 2022